Colleagues Praise
Mike Resnick

"The most versatile and entertaining madman writing science fiction today."
—Jack L. Chalker

"Resnick is a reader's writer, one who can be counted upon to deliver a dependably entertaining read."
—Michael P. Kube-McDowell

"Mike Resnick delivers pure entertainment and a rollicking good time."
—Alan Dean Foster,
bestselling author of
Quozl and *Cat*A*Lyst*

"His name on a book guarantees a solid story . . . Most important of all, it guarantees entertainment."
—Raymond E. Feist

"Resnick may well be on his way to becoming the Stephen King or John D. MacDonald of science fiction."
—Edward Bryant

"Mike Resnick spins a great yarn!"
—Jerry Pournelle

Ace Books by Mike Resnick

SOOTHSAYER
ORACLE
PROPHET

MIKE RESNICK
PROPHET

ACE BOOKS, NEW YORK

This book is an Ace original edition,
and has never been previously published.

PROPHET

An Ace Book / published by arrangement with
the author

PRINTING HISTORY
Ace edition / June 1993

All rights reserved.
Copyright © 1993 by Mike Resnick.
Cover art by Keith Birdsong.
This book may not be reproduced in whole or in part,
by mimeograph or any other means, without permission.
For information address: The Berkley Publishing Group,
200 Madison Avenue, New York, New York 10016.

ISBN: 0-441-68329-0

Ace Books are published by The Berkley Publishing Group,
200 Madison Avenue, New York, New York 10016.
The name "ACE" and the "A" logo
are trademarks belonging to Charter Communications, Inc.

PRINTED IN THE UNITED STATES OF AMERICA

10 9 8 7 6 5 4 3 2 1

To Carol, as always,

and to Doug Roemer,
keeper of the flame

Contents

	Prologue	1
Part 1	**The Gravedancer's Book**	3
Part 2	**The Iceman's Book**	63
Part 3	**The Silicon Kid's Book**	121
Part 4	**The Anointed One's Book**	171
Part 5	**The Prophet's Book**	219
	Epilogue	241

PROPHET

Prologue

It was a time of giants.

There was no room for them to breathe and flex their muscles in mankind's sprawling Democracy, so they gravitated to the distant, barren worlds of the Inner Frontier, drawn ever closer to the bright Galactic Core like moths to a flame.

Oh, they fit into human frames, most of them, but they were giants nonetheless. No one knew what had brought them forth in such quantity at this particular moment in human history. Perhaps there was a need for them in a galaxy filled to overflowing with little people possessed of even smaller dreams. Possibly it was the savage splendor of the Inner Frontier itself, for it was certainly not a place for ordinary men and women. Or maybe it was simply time for a race that had been notably short of giants in recent eons to begin producing them once again.

But whatever the reason, they swarmed out beyond the farthest reaches of the explored galaxy, spreading the seed of Man to hundreds of new worlds, and in the process creating a cycle of legends that would never die as long as men could tell tales of heroic deeds.

There was Faraway Jones, who set foot on more than five hundred new worlds, never quite certain what he was looking for, always sure that he hadn't yet found it.

There was a shadowy figure known only as the Whistler, who had killed more than one hundred Men and aliens.

There was Friday Nellie, who turned her whorehouse into a hospital during the war against the Setts, and finally saw it declared a shrine by the very Men who once tried to close it down.

There was Jamal, who left no fingerprints or footprints, but had plundered palaces that to this day do not know they were plundered.

There was Bet-a-World Murphy, who at various times owned nine different gold-mining worlds and lost every one of them at the gaming tables.

There was Backbreaker Ben Ami, who wrestled aliens for money and killed Men for pleasure. There was the Marquis of Queensbury, who fought by no rules at all, and the White Knight, albino killer of fifty Men, and Sally the Blade, and the Forever Kid, who reached the age of nineteen and just stopped growing for the next two centuries, and Catastrophe Baker, who made whole planets shake beneath his feet, and the exotic Pearl of Maracaibo, whose sins were condemned by every race in the galaxy, and Father Christmas, and the One-Armed Bandit with his deadly prosthetic arm, and the Earth Mother, and Lizard Malloy, and the deceptively mild-mannered Cemetery Smith.

Giants all.

Yet there was one giant who was destined to tower over all of the others, to juggle the lives of men and worlds as if they were so many toys, to rewrite the history of the Inner Frontier, and the Outer Frontier, and the Spiral Arm, and even the all-powerful Democracy itself. At various times in her short, turbulent life she was known as the Soothsayer, and the Oracle, and the Prophet. By the time she had passed from the galactic scene, only a handful of survivors knew her true name, or her planet of origin, or even her history, for such is the way with giants and legends.

But she had an origin, and a history, and a name.

This is her story.

PART 1

—————
—————
—————
—————
—————
—————
—————
—————
—————
—————

The Gravedancer's Book

1

A hot, dry wind swept across the surface of Last Chance, a remote world on the edge of the Inner Frontier. Dust devils swirled up to heights of sixty feet, breathing became almost impossible, and the few indigenous animals burrowed into the ground to wait out the dust storm.

A lone figure, his clothing nondescript, his face protected against the elements by a dust mask, walked down the main street of the planet's only Tradertown, looking neither right nor left. The door of an abandoned building suddenly buckled from the force of the wind, and he quickly crouched, withdrew a hand weapon, and fired at the source of the noise. The door briefly turned a bright blue and then vanished. The man remained motionless for a moment, then holstered his weapon and continued walking toward the brightly lit building at the end of the street.

He came to a stop about twenty yards from his destination, then placed his hands on his hips and studied the structure before him. The walls were made of a titanium alloy with a tight molecular bonding, finished to look like wood. The front veranda possessed two large doorways, both leading to the crowded interior of the End of the Line. From where he was standing, he couldn't tell which section was the bar and which was the casino, though he suspected the casino was at the back, where it could be more easily protected against potential robberies.

A door slid open for a moment, and the man ducked behind a vehicle and withdrew his weapon again as a tall woman emerged, took one step into the dust, then shook her head and went back into the building, coughing heavily.

The man strode back out into the middle of the street and continued staring at the building. Finally he began walking again, turning to his left after a moment and circling the entire building. There weren't any windows, which didn't surprise him given the force of the dust storm, but he hadn't survived this long by not being thorough, and he methodically checked out every means of ingress. All the various doors were closed, probably locked, certainly tied into a security system. Briefly he considered climbing to the roof—it was not beyond his capabilities to scale the side of the building, made rough by the abrasive action of the wind and the dust—but he couldn't see any advantage to be gained, and he rejected the idea.

He finally decided that he had no choice but to enter through one of the doorways at the front of the building. He was unhappy about it—not that he minded being identified after his work was done, but he preferred not to call any attention to himself before he'd earned his money—but no viable alternative had presented itself, and the dust mask made him feel constricted, even claustrophobic.

He realized that he was still holding his weapon in his hand, that he had been holding it since the woman had temporarily emerged from the building, and he once again replaced it in his holster. Then he climbed the three stairs to the veranda, walked across it, entered the End of the Line, and removed his mask. He would get the feel of the place, spot his quarry, wash the dust in his mouth away with a beer or two, and then go to work.

The place was as crowded as he had anticipated. A long chrome bar lined the left side of the front room, with perhaps a dozen tables scattered around the right side. The clientele was primarily human, for this was a human outpost world, but here and there were Canphorites, Lodinites, and a pair of beings of a type he had never seen before.

The back room was as large as the tavern, and even more crowded. There were roulette tables, dice tables, poker tables, two tables boasting alien games of chance. He scanned the faces at the tables, wondering which of them, if any, was his quarry. Then, finally, he turned and walked over to the bar.

A balding, overweight man with a slight limp approached him from the other side of the bar.

"Good evening," he said. "What can I get for you?"

"A beer."

"Coming right up," said the man behind the bar, placing a mug under a tap and activating it. "I haven't seen you around here before."

"I just got here."

"Sorry we have such lousy weather today," continued the bartender. "Usually Last Chance is a pretty pleasant place, even a bit on the cool side."

"I didn't come here for the weather."

"Good. Then you won't be disappointed."

The man lifted the mug to his lips and downed half of it in a single long swallow.

"I need a little information," he said, wiping his mouth with the back of his hand.

"If it's mine to give," replied the bartender.

"I'm looking for someone."

"Well, I know almost everyone here. Who is it?"

"A man named Carlos Mendoza. Some people call him the Iceman."

"Mendoza, eh?" said the bartender. He looked around the room. "You owe him some money? I can give it to him for you."

"Just point him out to me."

"I hope you're not looking for trouble," said the bartender. "They say Mendoza is a pretty tough customer."

"What I'm looking for is none of your business," said the man coldly.

"Fine by me," said the bartender with a shrug. "I just figured that since you don't know him, probably you've been hired by someone who *does* know him. Thought I could save you a little misery."

"Save your thoughts for Mendoza."

"Well," said the bartender with another shrug, "at least you've been warned."

"All right, I've been warned," said the man. "Now, point him out to me."

"See that fellow sitting by himself in the corner?" asked the bartender. "The one dressed all in black?"

The man nodded. "He's armed like he's going into battle," he said. "Laser pistol, sonic gun, projectile pistol. Probably got a knife tucked into that boot, too."

"Actually, he's got a knife in *each* boot," said the bartender. He paused. "Are you really sure you want to go through with this?"

"It's my work," said the man, turning to face his prey.

"You could talk," suggested the bartender. "The Iceman's always willing to talk instead of fight."

"He is, huh?"

"That's what I hear."

"I don't get paid to talk," answered the man.

He took a few steps toward the man in black, then stopped. "Mendoza!" he said in a loud voice.

Most of the action at the gaming tables stopped as the man in black looked up at him curiously.

"Are you talking to me?"

The man's fingers hovered above the hilt of his sonic pistol.

"Time to die, Mendoza."

"Do I know you?" asked the man in black.

"All you have to know is that I'm the last thing you're ever going to see."

Suddenly the newcomer flinched, and a puzzled expression crossed his face. He blinked his eyes rapidly, as if trying to comprehend what had happened, then groaned once and pitched forward on his face, a large knife protruding from his back.

The bartender limped over to him, withdrew the knife he had thrown with deadly accuracy, and wiped it off on a bar towel.

"They get younger and dumber every week," he said, turning the dead man onto his back with a foot. "No problem, friends," he announced, raising his voice. "Just our weekly visitor from wherever."

And because of who he was, most of the patrons took his word for it and returned to their drinks and their gambling.

The man in black walked over and stared at the corpse.

"Ever see him before?" asked the bartender.

"No," said the man in black. "You know who he is, Iceman?"

The Iceman shook his balding head. "No idea. But that's four of them this month. Somebody *really* wants me dead." He paused. "I just wish I knew why. I haven't been off the planet in damned near four years."

"If you hadn't killed him, maybe we could have found out," said the man in black. "After all, that's what you hired me for. You're not making my job any easier."

"I *made* your job easier," replied the Iceman. "He would have taken you."

The man in black frowned. "What makes you think so?"

The Iceman knelt down, gripped the corpse's left hand in his own, and displayed the index finger.

"Prosthetic," he said. "I spotted it at the bar, and when he turned his back, I saw the power pack under his shirt. While you were drawing your weapon, he'd have just pointed at you and burned a hole right through your chest."

"Well, I'll be damned!" muttered the man in black. "I guess you did make my job easier, at that."

"I'll take it out of your pay," said the Iceman wryly.

"You know, one of these days someone's going to come out here who knows what you look like," said the man in black. "What are you going to do then?"

"Duck, I suppose," replied the Iceman. "In the meantime, let's move our late friend here into my office and see what we can learn about him."

"I have a feeling he's going to be just like the others you described to me," predicted the man in black. "No identification, no fingerprints, surgically altered retinagram."

"Probably," agreed the Iceman. "But let's do it, anyway."

The man in black shrugged and gestured for a couple of other men to pick up the corpse. They began carrying it toward the casino.

The Iceman immediately barred their way. "Out the front and around to the side," he said. "We've got customers here. How would *you* like it if someone dragged a dead body right in front of you while you were drinking?" He paused, then sighed deeply. "Don't answer. Just do it."

They reversed their direction and carried the dead man out the front door.

"Well," said the man in black, "are you finally going to tell me what this is all about?"

"I wish to hell I knew," answered the Iceman, limping back to the bar and pouring himself a beer. He offered one to the man in black, who turned it down.

"Don't kill the next one and maybe you'll find out."

"Anyone who comes after me on Last Chance dies," answered the Iceman firmly. "That's part of the myth I spent three decades creating. If I let even one of these bastards live, the myth becomes a fairy tale and they'll be coming after me every hour instead of every week. Lord knows I've made enough enemies over the years."

"Then why did you hire me at all?" asked the man in black in frustrated tones.

"As you say, one of them may know who I am—and I happen to be a seventy-one-year-old man with a beer belly and an artificial leg. When I finally need you, you'll earn your money, never fear."

"You ought to let me cripple one of them," said the man in black. "Then we'd get some answers."

"You want to cripple one?" asked the Iceman. He gestured to the door. "You've got the whole damned planet on which to do it. But once they walk through that door, my first concern is staying alive." He finished his beer. "Now, if you want to practice on men who are here to kill *you*, that's your privilege, and good luck to you—but I didn't get to be this old by taking chances."

"They say there was a time when you took chances," replied the man in black. "Lots of 'em."

"I was young. I learned better."

"That's not the way I heard it."

"Then someone must have lied to you," said the Iceman.

"They even say," continued the man in black, "that you're the only man who ever took on the Oracle and won."

The Iceman grimaced. "I didn't win anything."

"Is she still alive?"

"I suppose so," replied the Iceman. "I can't imagine anything being able to kill her."

"Has the thought crossed your mind that she's behind all this?"

"Not for an instant."

"Why not?"

"Because if she was, I'd be dead," said the Iceman with absolute certainty.

"You faced her before, and you're still alive," persisted the man in black.

"Forget about her," replied the Iceman. "She's got nothing to do with this."

"You're sure?"

"To her, I'm about as insignificant as a grain of sand on a deserted beach." He paused. "If she's still alive, she's got more important things on her mind."

"What kind of things?"

"I hope to hell I never find out," answered the Iceman seriously. "Come on," he added. "Let's take a look at the body."

They walked over to his office and entered it, where they found the corpse laid out on a broad wooden desk.

The man in black examined the corpse's fingers closely.

"No prints," he announced. "Damned nice job on that fake finger. I never spotted it." He looked down at the dead man's face. "Got an ophthalmoscope?"

"A small one, inside the center drawer of the desk," said the Iceman, going over the body for scars or identifying marks. "But it's not tied into any computers."

The man in black walked to the desk and returned with the instrument. "I have a feeling that tying into a computer won't do you a bit of good with this guy—but let's see." He stared through the scope for a moment, then put it away. "Yeah, there's some scar tissue on the rods and cones. Five'll get you ten they're not on record anywhere in the galaxy."

"No serial numbers on any of the weapons, either," noted the Iceman. "Strange. Out here on the Inner Frontier, most killers pick colorful names and brag about their accomplishments. But this is the fourth one in a row who has no name, no identification, no reputation."

"Nice boots, though," said the man in black.

"I suppose so."

"Very nice."

"I checked for labels or manufacturer's marks," said the Iceman. "There aren't any."

The man in black continued staring at the boots.

"Do you see something I'm missing?" asked the Iceman, suddenly interested.

"It's possible," said the man in black, taking a boot from the corpse's foot and examining it.

"Looks sort of blue when the light hits it," commented the Iceman.

"I know," said the man in black. He handed the boot to the Iceman. "There aren't a lot of blue reptiles on the Inner Frontier—and I only know of one that's got this circular pattern of scales."

"Oh?"

The man in black nodded. "Big sonuvabitch. It lives on a world called Greycloud, out by the Quinellus Cluster." He paused. "They call it a Bluefire Dragon. It could swallow you whole and then look around for the main course."

"How big a world is Greycloud?"

"About the size of Last Chance, maybe a little smaller."

"Oxygen world?"

"Yes."

"Any sentient life-forms?" asked the Iceman.

"Not since we pacified it a few centuries ago," answered the man in black.

"How many Men?"

"Maybe seven thousand, mostly miners and aquaculturalists. It's mostly freshwater ocean, with a batch of islands and one very small continent."

"Does it do much exporting?"

The man in black shook his head. "Too small. Probably doesn't get a mail or cargo ship more than seven or eight times a year."

"So," continued the Iceman, "if our killer was wearing boots made from the local lizard . . ."

"There's a pretty good chance that he bought them there," concluded the man in black.

"They look relatively new," said the Iceman, studying the boots. "I think maybe you'd better pay a little visit to Greycloud. Take a couple of holos of our friend here before we bury him, and see if anyone knows who he was or who he worked for."

"I assume you'll be all right while I'm gone?"

"I'll make do," replied the Iceman dryly. "By the way, if Greycloud is so far off the beaten track, how come you know about this Bluefire Dragon?"

"I've been there."

"When?"

The man in black shrugged. "Oh, about eight or ten years ago."

"On business?"

"In a manner of speaking," said the man in black noncommittally.

"Good," said the Iceman. "You'll have some contacts there, some people you can talk to."

The man in black shook his head. "Everyone I knew there is dead."

"Recently?"

"About eight or ten years ago."

The Iceman smiled in grim amusement. "No wonder they call you the Gravedancer."

2

His real name was Felix Lomax, and he used it for the first twenty-six years of his life. But names have a way of changing on the Inner Frontier, metamorphosing to fit the natures of the men and women they're attached to.

Originally he'd been a Pioneer, one of that group of highly trained specialists that opened new worlds for the Democracy, terraforming them when necessary, cataloging the various life-forms, designing settlements, analyzing soils and minerals and water samples to determine exactly what type of colonists would be the most productive: miners, farmers, aquaculturalists, whatever. His specialty was pacification, a euphemism for decimating native populations until such time as they were willing to allow colonization—or, in some instances, until there were none left to object.

During that period of his life he had been known as Double X, an easily identifiable code name based on the spelling of his given name. (It was best not to use one's true name, just in case there were some survivors of the pacification process that resented the instrument of the policy rather than the formulators who were in their mile-high offices back on Deluros VIII, the capital world of Man, snug and secure in the heart of the Democracy.)

After four years of pacifying alien populations, something happened on the planet of Innisfree. He never spoke of it, never referred to it in any official document, but right in the middle of the campaign he quit and went off to the Inner Frontier. He bought a large ranch on Backgammon II and spent the next two years raising mutated cattle, huge, 3,000-pound specimens that

13

he sold to the Navy. During this time he was Felix Longface, for he never smiled, never joked, never seemed to take much of an interest in anything.

Then he finally put whatever demons were bothering him to rest and went farther into the Inner Frontier, returning to the trade he knew best: killing. For a while he was known as the Man in Black, for it was the only color he ever wore, but there were four other Men in Black on the Frontier, and before long he picked up the sobriquet of Gravedancer, and that was the name that stuck. Not that he ever danced or visited cemeteries, but when he landed on a planet, it was only a matter of time before *someone* would be visiting a graveyard, never to return.

His personality didn't change much. He still didn't smile, and he seemed to take no pride in his craft—which was strange for a man in his occupation—but before long his reputation preceded him, and he didn't lack for customers. He picked and chose those that interested him, which was how he came to work for the Iceman, who was as close to a living legend as a man could become on the Inner Frontier, where most legends died just about the time that they were recognized *as* legends.

He didn't know much about the Iceman—no one did—but he knew that he had, in his day, faced both the Soothsayer and the Oracle and had lived to tell about it, which was more than anyone else could claim. He would have thought that the Iceman would be the very last person on the Frontier to require protection, so when the offer came, his interest was sufficiently aroused to accept the commission. He hadn't realized at the time that it would require him to pay a return visit to Greycloud, but it wouldn't have made any difference to him if he had known it.

As his ship braked to sublight speeds and the water world came up on his viewscreen, he checked out his arsenal, selected those weapons that he thought would be most effective in this environment, and requested permission to land on the single continent's tiny spaceport.

"Please identify yourself," said a metallic voice, crackling with static.

"This is the *Peacekeeper,* Felix Lomax commanding, five days out of Last Chance."

"Permission denied."

"Why?"

"You are the Felix Lomax who is also known as the Grave-dancer, are you not?"

"I've been called that, yes."

"There are nine outstanding arrest warrants in your name, each for the crime of murder."

"All the more reason why you should want to get your hands on me," replied Lomax.

"We have no one here capable of taking you into custody against your will, Gravedancer," said the voice. "I assume you have not come to give yourself up to the authorities."

"A fair assumption."

"Then permission to land is denied. If you attempt to land on Greycloud, we will fire on your ship and destroy it before it can touch down."

"One moment," said Lomax, breaking the connection.

He had his computer scan the spaceport and surrounding vicinity, searching for weaponry. It found none, nor had he expected so thinly populated a world to have any defensive capabilities.

"Nice try, Greycloud," he said, reactivating his radio. "Now please give me landing coordinates."

"Denied."

"I'm landing whether you like it or not. If you won't give me coordinates, you'd better clear the sky or risk a collision over the landing field. This is the *Peacekeeper,* over and out."

He broke out of orbit and entered an elliptical path toward the spaceport, touching down about twenty minutes later. Once on the ground, he had the ship's sensors scan the area for armed personnel, found none, activated a number of security devices, and finally emerged through the hatch, the boots and a holograph of the dead man secured in a leather holdall that he slung over his left shoulder.

He walked about half a mile, past two small hangars, to the main traffic control and reception building, and entered warily. There were four clerks going about their business, one man and three women; none of them looked up at him or gave any indication that they were aware of his presence until he cleared his throat and three of them fidgeted nervously. He walked up to the fourth, a gray-haired woman, and stood before her.

"Yes?" she said coldly.

"I need transportation into town," he said.

"Do I look like a chauffeur?" she demanded.

"If I can't find one, you'll do."

"Go away and leave me alone, Mr. Lomax," she said. "I want nothing to do with you."

"Do I know you?" he asked.

"No, but *I* know you," she said, her eyes reflecting her hatred.

"Then tell me where I can find a ride into town, and you won't have to keep looking at me."

"I wouldn't help you if you were bleeding to death on the street," she said.

He stared at her for a long moment.

"Have it your way," he said at last. "Before I leave, though," he added, "I should point out that if anyone touches my ship, the ensuing explosion will flatten the spaceport and everything else within a radius of two miles."

Then he turned on his heel and walked out the main entrance. The parking lot was almost empty—the planet had a tiny population and relatively little commerce with the rest of the galaxy—but as he stood, hands on hips, wondering what to do next, a small groundcar pulled up. He walked over to it before the driver could get out, and opened the passenger's door.

"What's going on here?" demanded the driver, a young man in his early twenties.

"I'm paying you fifty credits to take me into town," said Lomax.

"The hell you are!" snapped the young man. "I've got a shipment of computer parts to pick up."

"They can wait."

Lomax sat down next to the driver, pulled out a sonic pistol, and pointed it at him.

"That wasn't a request," he said calmly.

"Who are you?" demanded the driver. "What the hell is this all about?"

"I'm just a guy who needs a ride to town," said Lomax. "Now, drive."

"Why don't you take an aircab?" said the young man, turning the car around.

"I wasn't aware you had any."

"We do. I can drive you to their hangar."

"I wouldn't want to put you to the trouble," said Lomax. "Just get going."

The young man stared at him, and suddenly his expression changed.

"You're *him,* aren't you?" he said.

"I'm whom?"

"The Gravedancer."

"Some people call me that."

"Damn!" said the young man, grinning and slamming his hand against the dashboard. "The Gravedancer himself, in *my* groundcar!" He turned to Lomax. "What are you here for?"

"Business."

"Who are you going to kill?" asked the young man eagerly.

"No one."

"You can tell me," persisted the young man. "I'm on *your* side."

"I'm just here to talk to the local bootmaker."

The young man snorted contemptuously. "Come on, Grave-dancer—do you expect me to believe you flew all the way to Greycloud for a pair of boots?"

"What you believe makes no difference to me," said Lomax. "Just take me where I want to go." He paused. "You can start by driving into town."

The young man put the vehicle in motion, and a moment later they were traveling on a road that paralleled an ocean shoreline.

"I've been wondering if you'd ever come back."

"You're too young to remember me," said Lomax.

"I was twelve when you were here the last time," replied the young man. "I saw you take on nine men at once." He paused, then extended his hand. "My name's Neil. Neil Cayman."

Lomax looked at his hand for a moment, then took it briefly.

"I'm Felix Lomax."

Neil shook his head. "You're the Gravedancer." He paused. "Where are you going from here?"

Lomax shrugged. "It all depends on what I learn while I'm here."

Neil seemed lost in thought for a moment, then spoke up. "Do you want some company?"

"Where?"

"Out *there,*" he said, waving his hand toward the sky. "I've spent my whole life on this world. I'd like to see something different."

"I work alone."

"I could be useful to you."

"Every damned world I touch down on, there's always some kid who wants to go out and make a name for himself on the Inner Frontier," answered Lomax. "Most of 'em die before the undertaker knows what name to put on their headstones."

"I'm different," said Neil.

"Yeah, I know," said Lomax. "You're all different."

"I've spent my whole life on Greycloud," continued Neil. "I want to see what's out there."

"Book passage with a tour group," answered Lomax. "You'll live longer."

"I don't want to see what tourists see," persisted Neil. "I want to see the way the worlds really are, the way the people really live." He paused. "I've got some money saved. I could be ready to go by this afternoon."

"Not with me," said Lomax.

"I'd do any kind of work you asked me to do, anything at all."

"Not interested."

The road turned inland, and was now lined by thick tropical foliage, which began thinning out as they moved farther away from the ocean.

"There have to be places where your face is known, where people run when they see you coming. *I* could go to those places and get information for you."

"Today is an exception," said Lomax. "Usually I'm after men, not information."

"I could spot them for you, let you know what their habits are, where they're likely to be. I wouldn't ask for any pay or anything like that," continued the young man. "Just a chance to get off this boring little world and travel with someone like you."

"I admire your persistence," said Lomax. "But the answer is the same."

"You're making a mistake, Gravedancer."

Lomax shrugged. "It's possible. I've made 'em before."

"Then let me come with you."

"I've also learned to live with the consequences of my mistakes," said Lomax. "The subject is closed."

They came to a tiny town, composed of a broad single street lined with some four dozen stores and shops, an old hotel, and a pair of restaurants, one of which was serving its customers in a shaded outdoor patio area. Neil drove more than halfway down the street and pulled up to a storefront.

"I'll wait here for you," he announced.

Lomax left the groundcar without a word and entered the store, a warm, dusty, single-story building that displayed a number of leather goods in the windows: coats, jackets, belts, hats, boots. Toward the back were sheets of various leathers, and hanging carefully from the walls were a number of pelts.

"Yes?" said a thin, balding man, walking out from a back room. "Can I help you?"

"Possibly," said Lomax, reaching into his leather holdall and withdrawing one of the dead man's boots. "Do you recognize this?"

The old man held it up to the light for a moment.

"Made from a Bluefire Dragon," he said.

"You made it?"

"If anyone else on the Frontier makes 'em, I sure as hell haven't heard about it." He examined it further. "This was a custom job, too. My label's not in it."

"How many custom boots do you make in a year's time?"

"Oh, maybe fifty."

"From Bluefire Dragons?"

"Maybe two or three."

"Good," said Lomax, pulling out the holograph and handing it over to the old man. "Do you recognize him?"

"Looks dead," noted the old man.

"He is. Do you know him?"

The old man nodded. "Yeah, I made some boots for him maybe seven, eight months ago."

"What can you tell me about him?"

"He wasn't real talkative," said the old man. "Seems to me he spent most of the day waiting in the bar across the street, then picked up his boots, paid for 'em, and left."

"Did he have a name?"

"Let me check my records," said the old man, activating his computer. "Yeah. His name is . . . was . . . Cole. Jason Cole."

"Did he pay cash?" asked Lomax.

"Yes."

"So you don't know what world he banked on?"

"Probably Olympus," answered the old man. "That's . . . let me think, now . . . Alpha Hayakawa IV."

"What makes you think he did his banking on Olympus?"

"He liked the boots so much he ordered a second pair. Had me ship them to an address on Olympus."

"What address?"

"Well, now, that's privileged information, isn't it?" said the old man, staring at Lomax.

"I'd call it *expensive* information," said Lomax, placing a pair of two-hundred-credit notes on the counter.

"Well, considering that the poor man has passed on, I suppose there's no harm in it," said the old man, greedily snatching up the money and stuffing it into a leather pouch that he wore around his neck. "Computer, print out Jason Cole's address."

The address emerged an instant later, and the old man handed it to Lomax.

"I'd say good hunting," said the old man. "But it appears to me that your hunting is already done."

"I have a feeling it's just starting."

"Well, in that case, good luck, Gravedancer."

"You know me?" said Lomax sharply.

"It'd be hard to forget you," said the old man. "You were the only exciting thing to happen to Greycloud in half a century." He paused. "Don't worry about me alerting the authorities or nothing. First, they probably couldn't stop you from whatever you're doing; and second, most of them you killed deserved what they got."

"Thanks."

"But let me give you a word of advice, Gravedancer."

"What is it?"

"Would I be right in figuring you plan to take a trip to Olympus next?"

"You might be."

"I'd be real careful there if I were you."

"Oh?"

The old man nodded. "Now and then I hear things from people who are passing through."

"What kind of things?"

"Oh, I don't put much stock in the details," answered the old man. "You know how people tend to exaggerate out here. But those who are willing to talk about it at all don't make it sound like a real friendly place."

"I'll keep it in mind," said Lomax, walking to the door.

"Can I interest you in a pair of boots while you're here?" the old man called after him. "Or maybe a new holster for all those weapons?"

"Maybe next time," answered Lomax.

"Men in your line of work don't usually live long enough for there to be a next time," said the old man with a half-amused smile. "This is your second trip here, so you're already on borrowed time."

"Next time," repeated Lomax, walking out into the street.

Neil was waiting for him and opened the door.

"Did you find out what you needed to know?" he asked.

"Possibly," said Lomax, settling back on his seat. "At least I know where I'm going next."

"Where?"

Lomax looked over at him and smiled. "Elsewhere," he said.

They drove to the spaceport in silence. Then Neil parked the groundcar.

"You're sure you won't take me?"

"You'll live longer on Greycloud, kid."

"I thought the quality of life was supposed to be important," said Neil sardonically.

"You've been misinformed."

Neil left the vehicle and walked to the cargo area while Lomax entered the main building.

The gray-haired woman who had refused to help him earlier glared at him, but beneath the mask of hatred he thought he saw a certain smugness, a brief look of triumph before the mask was fully in place.

He walked slowly to the door leading to the landing field, scrutinizing the area carefully. A pair of lead-suited mechanics were gingerly bringing out a small packet of plutonium to fuel an ancient cargo ship that was still powered by a nuclear pile, and a crew of three men were fixing a couple of cracks and potholes at the adjoining landing strip, but otherwise the place seemed deserted. Then, suddenly, he saw a brief movement out of the corner of his eye, coming from the roof of a hangar. He turned to face it, but couldn't spot anything out of the ordinary.

He lit a cigar, leaned lazily against a wall, and continued scanning the strip. A moment later the sun glinted off some metal on the roof of another hangar.

He walked to a vidphone directory and picked out a name at random, then approached the gray-haired woman.

"Call Jonathan Sturm and tell him that the Gravedancer's on his way," he said, walking out the front entrance before she could utter a reply or a refusal. "He's got until dark to put his affairs in order and make his peace with whatever god he worships."

He walked directly to the groundcar, entered it, and waited for Neil Cayman to emerge from the cargo area, carrying a box of computer parts.

"I thought you'd be gone by now," said Neil, surprised.

"Change of plans," said Lomax. "Do you own a ship?"

Neil seemed amused. "Where would I get a spaceship?"

"How about your parents or your employer?"

"Well, yeah, my boss has a little four-man job."

"Here?"

"Yes," said the young man. "It's in one of the hangars."

"Will they let you move it out to the landing field?"

"I suppose so."

Lomax peeled off five large-denomination notes. "It'll be sundown in about three hours. Do it then."

"Once they find out that I helped you, I'll be arrested."

Lomax shook his head. "You'll have plenty of time to fabricate an alibi. Almost every cop on the planet is going to be waiting for me at Jonathan Sturm's house."

"Sturm? What have you got against him?"

"Nothing," answered Lomax. "I never met the man."

"Then why—?"

"Just do what I said, okay?"

Neil stared at him. "I take it they've set a trap for you?" he asked at last.

Lomax nodded. "Will you help me?"

"I can't believe someone like you couldn't take them all out."

"Maybe I could," agreed Lomax. "But no one is paying me to do it, and when you put your life on the line often enough, you learn just how valuable a commodity it is. If I have to fight my way to my ship, I will—but if there's an easier way, I'll take it." He paused. "I need to hide until sunset, and then I need you to move your ship." He stared at the young man. "Now, are you going to help me or not?"

"Yeah, I'll help you, Gravedancer."

"Good."

"On one condition," added Neil.

"Oh?"

"Take me with you. I've had it with this planet."

"I told you . . ."

Neil handed the money back to him. "That's my price."

Lomax grimaced.

"All right, it's a deal," he said at last.

Neil withdrew all his money from his bank, then parked in a secluded spot, where he and Lomax waited until nightfall.

Then they drove back to the spaceport, where Neil approached the hangar and had them bring his employer's ship out onto the reinforced pavement of the takeoff strip. While the ship's computer was waiting for takeoff clearance, the young man raced out of the cockpit and stopped the first security man he could find.

"Something's wrong!" he panted.

"What?" asked the man.

"Someone's hiding in the cargo compartment of my ship; the computer spotted the extra weight. I just got a glimpse of him. He's dressed all in black."

"You keep away from the ship," the security man instructed him. "We'll take it from here."

Lomax watched from the shadows until he was convinced all the security personnel had surrounded Neil's employer's ship. Then he walked, briskly and silently, to his own ship, where he found the young man waiting at the hatch.

"Nothing to it," grinned Neil as Lomax uttered the proper code words to open the hatch without detonating the security system within the ship.

"Let's go," said Lomax, entering the ship. "The second I activate the ignition, they're going to know they were duped. Grab a seat, strap yourself in, and keep your fingers crossed that no one is approaching on our exit path."

"No one *ever* comes here," said Neil, seating himself in the cramped cockpit. "That's why I want to get the hell out of here."

Lomax fed the coordinates of Olympus into the navigational computer, waited until it had chosen a flight path, then hit the ignition. As he had predicted, it brought all the armed security men back from the other ship, but he managed to take off before they could get off any damaging shots.

"So where are we going?" asked Neil Cayman when they had left the system and achieved light speeds.

"Olympus," answered Lomax.

The young man had the computer cast a cartographic hologram in the air above his seat. "I can't find it," he announced after a moment's scrutiny.

"Try Alpha Hayakawa IV," suggested Lomax.

"Right. Here it is. I wonder why the difference in names?"

"Standard," replied Lomax. "Most of the planets are named after the head of the Pioneer team that opened them up. Roman numerals indicate how far out from the sun it is; any other number tells you how many prior planets the man had opened."

"I don't follow you."

"This is Alpha Hayakawa IV," explained Lomax. "That means it was first charted by a man or woman named Hayakawa, and that it's the fourth planet from a binary sun. But if you look elsewhere, you might also find that it's Jones 39 or Jones 22, which means that it's the thirty-ninth or twenty-second planet opened up by some guy from the Pioneer Corps named Jones." He paused. "And of course, the first thing the settlers did was change the name. Probably it's got some mountain that looks like a holo of Mount Olympus back on Earth, or maybe the first governor was a Greek scholar, or maybe they had a civil war and the general on the winning side was named Olympus."

"It gets confusing, doesn't it?" said Neil. "All these names to learn."

"Even moreso when the native life-forms have their own name for their world," said Lomax with a smile. "You get the hang of it after awhile."

"I *like* the notion of the inhabitants choosing their own name for their world," said Neil. "Now that I'm going out to the Frontier, I want to pick *my* own name."

"You've got one."

"I don't like it. I want something colorful, like Gravedancer or Catastrophe Baker or Cemetery Smith."

"That's your right, I suppose." Lomax converted to autopilot, unstrapped himself, and stood up, stretching his arms.

"You suppose?" asked Neil, following him back to the cargo area, which he had converted into a small lounge, with a pair of comfortable chairs secured to the deck.

Lomax sat down and lit a thin cigar. "If you're any good at anything, usually you'll find someone has picked your name for you, and you're pretty much stuck with it whether you like it or not."

"I could wait a long time," said the young man ruefully as he sat down opposite Lomax. "The only thing I'm really good at is wishing I was somewhere else."

"That's a start."

"It is?"

"Ever hear of Faraway Jones?" asked Lomax.

"No. Who is he?"

"An old man who's probably been to six, seven hundred worlds."

"Is he an explorer?"

"No."

"A cartographer?"

Lomax shook his head. "People say that when he was as young as you are, he fell in love with a girl on Binder X. Nobody knows what happened, but evidently he did something to make her leave him, and he's been hunting for her ever since." Lomax paused. "He must have been searching for her for, oh, close on to seventy years now."

"Do you think she's still alive?" asked Neil dubiously.

"Probably not. Seventy years is a long time for anyone to survive on the Inner Frontier."

"Then why does he keep looking?"

Lomax shrugged. "You'd have to ask him."

"Will I ever see him?"

"Hit enough worlds out there and you'll run into him sooner or later."

"Who else will I see?" asked the young man eagerly.

"I don't know. Who do you *want* to see?"

"Everyone. All the colorful characters I've heard about and read about." He smiled at Lomax. "They all seem so much bigger than life."

Lomax returned the smile. "I know how you feel. When I was your age, I wanted to go out to the Frontier and see all my heroes, too." He paused. "After awhile, you learn that they all bleed and they all die."

"What about the Prophet?"

"Who's he?"

"I don't know. Just someone I heard about on the video."

"This year's outlaw hero," snorted Lomax. "Take my word for it, kid: some bounty hunter will bring him down, just like they brought down Santiago and all the rest of 'em."

"Still, I want to see them all for myself." Neil paused. "You're the only famous person I've ever met."

Lomax smiled ruefully. "Let me tell you, fame isn't everything it's cracked up to be—especially out on the Frontier."

"You say that because you see famous people all the time," protested the young man. "But no one else special has ever come to Greycloud."

"There's nothing very special about pointing a weapon and killing people," said Lomax.

"Sure there is," argued Neil. "How many men can do it?"

"Too damned many."

"Still, I want to go out there and see them for myself."

"You may be disappointed," said Lomax.

"I doubt it."

"What do you think—that there are a couple of thousand worlds out there populated only by killers and folk heroes? Kid, the Inner Frontier is filled with miners and farmers and merchants and doctors and everything else you need to run a planet."

"I know that," said Neil irritably. "But they're not the ones who interest me."

"Something tells me that you'll find all the colorful characters you're looking for." Lomax paused. "Kids like you usually do."

"Maybe I can even become one myself," said Neil, trying to hide his eagerness.

"If you live long enough," said Lomax. "Now let's start taking care of business."

"What business do we have before we reach Olympus?"

"Well, to begin with," said Lomax, "they've probably issued a kidnapping warrant for me. I want you to radio Olympus and tell them you've come with me of your own volition."

"They won't believe me."

"Perhaps not, but I want it on the record."

Neil nodded. "All right."

"And then, since you're going to have to start earning your keep, I want you to go into the galley and make me up some dinner." He paused. "Soya products only. No red meat, no dairy products."

"I don't see how that makes you a better killer," said Neil.

"It makes me a healthier one," responded Lomax. "I've got high blood pressure and a high cholesterol count. No sense letting these control patches I wear do all the work."

The young man smiled. "You're kidding."

"Why should you think so?"

"I just can't imagine the Gravedancer sticking medical patches in his body for that stuff."

An amused smile crossed Lomax's face. "You probably can't imagine that I've got a prosthetic eye and that my current set of teeth is three years old, either."

"Is that true?"

"Kid, there are very few whole men walking around the Inner Frontier," answered Lomax. "Now go send those messages."

Neil activated the radio and spoke briefly to his father, who was alternately distressed and enraged, but finally realized that there was nothing he could do about the situation, and even volunteered to send some money ahead to Olympus, an offer the young man refused.

Then they ate, the young man insisting on having the same bland food as Lomax.

Finally they strapped themselves into the bunks that folded out from the bulkhead in the short corridor between the galley and the cargo area, and went to sleep.

Lomax awoke with a start an hour later.

"Shit!" he muttered.

"What is it?" asked Neil, sitting up abruptly.

"I put us on autopilot, but I forgot to activate the avoidance sensors. We're probably okay, but it'd be just my luck to smash into the only damned meteor within five parsecs."

"I'll take care of it," said Neil, walking to the control panel.

"Wait a minute and I'll hit the lights," said Lomax.

"Not necessary," came the answer.

"Even if you know where the sensor control is, you still have to be able to see it to make the adjustment."

"It's done," said Neil, returning to his cot in total darkness.

"How the hell did you do it?" asked Lomax.

"I thought I told you: I work with computers. I was picking up some parts when I met you."

"So?"

"A couple of years ago I programmed a pair of microchips for infrared vision and had them surgically inserted in my eyes."

"You can really see in the dark?"

"Sure," said Neil.

"Amazing!" muttered Lomax.

"Oh, that's nothing. I've got chips in me that enhance my hearing and my sense of smell, too."

"You designed 'em yourself?"

"It's what I do."

"I suppose if you had to, you could probably design one that would speed up all your reactions," said Lomax.

"Given enough time, I probably could. Why?"

"It might prove useful where you're going."

"You know, it never occurred to me," admitted Neil thoughtfully.

"Well, it's an idea, anyway," said Lomax, lying back down on his cot.

"It's a damned *good* idea, Gravedancer," said Neil. "If I'm going to live on the Frontier, I ought to be ... well, *prepared*."

"Nothing wrong with that," agreed Lomax. "Out here you need any edge you can get. I just went up against a man who had a laser built into a fake finger. Never spotted it. If the fat old man I'm working for hadn't been a little more alert than I was, I wouldn't have lived long enough to get to Greycloud."

"A weapon in a prosthetic finger ..." mused Neil. "*I* could do that." He considered the proposition. "Hell, I could turn my whole body into a killing machine."

"Who do you plan on killing?" asked Lomax.

"No one."

"Then why bother?"

"Because one of these days someone may want to kill *me,* and it's best to be prepared."

"Contrary to what you may have seen on the video, life on the Inner Frontier isn't one prolonged gunfight," said Lomax.

"Yours is."

"My life is like anyone else's in my profession," replied Lomax. "Endless stretches of boredom, punctuated by very brief periods of danger that make you wonder what was so wrong with the boredom in the first place."

"Well, it can't hurt to be prepared," said the young man stubbornly. "After all, you suggested it."

"I know," said Lomax sleepily. "You do what you want to do."

"I'll start designing what I need on the ship's computer in the morning."

"Fine," yawned Lomax. "At least I know what to call you now."

"You do?"

"Yeah. From this day forward, you're the Silicon Kid."

Neil smiled happily in the darkness. "I *like* that!"

"Somehow I thought you might," said Lomax.

4

Olympus was a rugged little world, filled with too many mountains and too little farmland, saltwater oceans that tended to produce tidal waves and freshwater lakes and rivers that tended to dry up every summer. At first view there was no reason why anyone should have wanted to settle there, let alone produce a sprawling megalopolis between two of the larger mountain ranges, but it happened that the planet was almost ideally located between the Democracy and that section of the Inner Frontier dominated by the Binder system. Originally it housed a single Tradertown, but as commerce grew between the Democracy and the worlds of the Inner Frontier, the Tradertown began growing in all directions—including *up*—and one day, without anyone knowing quite how it had happened, it had become a huge city encompassing almost two million humans and perhaps fifty thousand aliens of various races, a shipping and trading center of truly Homeric proportions. There were four spaceports, two orbiting hangars each capable of accommodating more than one thousand ships that were too big or too heavy to land on the planet's surface, and some forty square miles, just to the north of the city, for storing grain that was en route to the Democracy.

The city was named, appropriately enough, Athens, and most of the major thoroughfares bore names taken from *The Iliad* and *The Odyssey*. It possessed many of the conveniences of the Democracy, but despite its size and affluence, it still retained more than a little of the feel of a Tradertown. Gaily costumed miners and gamblers rubbed shoulders with conservatively clad businessmen, grim-faced bounty hunters and killers inhabited the bars and drug dens, entrepreneurs of all types were constantly scheming to share in some of the billions that sat in the vaults of two dozen major and minor banks.

"This is some place, this Olympus!" said the Silicon Kid as he and Lomax rode a slidewalk down one of the main thoroughfares. "Look at these buildings, Gravedancer!"

"They're just buildings," said Lomax with a shrug.

"You aren't impressed?"

"They blot out the sun." Lomax paused. "It looks like any other gateway world."

"Gateway world?"

"Between the Inner Frontier and the Democracy," answered Lomax. "There are about fifty of 'em."

"Well, I've never seen anything like this."

"One world's pretty much like the next," replied Lomax. "This one's a little warm for my taste. Could use a touch more gravity, too."

"I *like* the lighter gravity," enthused the Kid. "I feel like I'm floating." Suddenly he paused. "You have to make adjustments every time the gravity changes, right?"

Lomax nodded. "On a world like this, your tendency is to shoot too high."

"Yeah," mused the Kid. "I hadn't thought of that." Another pause. "Maybe I can come up with some chips that will make all the worlds feel the same to you."

"You come up with a chip like that and you'll never run out of friends," replied Lomax.

"Where are we going?" asked the Kid, watching a monorail race above them.

"To see where Jason Cole used to live."

"He's the guy with the laser in his finger?"

"That's right," said Lomax.

"Then what?"

"Then I ask some questions." Lomax turned to the Silicon Kid. "You don't have to come along. We can make an arrangement to meet somewhere."

"And miss the chance of seeing you in action?" said the Kid, watching a pair of silent hovercrafts race for a single landing space atop a nearby roof. "Not a chance."

"Not much action involved in asking questions."

"What if they don't answer?"

Lomax stepped aside as two young boys raced past him, toy guns blazing. "Cole's dead. Why shouldn't they?"

"Maybe whoever he lived with will be just a little upset that you killed him," answered the Kid.

"I didn't kill him."

"Maybe they won't believe you," said the Kid. "After all, you're the Gravedancer."

Lomax grimaced. "If he lived with anyone, they must have known what kind of work he did." He lit a thin cigar. "In this business, if you go out often enough, there comes a time when you don't return. That's a given."

"I'll come along, anyway," said the Kid. "You just might need some help."

Lomax shrugged. "It's been known to happen."

The Kid frowned as they passed a multi-environmental hotel that seemed to specialize in chlorine-breathers. "You know," he said, "every time I think I've got you pegged, you come up with an answer that throws me."

"Oh?"

"You're the *Gravedancer*! You shouldn't want help from anybody."

"You see enough men get blown to bits and before long you find that you're willing to take all the help you can get," answered Lomax, checking each street sign as they came to it.

"Well, it *seems* wrong."

"I suppose it'd make a lousy video," agreed Lomax with an amused smile.

"It sure as hell would," agreed the Kid seriously.

"Welcome to the real world."

They rode in silence for a few more minutes, until Hector Boulevard crossed Helen Street. Lomax managed the change of slidewalks easily, but had to reach out and steady the Silicon Kid, who had never been on a slidewalk before and almost lost his balance.

"Thanks," muttered the Kid. "That'd be a hell of a way to get killed, my first day on a new world."

"Don't jump," Lomax cautioned. "Just step onto the thin strip of pavement between them with one foot, and then step onto the next slidewalk."

"Stupid way to travel."

"Easier than walking five miles," answered Lomax.

"Do all the Frontier worlds have these things?"

"Hardly any of them do," said Lomax. "Olympus isn't really a Frontier world."

"The charts say it is."

"Oh, it's in the Inner Frontier," agreed Lomax. "But it's too built up, too civilized. The *real* Frontier keeps moving toward the Core, while the Democracy keeps absorbing the worlds on the outskirts."

"That's what I want to see," said the Kid. "The real Inner Frontier."

Lomax jerked his thumb in the direction of a travel agency they were passing. "Be my guest."

"I can wait a few days."

"How comforting." Lomax checked a street number. "We're coming to another change of slidewalks. Get ready."

This time the Kid moved as gracefully as Lomax, and after a short interval they stepped onto the pavement in front of the Hotel Apollo.

"Is this the place?" asked the Kid, looking at the steel and glass structure confronting them.

"If my information is correct," said Lomax.

The Kid grimaced. "Who could live in buildings like this? There's no room to turn around."

Lomax looked amused. "Oh, no more than thirty or forty trillion people. You belong to a race of social animals, Kid."

"Not *me*," answered the Silicon Kid. "Living like this would drive me crazy."

Lomax walked up to the main entrance. The Kid was about to try to step into the lobby, but Lomax reached out a hand and restrained him.

"What's the matter?" asked the Kid.

"Wait," said Lomax. "You're not on Greycloud any longer."

An alien doorman, reddish and mildly humanoid, nodded a pleasant greeting and uttered a single command, dispersing the energy field that protected the entrance.

"Welcome to the Hotel Apollo, the finest hostelry on all of Olympus," it said in heavily accented Terran. "How may I be of assistance to you?"

"We've come to visit a friend," said Lomax.

"Excellent," said the doorman. "Everyone should have friends."

"His name is Jason Cole."

"Alas, Jason Cole is not in residence at this moment."

"We'll wait."

"He has been gone for twenty-three days," answered the doorman. "He may be gone for twenty-three more."

"No problem."

"I am afraid that we empty the lobby every night at midnight," continued the doorman. "You cannot wait here."

"That was never our intention," said Lomax. "We'll wait in his room."

"That is not permitted."

"Sure it is," said Lomax, pulling out a large bankroll and thumbing through it.

"Hardly ever," said the alien.

"You're sure?" asked Lomax, peeling off a pair of bills.

"I am almost certain."

"What a shame," said Lomax, adding a third bill to the two.

"Except on special occasions," answered the alien, grabbing the bills and tucking them into its uniform. "How lucky for you that this is a special occasion."

"What's his room number?"

"I will take you there myself," said the doorman.

"It's not necessary."

"Ah, but it is."

"Why?"

"Because if you do not need my help to gain entrance to Jason Cole's room, then I cannot permit you to wander the corridors of our establishment without supervision."

Lomax smiled. "We'll follow you."

"This way, please," said the alien, waddling off to the airlift. They floated up to the forty-third floor, then emerged into a slow-moving corridor that took them past a number of rooms until they reached the one they wanted and stepped off.

"We are here," it announced, allowing the door's sensors to examine his palm and retina. Finally it uttered a code in its own tongue, and the door dilated, revealing the interior of a small apartment.

"I will leave you now," said the alien. "But I must warn you that I will have our security forces monitor your movements once you emerge from Jason Cole's apartment."

Lomax nodded. "I would expect no less from the finest hostelry on all of Olympus."

The alien bared its teeth in what passed for a grin.

"One question," said Lomax as the alien was about to leave.

"Yes?"

Lomax held up another bank note. "Who is Jason Cole's employer?"

The doorman eyed the note with almost human sadness. "I do not know, sir."

"Pity," said Lomax, putting the bill back into one of his many pockets.

He and the Kid entered the room, and a moment later the door closed behind them.

"Well," he said, "let's see what we can learn about the late Mr. Cole."

Lomax walked into the bedroom and checked the closet. There were two rather gaudy outfits there, and nothing else. The dresser had some undergarments, but three of the four drawers were empty. The bathroom looked like it had never been used; the medicine cabinet was completely bare.

He walked back into the living room, where he found the Kid going through a holodisk library.

"The guy liked pornography," announced the Kid. "If he had any other interests, you can't prove it by what's here."

"You checked the kitchen and the foyer?" asked Lomax.

"Yes."

"What do you find?"

"There's some beer in the kitchen, nothing else; and a pair of thermal garments in the closet. Either this world has a hell of a winter, or he sometimes goes to a planet that's a lot colder than this one."

Lomax double-checked the rooms the Kid had inspected. "As far as I can tell," he said at last, "he just used this as a mailing address, and maybe a place to spend an occasional night when he was on the planet." His gaze fell on a computer screen that was built into the wall. "Okay, let's check his mail." He walked over to the screen. "Computer, activate."

"Activated," replied a metallic voice.

"Please bring up all mail that you've received since I last activated you."

"There are eighty-seven parcels, Mr. Cole."

"Eliminate all advertisements."

"There are two parcels, Mr. Cole."

"Read the oldest of them."

"Working . . . 'Once you have proof that your assignment has been successfully carried out, report to me in person at my office, and payment will be made in the usual way.' "

"Who signed the letter?"

"There is no signature."

"Is there a return address?"

"No."

"Wonderful," muttered Lomax.

"I'm delighted that you are pleased," said the computer.

Lomax grimaced. "Now read the second letter."

"Dear Mr. Cole: This is to inform you that you have exceeded your credit limit of twenty-five hundred credits. Until this has been made good, we can no longer accept your custom. Please make arrangements to have the money transferred to our account #30337, First Planetary Bank of Olympus. Thank you for your prompt attention and payment."

"Is there a signature?"

"The Manager."

"Is there a return address?"

"The Blue Pavilion, 37 Achilles Street."

"Thank you. Deactivate."

"That's our next stop?" asked the Silicon Kid.

"I think so," said Lomax. "Did you notice anything peculiar about the wording of the first letter?"

"Not especially," answered the Kid. "Just that he's done business with this guy before."

"It sounded *formal*," said Lomax. "Like whoever wrote it is a businessman and makes this kind of assignment all the time."

"Probably he does," answered the Kid. "After all, killing's a business, just like any other."

Lomax shook his head. "That's not what I meant."

"Then I don't follow you."

"I have a feeling that my employer is up against a very professional organization," said Lomax, "the kind of organization that authorizes killings every day. Payment will be made in 'the usual way,' from some guy's *office*? That's the *last* place you'd want a killer to show up for his money—unless your primary business is hiring killers."

"That still doesn't tell us whether this guy is a middleman, or whether he's the one who initiated the assignment."

"I know."

"So what do we do now?" asked the Kid.

"Let's find out what Cole knew."

"How do we do that?"

"If we're lucky, we just ask the computer." Lomax turned back to the screen. "Computer, activate."

"Activated."

"Please bring up the last letter I posted from this address."

"Working . . . 'Tell the Anointed One I accept the assignment, for the usual price.' "

Lomax frowned. "The Anointed One?"

"That is correct."

"What is the address on the letter?"

"Electronic mailbox #804432J."

"In whose name is it registered?"

"Working . . . I am unable to retrieve that information, Mr. Cole. The owner of the box has asked that his name be unlisted."

"Is there any way I can find out who owns it?"

"If you are a legitimate creditor, you can go to Claims Court and fill out a Form 86-F. After an appropriate investigation, the authorities will release the name to you."

"There's no faster way?"

"No, Mr. Cole."

"Thank you, computer. Deactivate."

"The Anointed One?" repeated the Kid as the screen went dark. "You ever hear of anyone with that name?"

"Never."

"What about your employer?"

"He'd have told me if he'd ever come across it."

There was a momentary silence, which was finally broken by the Silicon Kid.

"Now we go to the Blue Pavilion?" he asked.

Lomax nodded his agreement. "Now we go to the Blue Pavilion."

5

The Blue Pavilion was a nightclub atop one of the taller buildings in the city. An enormous glass wall, some forty feet high, afforded a breathtaking view of Mount Olympus; the other three walls were covered with mirrors that reflected the deep blue sky, the mountain, and the huge pool that dominated the middle of the club.

The pool itself was filled with a dozen dolphin-like creatures that had been imported from Sylestria II; they were thought to be sentient, but as yet no common language had been developed, and, in common with all aquatic species, their inability to work with fire had hindered any attempts they might have made to develop a recognizable technology. Still, they were capable of intricate maneuvers that seemed almost like precision dancing, and just about the time the audience was becoming bored or jaded, twelve nude girls dove into the water, climbed aboard the creatures, and rode them as they performed yet another water ballet.

There was a long chrome bar on one side of the room, and a number of tables, most of them filled with patrons who were dressed more for show than for comfort. Obviously the Blue Pavilion was a place to see and be seen.

Waiters and waitresses, all in elegant silken outfits, moved rapidly about the room, filling empty glasses, taking orders, occasionally bringing out dinners as well as drinks. A six-piece orchestra hovered above the pool, their glittering platform floating in midair.

As Lomax and the Silicon Kid walked up to the entrance, a tall, formally clad man approached them.

"May I be of service to you, gentlemen?" he said, his expression displaying his disapproval of their clothing.

"We'd like a table, please," said Lomax.

"I'm afraid we have no available tables this evening."

"There are five empty tables," said Lomax.

"All reserved."

Lomax pulled out a hundred-credit note. "Not too close to the pool," he said.

"I'm afraid it's out of the question," said the man.

"Hey, this is the Gravedancer you're talking to!" snapped the Kid.

"I am aware of his identity," answered the man calmly. He turned to Lomax. "Your reputation precedes you, Mr. Lomax."

"Please excuse my friend," said Lomax, adding two more notes to the original one. "He's new to your world."

"You really must teach him some manners, Mr. Lomax," said the man, taking the bank notes and leading them to an empty table near the bar.

As they were being seated, Lomax laid three more notes on the table.

"We could use a little information," he said.

The man eyed the notes, then bowed deeply. "If it's mine to give."

"I gather that Jason Cole used to frequent this place."

"That's correct, sir," said the man, reaching for the notes.

Lomax covered the notes with his hand. "I know that," he said. "I need to know who he used to meet here."

The man looked nervously at the money. "I would love to help you, Mr. Lomax, but . . ."

Lomax added three more notes to the pile.

The man looked again, then sighed and shook his head. "He would probably kill me if I pointed him out to you. I'd love to do business with you, Mr. Lomax, but I'd love to wake up tomorrow morning even more."

"Tell you what," said Lomax, picking up the pile of notes and placing them into the man's hand. "You tell him that I know Jason Cole and I'd like to speak to him, and let *him* decide whether to come over and talk to me. Will that get you off the hook?"

"Admirably," said the man, pocketing the money. He signaled to a waitress, who immediately approached the table.

"What can I get you gentlemen to drink?" she asked as the maître d' walked off.

"Champagne," said the Kid.

"Champagne for him, fruit juice for me," said Lomax.

"What type?"

Lomax shrugged. "Whatever's available."

"You don't drink, either?" asked the Kid as the waitress walked away.

"Not when I'm working."

"I think it's almost criminal, coming to a place like this and *not* having a drink."

"You just watch the naked ladies and leave the thinking to me."

"I've *been* watching them," said the Kid. "We don't allow nudity on Greycloud. Is it common on the Frontier?"

"It varies from world to world," answered Lomax. "There are even a couple of colony worlds run by nudists."

"I'd like to see them."

Lomax shrugged. "Take it from me: most people look better with their clothes on."

"Still . . ."

"You do what you want. No one's keeping you here."

"Why do I get the feeling that you're trying to get rid of me?"

"Look," said Lomax. "I brought you here. That ought to be enough. Any minute now it could start getting dangerous."

"I can take care of myself," said the Kid. "You don't have to protect me."

"I have no intention of protecting you," said Lomax. "I just don't want you getting in my way."

"That's a hell of a thing to say," replied the Kid, more than half seriously. "I thought we were supposed to be friends."

"Friends aren't compatible with the business I'm in."

"What about the man you're working for?" persisted the Kid. "You make *him* sound like a friend."

"The Iceman? He's me thirty-five or forty years from now. If I survive."

"The *Iceman*?" repeated the Kid. "You're working for *him*?"

"Yeah."

"Why does he need you? He's the man who beat the Oracle!"

"He's an old man now, with a bum leg. If it's his leg at all; my guess is that it's prosthetic." Lomax paused. "And according to him, he didn't beat her. He seems to think he was lucky to come out of it alive."

"No, he beat her!" said the Kid firmly. "Everyone knows the story." He could barely contain his enthusiasm. "Just think of it—the *Iceman*! What I wouldn't give to meet him! Are all the other stories they tell about him true?"

"Probably not."

"They say he killed Three-Fisted Charlie, and that he found the Soothsayer when hundreds of bounty hunters couldn't, and—"

"Lower your voice and calm down," said Lomax in amused tones. "Or the band just might sue you for unfair competition."

"I'm sorry," said the Kid. "But the Iceman! He's one of my heroes." He paused. "What is he like?"

"He's a fat, balding old man with a limp," said Lomax. "But I'll give him this: he's sharp. He doesn't miss a trick."

"Why are you working for him? I would think that of all the men on the Frontier, the Iceman would be the last to hire someone like you."

"People get old, Kid. Even the Iceman."

The waitress returned with their drinks, and a moment later the maître d' approached them.

"I delivered your message, Mr. Lomax."

"And?"

The man shrugged. "And now it's up to the gentleman you wish to speak to."

Lomax nodded. "All right. You did your part."

"One more thing, Mr. Lomax."

"Yeah?"

"We are civilized people here, and Olympus is a civilized planet. The law is enforced very strictly here. If there is to be violence, it would be most unfortunate for all parties concerned if it were to occur in the Blue Pavilion." He looked meaningfully at the security cameras, which were clearly visible above each table.

"I'll keep that in mind."

"Thank you, Mr. Lomax."

The man retreated toward the kitchen, and Lomax took a sip of his juice, then made a face.

"Is something wrong?" asked the Kid.

"I've tasted this before," said Lomax. "Some kind of mutated citrus from the Altair system. It probably costs more than your champagne, but I can't stand the stuff." He pushed the glass to the middle of the table. "You want it?"

The Kid shook his head. "I'll stick with what I've got, thanks."

"That's up to you," said Lomax.

The Kid downed half his glass in a single swallow. "Good stuff."

"You ever drink champagne before?"

"Sure," said the Kid defensively. "Lots of times."

"Yeah, I could tell by the way you gulped it down." Suddenly Lomax tensed. "Take a walk, Kid."

"What?"

"You heard me."

"Why? What's going on?"

"I think I'm about to have a visitor," said Lomax, staring at a dapper, middle-aged man who was making his way across the floor toward their table.

"I'd rather stay."

Lomax stared at him. "All right. But you don't say a word, you don't contradict anything I say, and you don't make any sudden movements."

"You got it."

Lomax studied the man as he approached them. He was of medium height and build, with meticulously groomed gray hair and mustache, pale blue eyes, and an aquiline nose. There was a bulge in his pocket that he made no attempt to hide, but if it was a weapon, it looked like it would be very difficult to withdraw it without a great deal of fumbling around.

"You are Mr. Lomax?" asked the man, coming to a stop behind an empty chair.

"That's right. And this is my associate, Mr. . . . ."

"The Silicon Kid," interjected the young man.

"I don't believe I've heard of you, sir," said the man.

"You will," responded the Kid.

"I am Milo Korbekkian. May I sit down?"

"Please do," said Lomax.

Korbekkian seated himself. "Do you mind if I smoke?"

"Be my guest."

The dapper man lit up a thin cigar, and Lomax wrinkled his nose.

"It contains a mild stimulant," explained Korbekkian. "The odor is an unfortunate side effect. I can put it out if you wish."

"Suit yourself," said Lomax. "I can stand it if you can."

"Then, with your kind permission, I shall continue to smoke." Korbekkian leaned forward slightly. "I understand that you are an acquaintance of Jason Cole's?"

"That's right."

"Dear Jason," said Korbekkian, signaling to a passing waiter to bring him a drink. "The last I heard of him he was leaving for some little world on the Inner Frontier." He paused. "How is he getting along?"

"About as well as most corpses, I suppose."

"Poor boy," said Korbekkian with no show of surprise or regret.

"You should never send a boy to do a man's job," continued Lomax.

"Oh?"

"He never had a chance against the Iceman." Lomax stared into his eyes. "Neither did the other three you sent."

"What other three?" asked Korbekkian innocently, as his drink arrived.

"Mr. Korbekkian, we're never going to come to a satisfactory arrangement unless we put our cards on the table. I know you've sent four men to kill the Iceman. I know that all four are buried on Last Chance."

"Assuming that I *did* send four men out there, why should the notorious Gravedancer—if I may use your professional sobriquet—come all the way to Olympus to tell me that they've failed?"

"You can keep wasting your money sending cannon fodder out after the Iceman," said Lomax. "Or," he added, "you can buy the best, and get the job accomplished."

The Silicon Kid seemed about to say something, but Lomax stared him down.

"I see," said Korbekkian, finally lifting his drink to his lips and downing it in a single swallow. "You have come seeking employment."

"I've come to discuss the matter," replied Lomax. "I don't come cheap."

"No, I imagine you don't." He placed his glass down on the table and stared intently at it.

"On the other hand, you've seen what happens to those who do."

"A telling point, Mr. Lomax," agreed Korbekkian, looking across the table at Lomax. "A telling point indeed." He paused. "How much would you require, and when could you be ready to leave?"

"I'll want two million credits, or its equivalent in Maria Theresa dollars," said Lomax. "And I'll be ready to leave as soon as I've spoken to the Anointed One."

Lomax studied him carefully for a reaction—surprise that he knew the name of Korbekkian's employer, shock, fear, anything—but the man's face was an emotionless mask.

"That may be difficult to arrange, Mr. Lomax."

"No more difficult than terminating the Iceman, I'll venture," responded Lomax.

"The Anointed One does not like to be directly involved in such matters."

"I don't like dealing with middlemen."

"I assure you that I am far more than a middleman," said Korbekkian.

"What are your assurances worth?" asked Lomax.

"I don't believe I understand you, Mr. Lomax."

"If I deal directly with you, my fee is three million," said Lomax. "Now, is ten minutes of the Anointed One's time worth a million credits or not?"

Korbekkian stared at him for a long moment. "Why do you wish to see him?"

"I have my reasons."

"I will be happy to transmit them to him."

Lomax shook his head. "That's not the way I do business."

"May I give you a piece of friendly advice, Mr. Lomax?"

"I'm always happy to get advice," replied Lomax easily.

"If I were you, I would not make any demands or set any conditions that might annoy the Anointed One," said Korbekkian. "Even someone as accomplished as yourself cannot withstand his anger."

"I'm a lot more accomplished than the Iceman, and *he's* withstood it pretty well," noted Lomax.

"He is a minor irritant who probably does not even know of the Anointed One's existence," answered Korbekkian. "He lives on the Inner Frontier, and his influence on events is absolutely minimal."

"Then why have you gone to such lengths to have him killed?"

"That, Mr. Lomax, is none of your business."

"If I accept the Anointed One's commission, it is," said Lomax.

Korbekkian put out his cigar and immediately lit up another one.

"I do not think we can do business, Mr. Lomax," he said at last.

"Of course we can," said Lomax. "You just take my message to the Anointed One and bring me his answer."

Korbekkian shook his head. "I don't think so, Mr. Lomax. You ask too many questions, you make too many demands."

"I can be very demanding when it's my life that will be on the line," responded Lomax. "If the Iceman was easy to kill, he'd be dead by now."

"I don't see what killing the Iceman has to do with meeting the Anointed One," said Korbekkian irritably.

"You don't have to," answered Lomax. "*I* see it, and that's enough."

"I very much doubt that he'll speak to you, Mr. Lomax."

"Yes, he will."

Korbekkian made no attempt to hide his curiosity. "What makes you so certain, Mr. Lomax?"

"Because you're going to tell him that if he doesn't, I just might offer my services to the Iceman."

Korbekkian stared at him expressionlessly for a long minute. "Where can I get in touch with you?"

"Right here, tomorrow night."

The dapper man stood up. "I'll have an answer for you at that time."

He turned on his heel and walked out of the Blue Pavilion.

"You're not really going to hire on to kill the Iceman?" said the Kid.

"Don't be stupid."

"Then why didn't you kill him right here?"

Lomax smiled. "I promised the maître d' that we wouldn't get any blood on the tablecloths."

"What's to stop us from following him out right now and blowing him away?"

"Nothing but common sense," answered Lomax. "He's just a hireling. If I take him out, this Anointed One will just find someone else to hire his killers."

"So what do we do now?"

"I stay here and enjoy the show."

"What about me?"

"You?" said Lomax. "You take your see-in-the-dark eyes and follow Mr. Korbekkian."

"Where do I follow him *to*?" asked the Kid.

Lomax shrugged. "To wherever he's going."

"Then what?"

"Then remember how to find it, in case the Anointed One decides not to meet with me."

The Kid left the club, and Lomax, feeling he had put in a useful evening, settled back to watch the entertainment.

6

It was just after sunrise when the hotel room's vidphone began buzzing.

Lomax sat up, swung his feet to the side of the bed, and ordered the machine to activate. An instant later a holograph of Milo Korbekkian stared out at him.

"Good morning, Mr. Lomax."

"How did you find me?" asked Lomax. "I didn't use my real name when I checked in."

"I have my sources."

"What's up? I thought we were meeting at the Blue Pavilion tonight."

"That won't be necessary. I have spoken to him, and he has agreed to see you, Mr. Lomax."

"When?"

"I'll pick you up in front of your hotel at noon, precisely," said Korbekkian. "*Just* you; no one else. Have your luggage with you. You will not be returning."

"He's not on Olympus?"

"Just be ready, Mr. Lomax."

"Right," said Lomax.

"One more thing, Mr. Lomax," said Korbekkian.

"What is it?"

"I do not appreciate being followed. If your companion ever attempts to do so again, I cannot be held responsible for what happens to him."

Lomax allowed himself the luxury of a smile. "He's very young."

"If he wants to get older, he had best heed what I just said."

"I'll pass your message on to him." Lomax paused. "Do you want him to remain on Olympus?"

"Whether he stays on Olympus or not is of no import to me, Mr. Lomax. But he cannot accompany us."

Lomax nodded. "I'll see you at noon."

"At noon," echoed Korbekkian, breaking the connection.

Lomax got up, walked into the bathroom, took a brief shower, ran a comb through his hair, and began getting dressed. When he was finished, he left his room, took the airlift down two levels, rode the corridor to the Kid's room, and knocked at the door.

"Open," said the Kid's voice, and the door slid back.

"Good morning," said Lomax, walking into the room.

"Good morning," answered the Kid, who was fully dressed and watching a holographic video. He commanded the set to deactivate. "Was the address I gave you last night any use to you?"

"Not yet," said Lomax. He stared at the Kid. "You were spotted."

"Impossible!" said the Kid. "I was never within a hundred yards of him. I'll swear he never saw me!"

"Probably it was one of his bodyguards, then."

"He has bodyguards?" said the Kid, surprised. "I never saw any."

Lomax smiled. "They're the best kind."

"He told you that?"

Lomax nodded.

"When?" asked the Kid.

"He called me about ten minutes ago."

"How did he find you? We're using phony names."

"Olympus is his home world," replied Lomax. "If he wasn't good enough to find us, he wouldn't have lasted this long at his job."

The Kid stared at Lomax for a moment, then spoke. "So what's the story?" he asked. "Are we going to meet the Anointed One?"

"*I* am."

"What about me?"

"Korbekkian says no."

"What am I, then—a hostage?"

Lomax chuckled. "He doesn't need a hostage. He has *me*."

"Then what do I do?"

Lomax stared at him for a moment. "Do you really want to get involved in this, Kid?"

"I *am* involved."

"If you wanted to back out, this would be a good time," said Lomax. "Right now you're a civilian. You stay in, you become a warrior, and you're fair game."

"I'm in," said the Kid firmly.

"Okay," said Lomax. "Let's get some breakfast and discuss it."

They left the room, took the airlift down to the mezzanine level, and walked over to a small restaurant. The Kid ordered a full breakfast, while Lomax contented himself with a cup of coffee and a roll.

"I never saw a restaurant like this!" enthused the Kid, referring to the holographic representations of the various dishes that hovered above the table. "This is really interesting."

"Commonplace," said Lomax. "What you saw last night—printed menus and live waiters—is the rarity."

Their meal was conveyed to their table on an automated cart that waited until they had removed all their dishes, then rolled back to the kitchen.

"Well," said the Kid, "let's get down to business."

"Just a minute," said Lomax, pulling a small oblong mechanism out of one of his pockets.

"What's that?" asked the Kid.

"Just a scrambler," answered Lomax, activating it by pressing a small button. "There are security devices all over the main floor here," he continued, jerking his head in the direction of a camera that was positioned in a corner of the restaurant. "If anyone's trying to listen to us, this will stop them."

"You think someone's trying to monitor us?"

Lomax shrugged. "Who knows?" He paused. "You'll live a lot longer if you assume the worst and try to prepare for it."

"I'll remember that," said the Kid.

"See that you do." Lomax looked around casually, scanning the faces of passersby, trying to match them with anyone he had seen at the Blue Pavilion the night before. Finally he turned back to the Kid. "You're sure you want to get involved? There's still time for you to walk away from this."

"Not a chance," said the Kid.

"All right," said Lomax, taking a sip of his coffee. "There's nothing further to be learned on Olympus, so there's no reason for you to wait for me here."

"What do you want me to do?"

"You always wanted to meet the Iceman, didn't you?" said Lomax. "I want you to go to Last Chance and deliver a message."

"I want to meet him, sure," said the Kid. "But it sounds like you're sending me there just to make me feel useful. Why can't you just send it via subspace radio?"

"Personally, I don't give a damn whether you feel useful or not," answered Lomax seriously. "I'm sending you in person because it will almost certainly cost me my life if it's intercepted. Is that reason enough for you?"

"What's the message?" asked the Kid.

"I want you to tell him that no matter what he hears, I'm still working for him."

"What is he likely to hear?"

"If he hears anything at all, it'll be that the Anointed One hired me to kill him."

"Why should he believe me?"

Lomax took a ring off the little finger of his left hand. "Give him this. He knows it belongs to me."

"All right," said the Kid. He stared across the table at Lomax. "More to the point, why should he believe *you*?"

"Damned good question," admitted Lomax.

"Have you got an answer?"

Lomax grimaced. "Not really," he said at last.

"Sounds to me like you could have a problem on your hands," offered the Kid.

Lomax sighed deeply. "That's what I get paid for overcoming." He finished his roll and got to his feet. "I've got a couple of things to do. I'll pay for your room through noon; if you stay any longer, it comes out of your pocket."

"What about the hangar and exit fees?"

"I'll take care of them," answered Lomax. "I'll see you around, Kid."

"Right."

Lomax held a credit cube up to a scanner, waited until it registered, and then left the restaurant. He settled his bill at the hotel desk, then stopped by a vidphone and took care of the charges at the spaceport.

Then he checked the directory, paid a connect fee for the main branch of the planetary library, and accessed the newstape division.

"Bring up any information concerning the Anointed One," he ordered.

"There are six articles about the Anointed One, dating from 3445 G.E. to the present."

"Give me hard copies of all six."

"That will be an extra fee of 24 credits, 16.2 New Stalin rubles, or 4.78 Far London pounds. If your home bank deals in any other currency, there will be a three percent conversion fee. Do you accept the charges?"

"I do."

"Working . . . done."

The six articles emerged from a slot beneath the screen, and Lomax broke the connection.

He found a comfortable chair in a corner of the lobby, sat down, and started reading them.

The earliest mention of the Anointed One identified him as the leader of a small religious cult, far out on the Rim. He had been arrested for murdering one of his subordinates, but the case was dismissed for lack of evidence, when the two eyewitnesses disappeared.

Five months later he had moved his base of operations to the Spiral Arm, not that far from Earth itself, and now the Democracy was after him for the nonpayment of 163 million credits in taxes.

A year later he had set up temples and "recruiting stations" on some twenty planets in the heart of the Democracy and was said to have a following numbering in the millions. No mention was made of the disposition of the tax suit.

The final three articles, each spaced a month apart, concerned politicians and other public figures speaking out against the Anointed One, his sect's supposed excesses, his refusal to pay taxes (again), and his growing power. In the most recent article, there was a list of five people who had publicly opposed him and had since vanished.

There was no holograph or photograph of the Anointed One, nor any information or even conjecture about his origins. Lomax was mildly surprised that he hadn't heard about a man with such a large organization, but of course that organization had started on the Rim and had spread only to the Democracy, not yet reaching those worlds toward the Galactic Core that formed the Inner Frontier, and the men and women of the Frontier paid scant attention to those developments that didn't directly affect them.

The *real* question, decided Lomax, was not how the Anointed One had gathered such power so quickly, but rather what the Iceman, a saloon owner on an obscure Frontier world who himself hadn't set foot on a Democracy world in almost three decades, had done to attract the attention—and the obvious enmity—of a man who had yet to get within five thousand light-years of the Inner Frontier.

Lomax checked his timepiece, saw that he still had a couple of hours before he had to meet Korbekkian, and strolled out into the cool, crisp Olympus morning. He walked aimlessly for a few blocks, pausing to look at a window here, a holographic display there, a street vendor selling exquisite alien stone carvings, a psychic forecasting the fall of the Democracy, a street musician of an unknown race playing an atonal but haunting melody on a string instrument of strange design.

He stopped at a weapon shop, studied their display with an expert eye, saw nothing superior to his own armaments, and finally began walking back to his hotel. He noted with approval that Olympus, like most Inner Frontier worlds, disdained most of the new nanotechnology of the Democracy, and swept its streets with sleek machines rather than using the new dirt-eating microbes that had been developed on Deluros VIII.

He reached the hotel about twenty minutes before noon, had a quick cup of coffee, and stood just inside the front entrance. A few moments later a splendid, late-model groundcar pulled up. The door opened, and Milo Korbekkian summoned him with a gesture.

"Good morning, Mr. Lomax," said Korbekkian as Lomax entered the vehicle.

"Good morning."

"I assume you had the good sense to tell your young companion not to follow us."

"He's light-years from here by now."

"He had better be. We have your ship's registration number, and if we should encounter it during our voyage, we will not hesitate to blow it to pieces. Is that understood?"

"It's understood," said Lomax, leaning back on the plush seat.

"Have you any questions?" asked Korbekkian as his driver pulled the vehicle away from the hotel and into the light morning traffic.

"I'll ask them as I think of them."

"You will be thoroughly scanned before boarding my ship, and any weapons you are carrying will be confiscated." He paused. "If you reach an accommodation with the Anointed One, they will be returned to you."

"Fair enough."

"I think we understand each other," said Korbekkian with a satisfied smile.

"No reason why we shouldn't, Mr. Korbekkian," answered Lomax. "After all, we're going to be on the same team."

"I sincerely hope so," said Korbekkian. "I would relish working with a man of your qualifications."

"I think I can say the same about your boss."

Korbekkian looked idly at the oncoming traffic. "What do you know about the Anointed One?" he asked at last.

"Just what I managed to learn from the newstapes," said Lomax.

"I wouldn't believe everything I read in the public press, Mr. Lomax," said Korbekkian.

"No?"

"Definitely not."

"Does that mean he pays his taxes?" asked Lomax with a smile.

Korbekkian turned to Lomax. "One does not joke about the Anointed One, Mr. Lomax. The press doesn't begin to understand what they're dealing with."

"I got the impression that they thought he was a pretty powerful man, if not an altogether desirable or law-abiding one."

"If I told you the true extent of his political and financial power, Mr. Lomax, you would think me either a fool or a liar."

"It's possible," agreed Lomax pleasantly.

"If you believe nothing else I tell you, believe this, Mr. Lomax," said Korbekkian. "You would be wrong." He paused. "Dead wrong."

7

Lomax had been confined to his quarters aboard the ship, and hence had no idea of how many multiples of the speed of light they were traveling or how far they had gone, when the ship finally touched down.

"We have arrived, Mr. Lomax," announced Korbekkian, unlocking his door. "Please do exactly as you are instructed once we leave the ship."

"What about my weapons?"

"They will be returned to you after your interview."

"Your boss may want to see if I know how to use them."

Korbekkian smiled. "You are the Gravedancer. That is sufficient."

Lomax shrugged and walked out of his cabin.

"What's the gravity here?"

"Ninety-seven point two percent Standard. You will require no protective outfit, no breathing apparatus, no stimulants or depressants."

"I assume that if you wanted me to know what world I was on, you'd have told me," remarked Lomax.

"That is correct."

"Well, let's get going."

"Follow me, please."

Korbekkian led him to the hatch, and a moment later he found himself standing on a bleak, sun-baked patch of ground. There were enormous sand dunes in the distance, and the wind created reddish dust devils near the horizon. The air was hot and dry. It may or may not have been a desert world—probably there was an ocean somewhere, for the air had a fair oxygen content—but there was no question that he was in the middle of a desert, one that extended in every direction as far as the eye could see.

"You'll adjust to the heat," said Korbekkian. "If you should begin feeling light-headed, let me know."

"Where are we going?" asked Lomax. "It looks awfully empty."

"We're going to meet the Anointed One," answered Korbekkian. "Please bear with me, Mr. Lomax. Our transportation will arrive shortly."

Lomax moved out of the direct sunlight into the shadow of the ship and lit a small cigar. When it was half done, a sleek armored vehicle approached them, coming to a stop about ten yards away.

Korbekkian gestured Lomax to enter the vehicle, then joined him. It immediately took off at high speed, and Lomax settled back and relaxed, watching the seemingly endless desert landscape go by. Neither Korbekkian nor the driver said a word, and the silent journey continued for the better part of thirty minutes, at which time the vehicle suddenly slowed down and came to a stop.

Korbekkian and Lomax got out, and the vehicle immediately sped away.

"I take it we're here, wherever *here* is," said Lomax.

"That's right, Mr. Lomax."

Lomax stood, hands on hips, and surveyed his surroundings. They were at an oasis, whether natural or man-made he could not tell. There was a large tent some thirty yards away, made of a metallic fabric that seemed to soak up the sunlight and reflect it back in all the colors of the spectrum. Each time a breeze would pass over it, the colors would change, deepen, combine and then separate again, as if the tent itself were some kind of giant prism.

The tent was surrounded by some two dozen armed guards, each with identical sonic rifles but possessing no common uniform. About a mile to the west, on a flat strip of sun-baked ground that ran between two small dunes, was a large building, though Lomax could not tell if it was a garage or a hangar. There was no landing strip, but the ground was so flat and hard that he suspected none was really required. Atop the building was a very tall, cylindrical antenna, the sign of a subspace sending and receiving station, which was doubtless tied into the nearby tent.

"I expected something a little more elaborate," commented Lomax.

"This is only one of some fifty outposts we have throughout the Democracy and the Inner Frontier," answered Korbekkian. "It is merely a convenience." He paused. "I would be surprised if the Anointed One spends as much as three days a year at this location."

Lomax made no reply.

"Let's move to the shade of a tree, Mr. Lomax," said Korbekkian. "There's no reason why we shouldn't be comfortable while awaiting your audience."

"Makes sense to me," said Lomax, following Korbekkian as the latter sought out a shady spot beneath the sparse branches of a desert tree that grew a few feet from the water.

"Not that we shall have to wait long," added Korbekkian after a moment's silence.

"Oh?"

"I'm sure he will want to conclude your interview in time for us to depart from the planet before dark." He smiled. "There's no sense giving you a chance to see the stellar configurations and possibly determine where you are."

"I plan to be working for him long before dark," answered Lomax.

"I certainly hope so. I'm tired of sending overrated incompetents against the Iceman. The man should have been dead two months ago."

A young woman emerged from the tent and approached them.

"He will see you now," she said.

"Good," said Korbekkian, starting forward.

"Just Mr. Lomax," she added.

Korbekkian turned to him. "Good luck. I hope when you emerge that we are on the same team."

Lomax followed her to the doorway of the tent, where she stopped and turned to him.

"You will address him as 'My Lord,' " she said. "Because you are not yet a member of the faith, you will not be required to kneel before him," she continued. "You will bow when you are introduced, and you will never turn your back to him, and will back out of the tent when your meeting is concluded. Do you understand?"

"I understand," answered Lomax.

"Then enter," said the woman, stepping aside.

Lomax lowered his head and stepped through the doorway, where he was immediately greeted by two burly men who wore loose-fitting outfits of some gleaming metallic fabric. They indicated that he should walk between them, and they escorted him through another doorway to the inner section of the tent.

The floors were covered with exquisitely woven rugs from a dozen worlds, and the walls, composed of a titanium alloy which made the room virtually impervious to assault, displayed paintings and holograms from human and alien worlds. There was a faint scent of incense in the air, and the soft melody of an exotic alien symphony emanated from a silver cube that hovered a few feet above the floor near one of the holograms.

In the middle of the room was a jeweled chair, and upon it sat a tall, ascetic man with an aquiline nose, high protruding cheekbones, and large, coal-black eyes. He wore a robe of white, and around his neck hung a single gold chain, from which were suspended a number of jeweled religious charms.

Sitting next to the chair was a huge animal, basically feline in character, possessed of sleek, rolling muscles, wicked-looking claws, and enormous fangs. Its green eyes narrowed as Lomax approached, and it began uttering a series of deep growls. The man in the white robe uttered a sharp command, and the animal lay down, still glaring at the bounty hunter.

When Lomax finally came to a halt a few feet away, the man in the white robe stood up.

"Welcome to my humble quarters," he said in a rich, deep voice. "I am Moses Mohammed Christ, known to true believers as the Anointed One."

"I'm pleased to meet you, My Lord," answered Lomax, bowing deeply at the waist.

"Does my pet disturb you?"

"Not if he's a pet."

"No one else may approach him without losing a limb," said the Anointed One, gently stroking the creature's head. "But as you see, I touch him with impunity."

"So I see," said Lomax.

"If I were to tell him to attack you, he would tear your throat out in less than a second," continued the Anointed One.

"Perhaps," agreed Lomax. "But if you told him to attack me, who will you get to kill the Iceman for you?"

The Anointed One smiled. "I like you, Mr. Lomax."

"Thank you, My Lord."

The smile vanished. "Why do you wish to kill Carlos Mendoza?"

"I don't especially want to kill him," replied Lomax. "Killing people is dangerous work. I'd be just as happy to take a million credits from you not to kill him . . . but I don't suppose you'd care to pay me for not working, would you?"

"This is not a matter for levity, Mr. Lomax," said the Anointed One sternly, and the feline creature, sensing his anger, fidgeted uneasily. "It is essential that Carlos Mendoza be eliminated."

"Why?"

"That is none of your concern."

"Before I accept a commission, I always like to know *why* I'm being asked to kill someone."

"Thus far you have accepted commissions only from normal men."

"And you are not a normal man?"

The Anointed One opened his mouth. "Between my teeth is the space." He pointed to his ear. "On my left ear is the mole, on my right shoulder is the birthmark. I was born on the fourth day of the fourth month, and the sun was hidden by the moon. There can be no doubt that I am the Anointed One."

"Meaning no disrespect, My Lord," said Lomax, "but granting that you are the Anointed One, just what exactly does that mean?"

"I am he whom the race of Man has awaited for lo, these many eons. It is my destiny to unite the race, to bring order out of chaos, to expand Man's dominion to the farthest reaches of the galaxy."

"I thought the Democracy was doing just that."

"I forgive you your disrespect, for you are not yet a true believer," said the Anointed One. "But know that the Democracy is merely my forerunner, that now that I have arrived upon the scene, the Democracy's days are numbered. God has chosen me to be His conduit to the race of Man, to rule them as He wishes them ruled. Do you see the throne upon which I sit?"

"Yes."

The Anointed One's face took on a fanatical glow. "God has instructed me to rule the galaxy from this throne, to bring it with me to Sirius V and to Earth and ultimately to place it in a palace that I will build upon Deluros VIII, from which I shall finally fulfill my destiny and rule His vast domain."

"It sounds as if you've got your work cut out for you," said Lomax noncommittally.

"I am closer to completion of the Almighty's design than you might think," replied the Anointed One with absolute conviction. "More than two hundred worlds have already pledged their allegiance to me, and even as we speak, my followers are converting the masses upon thousands more."

"Why should a man who controls hundreds of worlds and tens of millions of followers, and who plans to take over the capital world of the Democracy, be concerned with a tavern owner far out at the edge of the Inner Frontier?" asked Lomax, honestly curious. "What kind of threat can the Iceman possibly present to you?"

"Mendoza?" repeated the Anointed One. "He himself presents no threat at all."

"Then why do you want him dead?"

"I told you before: it is not your concern."

"Perhaps not—but if you want me to kill him, you're going to have to tell me."

"Do you dare give orders to Moses Mohammed Christ?" demanded the Anointed One.

"No, My Lord," said Lomax, bowing once again. "Please be assured that I meant no offense." He paused. "I thought we could do business together. I was mistaken."

The Anointed One stared long and hard at Lomax. "Why should I believe that you can kill him when so many others have failed?"

"First, because I'm the best there is," answered Lomax promptly. "And second, because I've been to Last Chance before. My presence won't alert him."

"I can hire other men who have been to Last Chance."

"True," agreed Lomax. "But Last Chance is the Iceman's world, and he's well protected. They won't be able to kill him." He paused. "*I* will."

The Anointed One placed a fist to his chin and stared at Lomax again, even longer this time. Finally he spoke.

"If you carry out this assignment successfully," he said slowly, as if weighing each word, "there will be others. You will find that I can be as generous when rewarding success as I can be unforgiving when dealing with failure." He paused. "Because you cannot yet comprehend the true extent of my power, and because you are not yet conversant in the ways of the One Faith, and because Carlos Mendoza must die, I shall forgive you your transgression this one time, and tell you what you want to know."

"Thank you, My Lord."

"But thereafter, should you fulfill your commission, you will never question an order or an assignment again," continued the Anointed One. "Is that clear?"

"Perfectly, My Lord."

"Then listen closely, for I will not repeat myself," said the Anointed One. "Eventually the Democracy will yield to my will. Even the billion ships of its vaunted Navy will be unable to oppose me." He paused for a moment, looking at some distant point that only he could see. "In the entire galaxy, there is only one force capable of standing against me, of subverting the will of God and stopping me from bringing my throne to Deluros VIII."

"The Iceman?" said Lomax, frowning in disbelief.

"I told you to listen, not to speak," said the Anointed One harshly. "Carlos Mendoza presents no threat to me whatsoever. But he is the only person ever to survive an encounter with my only true opponent. If she has a reason to let him live, then I care not what that reason is—I want him dead."

"She?" asked Lomax.

"Like myself, she is committed to the death of the Democracy, and yet she has chosen to align herself against me as well, which will eventually cost her her life—but not before millions have spilled their blood," answered the Anointed One.

"Who are you talking about?"

"Her given name is unimportant," he continued, "but in the past four years she has emerged from obscurity and assumed her true identity. She is the Prophet."

PART 2

———

———

———

———

———

———

———

———

———

———

The
Iceman's
Book

8

The Silicon Kid, resplendent in a colorful new outfit and shining black boots, walked into the End of the Line Tavern, waited for the doors to slide shut behind him, and looked around. This was more what the Inner Frontier was supposed to look like, he decided: gamblers and whores, miners and adventurers, all of them armed, all of them real or potential killers. The Blue Pavilion really belonged in the Democracy; the End of the Line belonged exactly where it was, in a Tradertown on a tiny Frontier world called Last Chance.

He looked around the room once more, happily aware that a number of the clients were staring at him curiously, and nodded his head in satisfied approval. Finally he walked over to the bar.

"What'll it be?" asked the Iceman, limping over to serve him.

"A beer."

"Coming right up."

The Iceman took an empty glass over to a tap, murmured "Pour," waited a moment, ordered it to stop, and slid the glass down the bar to the Silicon Kid.

"Want to run a tab?" asked the Iceman.

"No, one beer's all I want," said the Kid, sliding some hexagonal coins down the bar. He paused and stared intently at the Iceman.

"Is something wrong?" asked the Iceman, eyeing the Kid suspiciously.

"That's funny," said the Kid.

"What is?"

"You sure as hell don't look like a living legend."

"Well, to tell you the truth, I don't feel much like one," answered the Iceman. "But just out of curiosity, what does a living legend look like?"

"I don't know," said the Kid. "But not like you." He paused. "Still, you must be as formidable as they say, just to *get* as old as you are."

"Son, let me give you a little friendly advice, if I may," said the Iceman, studying the Kid intently.

"What is it?"

"Whether or not I'm as formidable as they say, I'm formidable *enough*." He paused. "You can't see them, but there are four guns trained on you at this very moment, so my advice to you is not to do anything you might not live long enough to regret."

"Four?" said the Kid, surprised. He looked around the room once more. "Where are they?"

"That," said the Iceman with a grim smile, "would be telling." He paused again. "And speaking of telling, perhaps you'd like to tell me just what you're doing on Last Chance?"

"I came here to find you."

"Okay, you found me," said the Iceman. "What now?"

"Now I deliver the Gravedancer's message."

The Iceman stared at him. "What do you know about the Gravedancer?" he asked at last.

"You might say that we're partners, in a manner of speaking," answered the Kid.

"No, I don't think I'd say that," replied the Iceman. "Men like Lomax don't take on partners."

"Well," said the Kid, mildly flustered, "he gave me his ship and he trusted me to deliver a message to you."

"Okay," said the Iceman. "What is it?"

"Right here?" asked the Kid. "At the bar?"

The Iceman looked amused. "There's no one within thirty feet of us. Would you rather tell me next to the roulette wheel—or maybe in the men's room?"

The Kid shrugged and leaned on the bar. "The man who put out the hit on you is a religious cult leader called the Anointed One."

The Iceman frowned. "I never heard of him. Why does he want me dead?"

"I don't know."

The Iceman began drying a glass with a bar towel while he considered what he'd been told. "Why didn't Lomax just radio me the message?" he asked. "Why send you?"

"He was going off to meet with the Anointed One, and, well . . ."

"And you weren't invited?"

The Kid nodded his head.

"Well, that's what comes of being a junior partner."

"There's more," said the Kid.

"Oh?"

The Kid pulled out Lomax's ring. "He said to show you this."

"All right, I've seen it," said the Iceman. "It's his. Now, what's the rest of the message?"

"That no matter what you hear on the grapevine, he's not out to kill you."

"*Am* I going to hear that on the grapevine?" asked the Iceman.

"He seems to think so."

"So he met with this Anointed One under the guise of a free-lance killer?"

"You're very quick."

"Well, let's hope the Anointed One didn't offer him so much money that he forgets where his loyalties lie."

"He wouldn't do that," said the Kid.

"You'd be surprised what people would do for money," said the Iceman. He pulled a bottle out from behind the bar, picked up a couple of glasses, and limped over to an empty table not too far from the doorway. "Come on, young man," he said. "We've got some talking to do."

The Kid followed him to the table and sat down opposite him.

"Have a drink," said the Iceman, filling both glasses and shoving one over to the Kid. "On the house."

"Thanks. What is it?"

"A whiskey they make over in the Binder system."

The Kid took a sip. It burned his tongue and throat, but he forced a smile to his face. "Good," he muttered.

"Don't ever take a job as a diplomat or a politician," said the Iceman wryly.

"I beg your pardon."

"You're a lousy liar."

"I said I liked it," said the Kid irritably, downing the rest of the drink in a single gulp, then fighting unsuccessfully to stifle a strangled cough.

"How the hell did Lomax ever hook up with you?"

"What is *that* supposed to mean?" demanded the Kid.

"It means I want to know how the hell Lomax hooked up with you," the Iceman repeated calmly.

"I did him a favor back on Greycloud."

"What kind?"

"I saved his life."

The Iceman stared at him. *"You?"* he said with open disbelief.

"Me."

"I'd ask how, but you'd probably tell me."

"You think I'm lying?" asked the Kid heatedly.

"Let's just say that I think you're exaggerating," said the Iceman. "You'd better be," he added. "If Lomax needed you to save his life, I hired the wrong man—and I didn't get to be this old by misjudging the people I hire." He paused. "Where did you come across the Anointed One?"

"We didn't. We made contact with one of his men on Olympus, but I don't know where the Anointed One himself is."

"What *do* you know about him?"

"Not much. Just that he's some kind of cult leader, and he wants you dead."

"You're sure it's a *he* you're talking about, and not a *she*?" asked the Iceman, finally taking a sip of his drink.

"Yeah. At least, Korbekkian—that's his man on Olympus, the guy who keeps hiring men to kill you—Korbekkian kept calling him *he*. Why?" asked the Kid. "Is there some woman with a grudge against you?"

"Anything's possible," said the Iceman. "I just want to make sure she's not calling herself the Anointed One these days."

"So there's a woman out there somewhere who wants to kill you," repeated the Kid, his face alight with interest. "What did you do to her?"

"It's a long story," said the Iceman, downing the remainder of his drink.

"I'm all ears."

"It's also none of your business," said the Iceman.

"You know, you're not the friendliest guy I ever met," said the Kid.

"Look," said the Iceman. "I've had four men try to kill me in the past month, men I've never seen before. Now you show up out of the blue to tell me that some religious nut I've never heard of wants me dead, and that any day now I'm going to hear that the Gravedancer is working for him. Now, some people might feel friendly under these circumstances, but I don't happen to be one of them."

"But I'm here to help you," said the Kid.

"You?" said the Iceman with an amused smile. "What can *you* do?"

"You'd be surprised."

The Iceman shrugged. "Probably I would be." He paused. "What's your name?"

"They call me the Silicon Kid."

"Who does?"

The Kid swallowed hard. "Anyone who's met me since I left Greycloud," he answered lamely.

"All ten of 'em, eh?" said the Iceman. "Well, it's an interesting name, especially for a young man who seems to be all flesh and blood. How did you come by it?"

"The Gravedancer gave it to me."

"In that case, I'm properly impressed," said the Iceman. "*Why* are you the Silicon Kid?"

"I've got implanted chips that let me see in the dark, and into the infrared and ultraviolet spectrums. And while I was on my way here from Olympus, I created one that will give me the fastest responses of any man in the galaxy."

"You haven't had it implanted yet?"

"No, but it's simple outpatient surgery," said the Kid. "If you've got a doctor on Last Chance, I can have it done in less than an hour."

"We've got one," answered the Iceman, "but he hasn't been sober for the better part of ten years. If I were you, I'd wait until I hit a bigger world."

The Kid looked his disappointment. "I was kind of hoping to have it done here, so I could protect you."

"I thank you for the thought," said the Iceman, "but I don't *need* protection on my own world." He paused. "Besides, I'm leaving this afternoon."

"Oh? Where are you going?"

"Into the Democracy."

"Why?"

"Because if I stay here, I'm a sitting duck for this Anointed One's killers," answered the Iceman. "Maybe Lomax can handle the situation, and maybe he can't . . . but I don't plan to wait to find out."

"But why the Democracy?" asked the Kid. "I never said the Anointed One was there." He paused. "Hell, I don't know where he is."

"Neither do I," said the Iceman. "But I damned well intend to find out."

"And you think someone in the Democracy can tell you?"

"Oh, yes," said the Iceman with certainty. "There's someone there who can tell me."

"Why travel all that way?" asked the Kid. "Why not just send him a subspace message?"

"I didn't say he'd *want* to tell me," replied the Iceman. "Just that he could." He paused. "And he will," he concluded grimly.

"I'm coming along," said the Kid suddenly.

"I don't recall asking you to."

"There won't be any action here at all once you leave."

"Kid," said the Iceman seriously, "the graveyards are full of young men who came to the Inner Frontier looking for action. Believe me, you'll be much better off just waiting here until Lomax shows up."

The Kid shook his head. "There's a whole galaxy out there, just waiting to be seen." He smiled. "I plan to see it."

"Go tourist-class. You'll live longer."

"If you don't take me along, I'll just follow you in the Gravedancer's ship," said the Kid.

"That's your prerogative," answered the Iceman. "Try not to wreck it."

"Damn it, Iceman!" said the Kid. "Why can't I make you understand that I'm on your side!"

"Kid, you don't even know what the game is."

"Do you?"

"No," admitted the Iceman. "But I'm going to find out."

"You might need me."

"I doubt it."

"Once I get my chip implanted, I'll be the fastest gun anyone ever saw."

"Fast is good," said the Iceman. "Accurate is better." He paused again. "And knowing when not to shoot is better still."

"If I'm with you, you can tell me when to shoot and when not to."

"Telling you what to do isn't my responsibility," said the Iceman. He stared into the Silicon Kid's eyes. "You don't know what you're getting into. If you have a brain in your head, you'll go back to Greycloud and stay there."

"You don't know what *you're* getting into, either," retorted the Kid.

"I'm *already* in it," replied the Iceman. "Four men have come out here to kill me."

"What makes you think they'll stop, just because you leave Last Chance?" said the Kid. "I could help you."

"Why?"

"Why what?" asked the Kid, confused.

The Iceman stared at him with open curiosity. "I never laid eyes on you until ten minutes ago. Why do you want to risk your life for me?"

"I've heard stories about you since I was a kid. You probably aren't going to believe it, but you're one of my heroes."

"I'm too old and fat and lame to be anyone's hero," said the Iceman.

"All the more reason why you need me. You may be invulnerable on Last Chance, but you're fair game once you leave."

"Look, Kid, even if you get your implant, all it means is that your reaction time is quicker."

"Isn't that enough?"

The Iceman looked amused again. "It means you can miss twice as many shots as most normal people."

The Kid got to his feet, picked up the bottle, and walked over to the bar. He placed it down at the far end, then returned to the table.

"Can you shutter the windows and kill the lights?" he asked.

"I've got a couple of dozen customers who won't appreciate it."

"Just for a few seconds."

"Why?"

"So I can prove to you that you need me."

The Iceman stared at him, then shrugged. "We're going to darken the room for just a moment," he announced to the assembled drinkers and gamblers. "There's nothing to worry about. If you've got cards or money on the tables, place your hands over them."

He waited a few seconds, then nodded to one of his men, who went into his office. A moment later the doors closed, the windows became opaque, and the lights went off.

"Now what?" asked the Iceman.

"Now I show you what I can do," said the Kid.

There was an instant of silence, punctuated by the explosive sound of a bullet being fired from a handgun, and then a crash.

"What the hell was *that*?" demanded the Iceman as a woman shrieked and a few men yelled obscenities.

The lights came on immediately, and the Iceman saw that about half his clients had drawn their own weapons.

"It's okay, folks," he said reassuringly. "Nothing to get excited about."

"Take a look," said the Kid proudly, pointing to the shattered liquor bottle on the bar.

The Iceman limped over to the bar and stood a few feet away from the bottle, staring at the glass shards that lay atop the bar. "You really can see in the dark?"

The Kid nodded. "And I can hit what I'm aiming at."

"How do I know you didn't just remember where it was?" asked the Iceman.

"Do you really think that's what I did?" asked the Kid. "We can do it again, and you can place it anywhere you want once the room's dark."

The Iceman considered the proposition, then shook his head. "No, it's not necessary. I believe you."

"Well?" said the Kid, grinning confidently.

"All right," said the Iceman. "I'm impressed."

"*How* impressed?" asked the Kid.

"From this moment on, you're working for me."

"What does the job pay?"

"It depends on what I want you to do," answered the Iceman. He pulled a wad of credits out of a pocket and handed them to the Kid. "This'll hold you for awhile."

"Thanks," said the Kid, taking the money. "When do we leave?"

"After I have lunch and pack my gear. You can meet me over at the hangar."

"Thanks, Iceman," said the Kid. "You won't be sorry."

"That remains to be seen," said the Iceman.

9

The name of the planet was Sweetwater, and it was a relatively new concept in interstellar real estate: a retirement world for the Very Wealthy.

Sweetwater boasted a golf course for every 50 of its 35,000 residents, indoor and outdoor pools in every house, quick home delivery from local stores, a doctor for every two hundred people, a guarantee of one mile of coastline along a freshwater ocean for every property owner, imported birds of every shape and color, daily spaceliner service to more than a dozen major worlds of the Democracy, literally hundreds of private hangars, half a dozen brokerage houses that were tied into every major stock market in the Democracy, high security fences around every piece of property, and a large but unobtrusive private security force for the entire planet.

"It must cost a bundle to set up housekeeping here," said the Kid as he and the Iceman emerged from their ship.

"Most of the people who live here can afford a bundle or two," replied the Iceman dryly.

"Who *does* live here?"

"Anyone who can afford it."

"Must not be a large population," remarked the Kid.

"There isn't," said the Iceman.

They walked through the spaceport, which housed an elegant restaurant and two very upscale gift shops, one of which dealt exclusively in rare and expensive pieces of alien art, then emerged into the bright sunlight and warm dry air of Sweetwater.

"The man I have to see isn't going to talk in front of strangers," said the Iceman, turning to the Kid. "Doctors aren't exactly an endangered species on this planet. Why don't you get your chip implanted while I take care of my business, and I'll meet you back here in front of the restaurant in about five or six hours. We can have a decent dinner before we take off."

"Suits me," agreed the Kid.

The Iceman pointed toward an airlift. "That leads to a monorail platform, from which you can get into what passes for a town in about ten minutes. You won't have any trouble finding a doctor once you get there."

"You're not going into town?"

The Iceman shook his head. "My man lives in the opposite direction. I'll rent a groundcar and drive out there."

"Okay," said the Kid. "See you later."

The young man walked off toward the airlift, and the Iceman made arrangements for his vehicle. In a few minutes he was driving through the carefully landscaped countryside, passing one oceanfront estate after another, until he finally came to the one he sought.

He turned into a driveway, proceeded for perhaps a quarter of a mile, and then came to a high-voltage electronic field.

"Who's there?" asked a mechanical voice emanating from a holographic imaging station.

"Carlos Mendoza."

"Checking files . . ." said the voice. "Positive identification made."

Then another voice was heard, a human voice. "Well, I'll be damned! Come on in!"

The field dissolved and the Iceman drove the remaining three hundred yards to an angular house constructed of an alien material that seemed to reflect hundreds of changing colors in a continuous pattern. It was surrounded by pools, decks, and exotic gardens filled with tinkling crystalline flowers, and one long glass wall offered a panoramic view of the blue-green ocean.

He brought the vehicle to a stop, then stepped onto a moving cushion of air that brought him gently to the second level of the house. When he arrived at the front door, he found it open, and he stepped into a mirrored foyer where an old, balding man with spindly arms and legs but sporting a small potbelly greeted him.

"Carlos Mendoza! It's been a long time!"

The Iceman nodded. "How have you been?"

"I can't complain," said the old man, leading him through the foyer into a large, circular room that afforded a fantastic view of the shoreline.

The Iceman's gaze swept the room, and he smiled. "They'd lock you away if you did. This is some place."

"Haven't you been here before?"

"Once, just when you moved in."

"Ah, yes—my retirement party." The old man paused. "Can I get you something to drink?"

"Why not?"

"What'll it be?" he said, walking to a bar that rose out of the floor as he approached it.

"Whatever you're having."

"Well, I've been saving a bottle of Cygnian cognac for a special occasion," said the old man. "Since you're my first visitor in more than a month, I figure that makes it special enough."

"Sounds good to me," said the Iceman, walking over to the window wall and looking out at the ocean. "Nice view."

"Isn't it?" agreed the old man with a show of pride.

"Nice world, for that matter. Makes me think I could learn to adjust to retirement."

"There are a couple of properties for sale up the road," said the old man. "No reason why you shouldn't consider it." He touched a button on his wristwatch and a shining metallic robot entered the room. "Two Cygnian cognacs, please, Sidney."

The robot bowed and left the room.

"Sidney?" repeated the Iceman with a smile.

"Beats the hell out of calling it Model AU-644," answered the old man. "Have a seat, Carlos."

The Iceman walked over and sat down on a chair that instantly adapted itself to his body, while the old man seated himself a few feet away. The robot reentered the room a moment later with two cognacs on a shining tray made of some alloy the Iceman didn't recognize.

"Thank you, Sidney," said the old man. "That will be all."

The robot bowed again.

"How much did the little piece of machinery cost you?" asked the Iceman.

"Plenty."

"Does it do anything besides serve you drinks?"

"It does—on those rare occasions when I can think of something else for it to do," answered the old man. He took a sip of his cognac. "Excellent! They still make it better in the Cygni system than anywhere else."

The Iceman sipped his own drink. "You'll get no argument from me."

There was a momentary silence as the old man stared at him.

"So, Carlos," he said at last, "are you really thinking of retiring?"

"I think about it all the time."

"No reason why not," agreed the old man. "You've certainly put in your time out there on the Frontier, and Lord knows you've made enough money. What's to stop you?"

"Four different men have tried to stop me in the last month," said the Iceman.

"I don't think I follow you."

"Someone's put a hit out on me," said the Iceman. "I thought you might be able to help me find out why."

"I've been retired for almost four years, Carlos," said the old man. "I don't know what's happening on the Inner Frontier—or anywhere else, for that matter."

"But you can find out."

"How?"

"I know the name of the party that wants me dead."

"I told you—I'm out of touch."

"Come on," said the Iceman. "You were in the service for half a century. You can't make me believe that they don't still call you to pick your mind, or that you haven't got a computer that's tied into the master computer on Deluros VIII."

The old man looked annoyed. "You're asking a lot for a man who just showed up out of the blue."

"I *gave* you a lot, 32," said the Iceman.

"I'm not 32 anymore," said the old man. "They retired my code name when I quit. These days I'm just plain Robert Gibbs."

"If I hadn't agreed to go up against Penelope Bailey six years ago, you'd have been fired before you had a chance to quit," said the Iceman firmly. "It was 32's fat I pulled out of the fire a little over six years ago, and it's 32 who owes me a favor. I'm here to collect it."

"You were well paid for that incident," said Gibbs.

"So were you, as your current surroundings go to prove." The Iceman paused. "You still owe me."

"I don't see it that way, Carlos," answered Gibbs. "I was working for the government. You were a free-lancer who extorted an enormous fee for your services."

"And gave you value received when no one else in the galaxy could have done so," said the Iceman. "And don't give me that holier-than-thou attitude just because you stayed in the service. I put in fifteen years with them before I went my own way. They got their pound of flesh and then some."

"Nevertheless . . ."

"Damn it, I wouldn't ask for this favor if I didn't need it!" snapped the Iceman. "I told you: there have been four attempts on my life!"

"You've made a lot of enemies over the years."

"True. But the Anointed One isn't one of them, and he's the one who's after me."

Gibbs looked at him, startled. "The Anointed One?" he repeated.

"That's right."

Gibbs got to his feet, walked over to the window, and looked out at the ocean. "Why does he want you dead?"

"That's what I want to know. I need whatever information you have on him."

"I don't have anything."

"But you can get it," said the Iceman.

Gibbs nodded. "I can get it."

Now it was the Iceman's turn to frown. "Why this sudden change of mood? I thought you were digging in your heels and telling me I had no business asking you for information."

"This is different," said Gibbs, turning to face him. "The Democracy's been after the Anointed One for close to three years."

"Why?"

"Because he's grown from a minor upstart into a serious problem," answered Gibbs. "The man may have as many as two hundred million followers."

"Why haven't I heard of him, then?"

"He began his operation on the Outer Frontier, out by the Rim and in the Spiral Arm. He just reached the Democracy about a year ago. That's why I'm surprised that he's after you: to the best of our knowledge, he hasn't made any inroads on the Inner Frontier yet."

"Tell me about him," said the Iceman, taking another sip of his cognac.

"He purports to be a religious leader," answered Gibbs, finishing his own drink and walking over to a small table, where he deposited the empty glass. "He had some tax problems, and one day the government's witnesses showed up dead. That's when we started keeping an eye on him."

"Go on."

"We don't know what his eventual goal is, but we can tie him to more than fifty murders. We know he's been buying arms at a phenomenal rate, we know he's got a fair-sized army in his employ, and we know he finances them through a number of illegal businesses. We've taken him to court on tax charges on more than eighty worlds, and ninety percent of those cases are dragging on through endless postponements while he claims that he's a tax-free religious institution." Gibbs snorted contemptuously. "How many religions do *you* know of that possess a sizable army?"

"What do you think he's after?"

Gibbs shrugged. "I don't know; hell, no one knows. At first we thought he actually planned to take over a number of worlds out on the Rim and set up his own little empire, but then he began expanding into the Democracy itself."

"Surely he doesn't plan to go up against the Democracy?"

"For a while we thought he did," said Gibbs, staring out at his terrace, where a trio of gold-and-purple avians had landed at an automated feeding station.

"But the Navy's got a billion ships," said the Iceman.

"And they're spread out over fifty or sixty thousand worlds. One quick strike at Deluros VIII could cause so much chaos that we might actually be willing to strike a deal with him."

"I very much doubt it."

"Well, that was our original assessment, anyway," said Gibbs. "In fact, we pulled the 23rd Fleet back to help defend the Deluros system against an assault, even though he's years away from having enough firepower to seriously consider it. But in the last year or so, he seems to have changed his focus."

"Oh?"

Gibbs nodded. "Yes. According to our informants, he seems obsessed with another religious figure called the Prophet, who is probably a rival in the cult business." He smiled and shook his

head in wonderment. "I don't know where they get these names—
or these followings, for that matter." He paused. "Anyway, these
days he seems to be skirting the Democracy and expanding toward
the Galactic Core, which means he'll reach the Inner Frontier
anytime now."

"Why?"

"I was hoping you might tell me," said Gibbs. "After all, you're
the one he's trying to kill."

"I never heard of the man until two days ago," said the Iceman,
staring through the window wall as two of Sweetwater's three
moons moved rapidly across the sky.

Gibbs shrugged again. "Well, I've told you everything I know
about him."

"But not everything the Democracy knows," said the Iceman.
"I want to know where he's at right now."

"If we knew, we'd go in after him."

"I still want to know what the Democracy knows," said the
Iceman. He stared directly at Gibbs. "I want his confidential
file."

Gibbs ordered Sidney to bring him another cognac. "I don't
think there is one."

"Come on," said the Iceman contemptuously. "I used to work
for the service, remember?"

"I'm not kidding, Carlos. They don't know a damned thing
about him."

"They've got to have photographs, holographs, a past history,
a list of current associates . . ."

"That's classified material, Carlos," said Gibbs, accepting the
cognac from Sidney. The robot bowed, picked up Gibbs's empty
glass, and retreated to another room. "I can't give you that."

"Sure you can. Just tie into Deluros and tell them you want it.
You're still cleared for it."

"There's bound to be some sensitive material that could embarrass the government and wouldn't help you at all," said Gibbs.
"The service is not without its own elements of corruption. If
there are any agents or officials under investigation who have
not formally been charged, I won't turn their names over to
you." He paused and stared at the Iceman. "That's my deal: if
I do get the file from Deluros, I insist that I go through it first—
and in private—and give you only what I think is safe for you to
have."

"Fair enough," replied the Iceman. "I'd like a file on the Prophet, too."

"Can't help you there, and that's the truth," said Gibbs. "We don't have a thing on him. In fact, if our informants hadn't mentioned that the Anointed One is obsessed with him, we wouldn't even know the Prophet existed."

"Obviously he considers the Prophet a threat," said the Iceman. "If a man of such power is worried about the Prophet, how the hell can the Democracy not know a thing about him?"

"Beats the hell out of me, Carlos," admitted Gibbs. "But if anything turns up on him, I'll make it available to you under the same conditions: I won't release any material that might embarrass the service." He paused. "That's the best I can do."

"All right," agreed the Iceman.

Gibbs left the room, walked down a long corridor, entered his study, activated his computer, and put through his request for the Anointed One's file, while the Iceman got out of his chair and walked around the room, admiring the pieces of alien and human art that Gibbs had acquired—or, more likely, had purchased from his decorator.

A few moments later the old man re-entered the room. "It should be just a couple of minutes," he announced.

"What I mainly want," said the Iceman, "is a list of the places I'm most likely to find him or his chief underlings, a couple of holographs, some material concerning his past, and a list of the hit men he's used in the past."

"I think he hires free-lancers whenever he can," answered Gibbs. "And I'll tell you right now: there aren't any photos or holos of him. He's always had his associates represent him in court."

"Then how do you know he's a male?" demanded the Iceman.

"Why do you think he's not?"

"Because no one seemed to have heard of him six years ago."

Gibbs paused, trying to follow the Iceman's train of thought, and finally smiled. "You think he's Penelope Bailey?"

"It's possible," said the Iceman, taking his seat again.

"You're wrong, Carlos. His name is Moses Mohammed Christ, which I think you will agree is a most unfeminine name. Also, we've taken a number of his followers into custody, and they've testified that the Anointed One is a male in his forties." He paused. "Besides, Penelope Bailey is dead."

The Iceman leaned forward intently. "Say that again."

"She's dead, Carlos."

"Not a chance," said the Iceman with absolute certainty.

"She was confined in a cell on Alpha Crepello III."

"Last time I saw her, yes," said the Iceman. "The locals called it Hades."

"Well, Hades no longer exists."

"What are you talking about?"

"It was struck by a huge meteor about eighteen Standard months ago," answered Gibbs. "There's nothing left of it except some dust and a bunch of asteroids in orbit around Alpha Crepello."

"You're sure?"

"Fly out there yourself if you don't believe me." Gibbs got to his feet. "The file should be here by now. If you'll excuse me . . ."

The Iceman sat, silent and motionless, for the entire time that Gibbs was censoring the Anointed One's file. Finally the older man re-entered the room and handed the Iceman a hard copy in a folder.

"I hope this file proves useful to you," said Gibbs. "I'm no longer empowered to make such assignments, but the Democracy would be very grateful if you found a way to terminate the Anointed One."

"The Democracy has got a bigger problem than some half-baked religious fanatic with delusions of empire," said the Iceman grimly. He stood up and walked to the door.

"What are you talking about?" asked Gibbs.

The Iceman reached the doorway and turned. "None of you ever understood what you were dealing with." He paused. "You still don't."

"Perhaps you'd care to enlighten me," said Gibbs, his voice reflecting his annoyance.

"Why bother? You won't believe me."

"Try me."

The Iceman stared at him. "Penelope Bailey is alive."

"You're mistaken," scoffed Gibbs.

"The hell I am," said the Iceman.

"I told you: Alpha Crepello III was destroyed by a meteor."

"I don't doubt it."

"Every living being on the planet was killed—including her."

The Iceman looked at Gibbs for a long moment and sighed deeply.

"You're a fool," he said, and walked out to his waiting vehicle.

10

The Kid was waiting in front of the restaurant when the Iceman returned to the spaceport.

"Everything go okay?" asked the Iceman.

"I'm a little bit sore," replied the Kid. "He used a local anesthetic, and it's starting to wear off."

"Small price to pay to be the fastest gun in the galaxy," said the Iceman wryly. "Now, if you were only the most accurate gun as well . . ."

"I'm working on it," the Kid assured him.

"It'll take a lot of practice."

"Practice is for losers. I'll do it with chips." Suddenly he grinned. "I'm the Silicon Kid, remember?"

"I'll try not to forget again," said the Iceman sardonically.

"How was *your* day?" asked the Kid after a momentary silence.

"Not good," said the Iceman, frowning. "Not good at all."

"Oh?"

"There's no sense standing here talking," said the Iceman. "Let's get some dinner, and then we'll take off."

He summoned the maître d', who led them past a multicolored fountain in the middle of the floor and escorted them to a secluded table toward the back of the restaurant.

The Kid immediately picked up a menu and studied it. "Everything seems imported," he noted. "You'd think a temperate world like this could grow its own food."

"That's not what this world was created for," replied the Iceman.

"But it's so expensive to do it this way."

"If you live on Sweetwater, you don't worry about prices."

"I suppose you're right," said the Kid, surveying his surroundings and toying with his crystalline wine and water glasses. "It's a pretty nice place."

"I've seen worse," said the Iceman. "See those shellfish in that tank?" he added, pointing to a saltwater tank that was discreetly placed against a wall.

"Yeah?"

"They're mutated," said the Iceman. "They come from the Pinnipes system." He paused. "I can't pronounce their name, but they're supposed to be the best-tasting seafood in the galaxy."

"I've never been a seafood fan."

"Well, take my word for it," said the Iceman. He looked across the room. "And those are real Hesporite paintings on the wall, not fakes," he continued.

"How can you tell?"

"Watch when a waiter passes in front of them," said the Iceman. "They'll glow wherever his shadow falls."

"How come?"

"They use the larvae of some phosphorescent insect in their paints," answered the Iceman. "They look like oils in the daylight, but they glow in the dark."

"I never knew that."

The Iceman smiled. "There are probably a lot of things you never knew. Live long enough and you'll learn some of them."

"I get the feeling that you don't have much use for anyone younger than the Gravedancer," said the Kid wryly.

"Not much," agreed the Iceman. He signaled a waiter and ordered an Antarrean wine, while the Kid requested a beer.

"You know, I'd never seen a live waiter until I left Greycloud," remarked the Kid. "Now I've seen them twice in a week."

"They're like most luxuries," responded the Iceman. "You pay for what you get—and you pay *plenty* at a place like this."

"Uh . . . until I figure out exactly what I'm going to do on the Frontier, I'm on a budget," said the Kid.

"No problem," said the Iceman. "When you travel with me or work for me—and right now you're doing both—I pick up the tab."

"Are you that rich?"

"As a matter of fact, I am."

"How does someone get to be as rich as you?" asked the Kid.

"Live a long time and don't do anything too stupid," replied the Iceman with a smile.

"There it is again," said the Kid.

"There *what* is?"

"This contempt for people my age."

"Not for all of them," answered the Iceman. "Right now the most dangerous person in the galaxy is a twenty-eight-year-old woman named Penelope Bailey. She's probably been the most dangerous person since the day she was born."

"I never heard of her."

"Yes, you did," said the Iceman. "You just never knew her real name."

"Who is she?"

"At various times she's been known as the Soothsayer and the Oracle."

"The Oracle?" asked the Kid, suddenly enthused.

"Right."

"Tell me about her."

"In a minute," said the Iceman as their waiter brought them their drinks and recited the day's special off-the-menu selections. The Kid requested a plain steak, and the Iceman ordered a shellfish in a cream sauce.

"Would you like to select your own, sir?" asked the waiter.

The Iceman shook his head. "I'll trust to your taste."

"Very good, sir."

"I *do* love seafood," said the Iceman when the waiter left. "You sure you don't want to have some? You can get steak anywhere."

"No, thanks."

"You're making a big mistake," continued the Iceman. "The sauce alone is worth the price of the meal."

"Get back to the Oracle," said the Kid impatiently. "What is she like?"

"She's a young woman with a gift," answered the Iceman. "I first met her twenty years ago, when she was just a frightened little girl—but even then, two hundred of the best bounty hunters on the Inner Frontier were no match for her."

"You're telling me an eight-year-old girl stood off two hundred armed bounty hunters?" said the Kid skeptically.

The Iceman smiled and shook his head. "You make it sound like she beat them in a shoot-out. Her gift doesn't work like that."

"How *does* it work?"

"She's precognitive."

The Kid frowned. "What does *that* mean?"

"It means she can see the future," said the Iceman. "More to the point, it means she can see a number of futures, and through her actions she can bring about the one that's the most favorable to her."

"How?"

The Iceman shrugged as a string quartet walked over to the fountain and started filling the room with their music. "I don't know how it works. I only know that it *does* work."

"Give me an example," said the Kid.

"All right," said the Iceman. "Let's say she's hiding from you in the cargo area here, and you've been hired to kill her." He paused and leaned forward. "Whatever approach you take, whatever entrance you use, she'll know it even before you do. She'll see an infinite number of futures. Maybe you kill her in all but three of them. She'll figure out what she has to do to bring one of those three favorable futures into being."

"How?" asked the Kid.

The Iceman shrugged. "Maybe it'll be something as simple as her walking out one door while you walk in through another. Maybe it will be more complex, like positioning you under a crate that will drop on you and kill you once in a million times, and doing whatever it takes to make that million-to-one possibility come to pass. Maybe she'll see that of all the possible futures, there's one in which you die of a sudden heart attack; she'll analyze every facet of that future, see how it differs from all the others, and do what she can to bring it into being."

"But surely there must be some futures in which she doesn't survive," said the Kid. "What if I surrounded the building with fifty gunmen?"

"Probably she'd still manage to find a future in which she escaped."

"Hah!" said the Kid, and one of the violinists glared at him.

"Keep your voice down," said the Iceman. "Most of the diners would rather hear the music."

"Sorry," said the Kid. "But you said 'probably.' What if she couldn't?"

"Then she'd surrender to you, and find some way to escape an hour or a day or a week from now." The Iceman paused. "Not all problems are capable of immediate solution. She was a prisoner of some alien bounty hunter, chained to a bed in his room, when a friend of mine first found her." He paused. "To this day, I still haven't decided whether my friend actually *found* her, or if she manipulated events so she would be found."

"That's some gift, that—what did you call it?—that precognition," said the Kid.

"That it is," agreed the Iceman. "That's why the Democracy was so set on exploiting it."

"The Democracy?"

"Who do you think hired all those bounty hunters?" said the Iceman. "Think of what someone who could not only see but manipulate the future could do. They'd never lose a war, or even a battle. They'd know exactly how to handle a galactic economy. They could probably just stand her on a new world and have her tell them whether it was worth the effort to set up mining operations or not." He paused, then smiled. "And of course, if they found a way to control her, they'd never lose an election, never make a bad investment in the market, never cheat on their spouses if there was a chance of being caught. They'd know *before* they contracted cancer or some other disease, and take whatever precautions were necessary to avoid it."

"I begin to see now," said the Kid. "Hell, she'd be worth *billions*."

"That's what *they* thought," answered the Iceman. "That's why they were so hot to get their hands on her."

"You make it sound like they were wrong."

"They didn't know what they were dealing with," said the Iceman, lowering his voice still further as the quartet's violinist began walking slowly throughout the room, playing romantic solos at those tables where he thought he might cadge a tip.

"What did they *think* they were dealing with?" asked the Kid.

"From their point of view, this was a little eight-year-old girl who just managed to elude their grasp. From mine—and I think time has proven me right—this was a child who managed to remain free despite the best efforts of the largest and most powerful government in history to capture her. A lot of legendary bounty hunters caught up with her at one time or another—Cemetery Smith, Three-Fisted Ollie, Jimmy Sunday—but when the dust cleared, they were dead and she was still free."

"She killed them all?" asked the Kid, his voice filled with disbelief.

"Not directly, but yes, she was responsible for their deaths as surely as if she had killed them herself." The Iceman paused again, thinking back to the first time he had encountered Penelope Bailey. "The thing was, she didn't *look* like the most dangerous human being in the galaxy. She looked like a frightened little girl who was always hugging a rag doll for comfort. But in the end, everyone who was associated with her—those who tried to capture or kill her and those who tried to protect her—was dead, and she was still free."

"What about you?"

"I was lucky." The Iceman patted his prosthetic leg. "Still, this used to be flesh and blood."

"But she didn't kill you."

"She was very young, and her powers weren't fully developed," answered the Iceman. "She left me for dead. She couldn't see far enough ahead then to know that I'd survive."

"And that was your experience with the Oracle?"

The Iceman shook his head. "She was just 'Penelope Bailey' back then, though some alien who had latched onto her—practically worshipped her, for all the good it did him in the long run—called her the Soothsayer, and for a while the name caught on."

The waiter brought their salads out. The Kid pushed his aside, while the Iceman began eating his own.

"Needs a little pepper," said the Iceman.

"Certainly, sir," said the waiter, supplying it and then walking off to the kitchen.

"How did she become the Oracle?" asked the Kid.

"Well, as I said, she was very young and her powers weren't mature," answered the Iceman. "She and her alien friend sought asylum on a planet called Hades. Somehow the race that lived there figured out what she was and managed to imprison her in a room protected by an impenetrable force field—as I said, her powers weren't fully developed at the time." He took another bite of his salad. "Anyway, they made a deal with her: they would feed her and keep her alive, and she would direct them in their attempt to remain independent of the Democracy. Over the next fourteen years pronouncements would come forth from her cell, and the government of Hades would act upon them; that's how she became the Oracle."

"How did you get involved with her again?"

The Iceman sighed. "It's a long story. Basically, a man named 32, who worked for the Democracy—he's the same man I saw earlier today—hired me to kill her." He took a last bite of his salad and pushed the bowl aside. "And since I knew what kind of threat she represented, I took the commission—but because she knew who I was, I farmed it out to someone who was younger and tougher than I was."

"You don't take any risks if you can avoid it, do you?" said the Kid.

"Not if I can help it," said the Iceman, showing no irritation at the question. "I didn't get to be this old by looking for trouble."

The waiter arrived with their dinners, and both men fell silent again until he left.

"Excellent!" said the Iceman, taking a mouthful of his shellfish. "I'm going to have to make a point of visiting 32 more often."

"Okay," said the Kid as soon as the waiter was out of earshot. "So you hired someone else to kill her. Where do you come in?"

"You had to go through a lot of Blue Devils—that's what we called the aliens—to get to her," said the Iceman, taking a taste of his meal and nodding his approval. "She was very valuable to them, so she had layer upon layer of protection. It was when I realized that my man was working his way to her too easily that I went there to try to stop him."

"To stop him?" repeated the Kid, frowning. "Why?"

"The fact that no one else had been able to stop him—or even appreciably slow him down—meant that she wanted him to succeed, not in killing her, but in reaching her prison. And if she wanted it, then I didn't."

"So you saved her life."

The Iceman shook his head. "Her life was never in danger. It probably hasn't been in danger since the day she was born."

"But if your killer made it to her prison . . ."

"You still don't understand," said the Iceman. "Stand her against that wall"—he gestured toward a wall of the restaurant—"and program a dozen laser weapons to fire randomly at her, and she'll know when each one will discharge and where each beam will hit, and she'll simply avoid them. And if you fired so many beams from so many weapons that she couldn't avoid them all, then she'd find a future in which one of the weapons was a dud and exploded in your face before you could activate the rest of them."

"So what happened on Hades?"

"My man had certain information she needed, something that could effectuate her escape. He was killed before she could make use of him." The Iceman stared blankly out the window across the landing field. "He was a damned good man."

"So she was still a prisoner on Hades?"

"That's right."

"And now she's free again?"

The Iceman nodded.

"When did she escape?"

The Iceman shrugged. "I have no idea. At least eighteen months ago."

"How does someone escape from a force field? I didn't know we'd even developed the technology."

"We haven't. The inhabitants of Hades weren't human; *they* developed it."

"So how did she escape from it?"

"I don't know."

"Where is she now?"

The Iceman shrugged again. "I had rather hoped she was the Anointed One, but I've got a feeling she isn't. Too many people have seen him and testified that he's a man in his forties."

"Just a minute," said the Kid. "You don't know when she escaped, you don't know how she escaped, and you don't know where she is. Is that right?"

"That's right."

"Then how do you know she's escaped at all?"

"Because a meteor crashed into Hades eighteen months ago and blew the whole damned world to smithereens. No survivors."

"Well, then, that's it. She died when the meteor hit."

The Iceman shook his head. "Not her. If there was one future in a trillion in which the meteor didn't hit Hades, in which it missed the planet or was blown to bits by a weapon or another meteor, she'd have found a way to make it come to pass."

"But that doesn't make any sense," said the Kid. "If she could make it miss the planet, how come the planet was demolished?"

"Because it was payback time," answered the Iceman with utter conviction. "Sometime before it hit, she found a way to escape from that force field . . . and just as she could have chosen a future in which the meteor missed Hades if she were still on the planet, she could also choose the one-in-a-million future in which it smashed into Hades once she had left. This was a race that had imprisoned her for close to two decades; there was no way she was going to let them off the hook with merely a reprimand."

The Kid considered what the Iceman had said. "You really think she had the power to do that?" he asked dubiously.

"I *know* she has," said the Iceman firmly.

The Kid finally tried a piece of his steak, and made a face.

"What's the matter?" asked the Iceman.

"It's cold."

The Iceman, who had been eating while they had been speaking, took the last bite of his own meal. "Pity," he said. "You probably won't eat this well again for months."

"You think she'll be coming after you?" asked the Kid, chewing on a piece of no-longer-warm meat.

"No," said the Iceman. "I'm no more to her than an insect. No man is."

"Good," said the Kid. "Leave her to the Democracy, and let's worry about the Anointed One."

"After twenty years, the Democracy still doesn't know what they're dealing with," said the Iceman. "Besides, they think she's dead."

"From the meteor?"

"Yes."

"Well, who knows? Maybe they're right and you're wrong."

"I'm *not* wrong!" said the Iceman angrily.

"Okay, you're not wrong," said the Kid. "What do you plan to do about it?"

"Nothing," said the Iceman. "Yet."

"You're not going to go after her?"

"Go where?"

"So it's like I said: let's concentrate on stopping the Anointed One."

"The Anointed One is nothing but a minor irritant," said the Iceman.

"A minor irritant who's paid five men to kill you," the Kid pointed out.

"Lomax will handle him," said the Iceman, dismissing the subject. "Or at least he'll warn me if anyone else is coming after me. We have more important things to worry about."

The Kid frowned. "Like what?"

The Iceman stared at him. "Haven't you heard a word I've said?" he demanded. "There is a monster loose in the galaxy, and no one else is aware of the threat she presents." He paused. "I've got to find out where she is, what name she's using, how well protected she is."

The Kid frowned in confusion. "I thought you just said you weren't going to go after her."

"I'm not. She knows who I am, what I look like. I'd be dead before I could get anywhere near her."

"Then what—?"

"Once I locate her, the next step is to find out what she's planning to do." He stared at the Kid. "That's when I send *you* in."

"Me?"

"You want to be a genuine Inner Frontier hero, don't you?" said the Iceman with a grim smile.

"Yeah," said the Kid, suddenly excited. "Yeah, I do."

11

"There it is," said the Iceman as his ship braked to light speeds in the Alpha Crepello system.

The Silicon Kid walked over to the viewscreen. "You mean, there it *isn't*."

The Iceman looked away from the whirling dust and rocks that were the only things left in Alpha Crepello III's orbit.

"I had to make sure," he said. "Well, now I'm sure."

"And this Penelope Bailey did this just by *wishing* it?" said the Kid, staring at the dust and trying to imagine a planet in its place.

"Essentially," replied the Iceman. "It's much more complex, but that's the gist of it."

The Kid let out a low whistle. "That's some lady," he said. "She makes you and the Gravedancer look like pikers."

"Have you got yourself a new hero now?" asked the Iceman, amused.

"Not me," said the Kid. "She scares the shit out of me." He continued to stare at the viewscreen. "People just can't *do* things like that."

"She's not a person," said the Iceman. "Not anymore. She hasn't been for a long time." He paused thoughtfully. "Maybe she never was."

"They say she killed the Forever Kid when she was the Soothsayer. Is that right?"

"Not exactly."

The Kid frowned, confused. "I don't understand."

"She didn't kill him," explained the Iceman. "She could have saved him, but she chose not to. Legally it's not the same thing; morally it is."

"All these legendary men and women—and you're the only one who survived," said the Kid. "What's your secret?"

The Iceman shrugged. "I was lucky."

"Maybe once was luck. Not twice."

"Kid, if I knew the answer to that, I'd be willing to go up against her again."

"Maybe you've got some kind of power, too," suggested the Kid. "One you don't even know about."

"If I had it, I'd know about it by now." The Iceman took one last look at where Hades had been. "She killed one hell of a lot of Blue Devils," he remarked. "A lot of Men, too."

"I didn't know any Men lived on Hades."

"They didn't—but Hades had three terraformed moons that were all populated by Men: Port Maracaibo, Port Marrakech, and Port Samarkand. You don't see 'em now, do you?"

"What happened to them?"

"They probably fell into the sun when the planet blew," answered the Iceman.

The Kid was silent for a long moment and then spoke. "Well, to be fair about it, she had some justification," he said. "She'd been a prisoner there for sixteen or seventeen years."

"And that justifies killing every living thing on Hades and all its moons?"

"They didn't have any reason to imprison her in the first place," said the Kid. "From what you told me, they just spotted her talent and locked her away."

"What would *you* have done?" asked the Iceman.

The Kid shrugged. "I don't know. Talked to her, tried to find out what her plans were, seen if there was any way to get her to work for me."

"You're a fool."

"How do you know that she doesn't plan to use her powers for good?"

"Whose good?" responded the Iceman. "Hers or ours?"

"They might be the same."

"They've never been the same," said the Iceman. "You're making the same mistake 32 and all the rest made. You think because she looks human and had human parents, she must *be* human." He paused. "Take it from me, Kid—she hasn't been a human being for a long, long time—if indeed she ever was."

The Kid turned in his seat to face the Iceman. "How can you be so sure of that?"

"Because I know the way her mind works—as much as any Man *can* know, anyway," answered the Iceman. "What frightens me—and what ought to frighten the shit out of you and everyone else—isn't that she has the power to blow Hades to bits; hell, the Navy can do that, too." He shook his head. "No, what frightens me is that I *know* she did it without a single regret or second thought. By the time she became the Oracle she had evolved past all human reference points: we mean no more to her than a grain of sand means to us."

"She was human once," said the Kid doggedly. "You told me she was just a frightened little girl when you first met her. There must be a shred of that humanity still remaining somewhere within her."

The Iceman sighed heavily. "Fine. *You* search for it."

"I plan to—if I get the chance."

"I wish you luck," said the Iceman, closing the subject. He commanded the ship's computer to break orbit and take them out of the Alpha Crepello system. "I've seen everything I needed to see. No sense staying here any longer."

"What do we do now?" asked the Kid.

"Now," said the Iceman, selecting a world from the holographic display of the Inner Frontier and directing the navigational computer to lay in a course for it, "we head for Confucius IV."

"Never heard of it."

"It's an ugly little world on the edge of the Frontier."

"Why are we going there?"

"Because you can usually buy information there."

"What kind of information are we after?" asked the Kid, staring at the holographic display until it faded into nothingness.

"We're trying to get a line on the Prophet."

"The Prophet?" said the Kid, surprised. "Isn't he some bandit on the Frontier?"

"Possibly."

"Possibly?" repeated the Kid. "You think it might be Penelope Bailey?"

"I don't know," answered the Iceman. "That's what I plan to find out." He walked carefully to the galley, pulled out an exotically shaped bottle, and poured himself a drink. "You want some?" he asked.

"Sure," said the Kid. "What is it?"

"Alphard brandy," said the Iceman, handing the bottle and a glass to the Kid. "Not as good as the stuff they make in the Terrazane system, but it keeps better at light speeds."

"Thanks," said the Kid, filling his glass and returning the bottle to the Iceman. "Do you mind if I ask you a question?"

"Go ahead."

"You didn't pick the Prophet out of a hat," said the Kid, taking a swallow of the brandy and deciding that he liked it. "There's hundreds of bandits with strange names out there. What makes you think the Prophet might be Penelope Bailey? Why not Father Christmas or Undertaker McNair or the Border Lord?"

"Well, the name fits," said the Iceman, returning to his seat and setting his glass down on a panel in front of the navigational computer. "But that's secondary; there have been Prophets before. There will be again." He paused. "It was something 32 told me."

"What?"

"That the Anointed One was thought to be building up his forces for some military action against the Democracy, but during the past year he seems to have changed his target. Now he's hunting for the Prophet."

"So what?"

"Think it through," said the Iceman, returning to his seat with his glass in his hand. "Here is this fanatic with two hundred million armed followers, all set to take on the Democracy—and suddenly he decides the Prophet is a greater threat." He stared at the Kid. "The Democracy's got a navy of almost a billion ships, and a standing army of maybe ten billion men. Now, what do you think could possibly pose a greater threat than that?"

"You make it sound logical enough," admitted the Kid. "But it's also possible that the Anointed One decided that he wasn't up to defeating the Democracy . . . or maybe he's out to assimilate all the Prophet's followers into his fold."

"What followers?" demanded the Iceman. "According to 32, the Democracy hasn't got any hard information on the Prophet. Don't you think they'd know if she had millions of men ready to fight on her command?" He paused again. "You say that the Prophet is just a bandit on the Frontier. All right. Who has she robbed? What sector is she operating out of?"

"I don't know," said the Kid. He stared at the Iceman. "But neither do you. For all you know, the Prophet is just some small-time bandit."

"Like I said, it's possible."

"Then why go on some wild-goose chase after her—or *him,* as the case may be?"

"I'm going after Penelope Bailey because the Democracy thinks she's dead. *They* sure as hell aren't going to go looking for her." He paused. "And the reason I'm going to try to find the Prophet is even simpler: I don't have any other leads." He took a deep breath and released it slowly. "And there's one other thing."

"Oh? What?"

"I've never met the Anointed One in my life," said the Iceman. "I never even heard of him until a couple of weeks ago."

"What has that got to do with the Prophet?"

"Maybe nothing," admitted the Iceman, picking up his glass and taking another sip. "But if we've never met and I haven't hampered him in any way, then I can think of only one reason he wants me dead." He paused again. "I'm the only person ever to meet Penelope Bailey and live to tell about it. That could imply that I'm working for her."

"But you're not," the Kid pointed out.

The Iceman smiled. "You know it and I know it, but the Anointed One has no reason to know it. The only thing he knows is that I've been in her presence a number of times, and I'm still alive."

"You're working with even less information than he is," responded the Kid, finishing his brandy in a single gulp. "Both in regards to the Anointed One's motives and Penelope Bailey's identity—if she's still alive."

"You're supposed to *sip* your brandy," said the Iceman.

"I'll remember next time," said the Kid.

"Please do. It's expensive stuff. If you're just thirsty, I've got water and beer."

"All right," said the Kid irritably. "I said I'd remember, and I will." He paused. "So how do we go about learning if you're right or wrong about the Prophet?"

"We assume that I'm right and that she's Penelope Bailey, and we proceed based on that supposition," said the Iceman. "We'll start on Confucius IV. I don't know anything about the Prophet, you don't know anything about the Prophet, even the Democracy doesn't know anything about the Prophet. But we do know that the Prophet exists. People have heard of her. People talk about her. *You've* heard of her. And we know that the Anointed One is searching the Inner Frontier for her." The Iceman paused and drummed his fingers on the computer panel. "So we start going from one likely world to another, until we find someone who knows something more about her than her name. Maybe we'll get a location, maybe the scene of a recent crime, maybe the name of an associate—but sooner or later we'll get *something*."

"And then?"

"Then we keep piecing together bits of information until we know if she's Penelope Bailey or not."

"I don't know about this," said the Kid doubtfully. "This whole scenario you've built, everything you've said—it's all supposition."

"True," agreed the Iceman. "But it *feels* right."

"So we're going all over the Inner Frontier chasing some bandit because it *feels* right?" said the Kid, displaying a sardonic smile.

"When you pay the bills, we'll do it your way," said the Iceman. "In the meantime, if you have any objections, I can let you off on the nearest oxygen world."

"No, I'll stay with you," said the Kid. "I've still got a lot of worlds to see. I might as well see them on salary." He paused thoughtfully. "And if she really *is* alive, I want to see her." Suddenly he smiled. "Who knows? Maybe I'll go down in history as the man who killed Penelope Bailey."

"I wouldn't bet my last credit on it," said the Iceman dryly.

12

Confucius IV wasn't much of a world. It consisted of three abandoned Tradertowns, a handful of mines which were mostly played out, some enormous flat fields that didn't have rich enough soil or get enough rain, and one small city.

The city, New Macao, was pretty unimpressive even by the standards of the Inner Frontier. Its cobblestone streets, created to be charming, were in dire need of repair and caused equal havoc to feet and tires. The major hotel resembled a steel and glass pagoda, and the rooms were furnished with the same lack of taste displayed by the architect. Another hotel resembled an emperor's palace, as conceived by someone who had never seen either an emperor or a palace. The streets were narrow and winding, with an abundance of bars and drug dens and an absolute minimum of official supervision.

"I *like* it," said the Silicon Kid as he and the Iceman walked down the main street, past the two hotels and a trio of overpriced nightclubs.

"It's filthy and dangerous," replied the Iceman.

"That's what I like about it. It's exotic."

"Your definition of exotic and mine differ considerably," said the Iceman wryly.

"Look at the men standing in the doorways of some of those buildings!" said the Kid excitedly. "I'll bet I've seen half of them on Wanted posters!"

"Probably," said the Iceman. "I suppose I should warn you that that doesn't necessarily make them desirable companions."

"I've been rubbing shoulders with farmers all my life," said the

Kid. "At least these guys figure to be more interesting."

"When's the last time a farmer took your wallet, cut your throat, and left you for dead in the street?"

"I'd like to see someone try it, now that I've got my implants," said the Kid confidently.

"You would?" said the Iceman with an amused smile. "Well, maybe I can accommodate you."

"What are you talking about?" asked the Kid, suddenly tense.

"When we turn off of this street, just keep twenty yards behind me. I guarantee you'll have a chance to try out the New Improved You."

"What about you?"

"Me? I gave up showing off half a century ago."

"No," said the Kid. "I mean, if this place we're going is so dangerous, why won't they go after you, too?"

"Because they want to live."

The Kid laughed. "You're a fat old man with a limp."

"That's right."

"Then why should they leave you alone?"

"Because I'm the Iceman," came the reply in such a cold voice that the Kid decided his aging companion was more formidable that he looked.

"So where are we going?"

"A place even the police don't go," answered the Iceman. "It's just a couple of more blocks."

"Has it got a name?"

"Nightmare Alley."

"Picturesque," remarked the Kid.

"Accurate," replied the Iceman.

They walked for another fifty yards, then turned down a narrow side street.

"This is Nightmare Alley?" asked the Kid.

"Soon," said the Iceman.

They walked past two dilapidated buildings, then came to a winding alleyway—and suddenly the character of the area changed from something that the Kid thought was exotic and Iceman thought was merely run-down, to something that both agreed was deeply weird.

Club after club lined the alley, most with their own barkers. There was a drug den, a betting parlor, a bar, another drug den, a pornographic stage show, a whorehouse for men, a whorehouse for women, a whorehouse for aliens, and a whorehouse for those desiring that most taboo of vices—interspecies sex. Taverns, each darker and more disreputable than the last, catered to all races. Shrill screams and raucous laughter came from the whorehouses, and terrified screams emanated from one of the drug dens. There were a pair of weapon shops, one specializing in laser pistols and rifles, the other in projectile firearms, and the Kid had the feeling that not a single weapon in either shop possessed a serial number.

Every fifteen feet or so they came to a body lying on the pavement. Some appeared drunk, others comatose; the Iceman paid them no attention.

"I think I just saw Lizard Malloy in that bar across the alleyway!" whispered the Kid excitedly.

"Well, this is a good place to stay when there's a price on your head," replied the Iceman.

A few faces peered out at the Iceman and the Kid from the interiors of the buildings they passed, but no one made any move to hinder them, and even the barkers stepped aside as the Iceman approached them.

"They seem to know you," said the Kid, impressed.

"They know enough not to bother me, anyway," answered the Iceman.

"I thought you hadn't left Last Chance in four years."

"That's right."

"You must have made quite an impression the last time you were here."

The Iceman made no reply, but began slowing down. "We're going in there," he said, gesturing toward a doorway. "Once we're inside, keep your mouth shut and your eyes open. Got it?"

"Right," said the Kid. He paused uncertainly. "What am I looking for?"

"You'll know it when you see it," said the Iceman.

He entered the doorway, followed by the Kid.

"Welcome to the House of Usher," said a tall man dressed in faded formal garb. He stared at the Iceman, and suddenly a look of recognition crossed his face. "It's been a long time, Mr. Mendoza. We heard rumors that you had been killed."

"I can only be killed with a silver bullet," replied the Iceman with a wry smile. "I thought everyone knew that." He pulled out a hundred-credit note and handed it to the man. "I'm renting a table near the bar. It's my office for the next two hours."

The man grabbed the note and nodded.

"There's another hundred credits for you for every person you bring to my office—if they have anything useful to sell."

"What are you buying?"

"Information."

"There's all kinds of information, Mr. Mendoza."

"Pass the word that the Iceman is interested in information about the Prophet."

The man rubbed his chin thoughtfully. "That may be more difficult than you imagine, Mr. Mendoza. I've only heard the Prophet mentioned twice in all the time I've been here."

"This is Nightmare Alley," said the Iceman. "Someone will know something." He pulled out two more notes. "Put the word on the street, too. Tell them I'll be here for two hours, and then I'm leaving Confucius."

"I'll pass the word as soon as I take you to your table."

"Don't bother," said the Iceman. "I know the way."

As the tall man walked out the door, the Iceman turned to the Kid.

"Follow me, and don't stare."

"At what?"

"At anything you see. It's in bad taste."

The Iceman led him through a labyrinthian corridor that passed a number of dimly lit rooms. In one, a number of men and women, all addicts of the alphanella seed, lay in various states of stupor and catatonia, their pupils dilated, their eyes wide open, their faces contorted in nightmarish smiles. In another, three green-skinned aliens, mildly apelike in appearance, sat naked on the floor, surrounded by perhaps two hundred blue-glowing candles. Each alien was dissecting a small animal. The Kid tried to ignore the little animals' screams of pain and wondered if he was observing a religious ritual or an illegal dinner, or both.

They passed three more cubicles, each with humans or aliens doing things that they were never meant to do, and finally they came to the bar. There were a dozen tables evenly spaced throughout the room, all but three of them occupied by a relatively equal number of humans and aliens, and the Iceman picked the one that was farthest from the corridor through which they had entered. The two men who were sitting there took one look at him and left hurriedly as he approached.

"Welcome back, Mr. Mendoza," said the bartender, a grossly obese bald man with a handlebar mustache that had been dyed a bright blue. "It's been a long time."

"Not long enough," said the Iceman distastefully, and the bartender chuckled. "Bring us a pair of beers."

The bartender nodded, and waddled over with their drinks a moment later.

"Sure I can't interest you in a Dust Devil or a Blue Giant?" he asked, panting from the effort of walking across the room.

"Just the beers," said the Iceman, tossing a pair of Maria Theresa dollars on the tray.

"Maybe later," said the bartender.

"Maybe," said the Iceman, and the bartender retreated to his station.

"This is some place!" said the Kid, unable to keep the excitement from his voice.

"You *like* it here?" asked the Iceman.

"Don't you?"

"The scum of the Inner Frontier, if they sink low enough, eventually wind up on Confucius IV—and the worst of them turn up in Nightmare Alley. If I didn't have business to transact, you couldn't pay me to spend two seconds in this place."

"It's got *atmosphere,*" said the Kid.

"Yeah," said the Iceman. "Well, if you scrub hard enough in the shower, most of it'll wash off."

"You've got no sense of adventure," said the Kid with a smile.

"This isn't an adventure, Kid. It's a business, and a deadly one at that."

The Kid lowered his voice. "See that woman at that table over there? The skinny one with the red hair?"

"Yes."

"I think it's Sally the Blade!"

"So what?"

"She's killed thirty men, maybe thirty-five!" said the Kid excitedly.

"I know."

"Do you know her personally? I'd like to meet her."

"Why don't you just walk over and ask for her autograph?" said the Iceman caustically.

"Maybe I will."

"Don't."

"Why not?"

"You don't come to the House of Usher to meet star-struck farm boys," said the Iceman. "You come here to conduct business. That man she's with isn't here just to buy her a drink and talk her into bed—and I don't think he'd appreciate having a stranger come up and start talking." The Iceman paused. "He might even think you had some notion of blackmailing him once Sally does what he's paying her to do."

The Kid considered the Iceman's statement. "All right," he said sullenly. "But you don't have to make fun of me."

"Just keep your mind on business," said the Iceman. "We're here to find out about a woman who destroys entire worlds as easily as Sally slits throats."

They sat in silence for perhaps ten minutes. Then a very small man, his face disfigured by some skin disease that had gone untreated, walked up to them and sat down.

"Word is that you're looking for the Prophet," he said in a hoarse voice.

"That's right," said the Iceman.

"What are you paying?"

"Depends what you're selling."

"For three hundred New Stalin rubles, I can put you next to a guy who works for him."

"On this planet?"

"No," said the man. "But he's not far from here. You can reach him in half a day."

"And when I find out he doesn't exist, or that he's never heard of the Prophet, how long will it take me to find *you* again?" asked the Iceman.

"Are you calling me a liar?" demanded the man heatedly.

"No, just a lousy salesman," said the Iceman. "Now, go away."

"I ain't going anywhere till you pay me something for my time," said the man.

"Kid," said the Iceman. "Give him something for his time."

The Kid drew his sonic pistol so fast that even the Iceman, who was expecting it, couldn't follow the motion. A fraction of a second later it was pointed directly at the man's head.

"You want the down payment now or later?" asked the Iceman.

The man glared at him, trying to keep the fear from his face, then muttered a curse under his breath and scuttled off toward the corridor.

"I assume that was what you wanted me to do?" said the Kid.

The Iceman nodded. "But don't shoot anyone unless I tell you to," he said. "We won't be able to do any business if word gets out that we're killing the customers."

"We don't need customers like him."

"We're passing the word to the dregs of humanity," replied the Iceman. "Five out of six customers are going to be exactly like him. Offer them enough for a drink and a fix, and they'll swear to anything, sell you any information you're looking for—and be long gone, or dead, by the time you find out they were lying."

"So how will you know who's telling the truth?"

"There are ways," said the Iceman.

He got to his feet, returned their empty glasses to the bar, and ordered two more beers. Before he could take his first swallow, a well-dressed man with long, flowing golden hair sat down next to him.

"You're the Iceman?" he asked.

"That's right."

"I know a little something about the Prophet."

"What about him?" asked the Iceman.

"First of all, it's a *her*."

The Iceman pulled out a roll of bank notes, peeled one off, and laid it on the table in front of the blond man.

"Keep going," he said.

"She's on the Inner Frontier," said the man.

"Where?"

"I'm not sure what world. At various times I've heard she was on Oceana, Port Raven, and Primrose."

The Iceman laid another note on top of the first.

"What's her game?"

"Word is that she's raising an army, that she wants to take over some of the Frontier worlds."

The Iceman didn't pull out a note this time.

"Word is wrong. She doesn't need an army."

"Hey, I'm just telling you what I've heard."

"What else do you know, or think you know, about her?"

"She must have access to some awfully powerful weapons," said the man. "They say she blew up some alien world."

"Old news," replied the Iceman, refusing to peel off another note. "You got anything else?"

"That's it," said the man, picking up the two bank notes.

"Just a minute," said the Iceman as the man started to get up.

"Yeah?"

"I'll double what you've got if you can give me a name."

"A name?" The man looked puzzled.

"The name of the person who told you the Prophet is a woman."

"Won't do you much good. He's dead."

"I'll pay a hundred credits for the name, anyway."

The man paused and stared at him curiously. "Zanzibar Brooks," he said at last.

"Who was he?"

"He did a little of everything, you know what I mean?"

"I know what you mean," said the Iceman. "Was there paper on him?"

"Yeah. Fifty thousand credits, dead or alive." He paused. "He died in some bar brawl on Port Raven a couple of months ago." Suddenly he smiled. "If I'd have known it was going to happen, I'd have shot him myself and cashed the reward."

"He actually saw the Prophet?"

"He said he did."

The Iceman gave him a final bank note. "Thanks."

"My pleasure," said the man. "If you have anything else to ask me, I'll be in one of those rooms down the hall."

He got up and left the table.

"Did you believe him?" asked the Kid.

"He answered the first question right," said the Iceman. "As for the rest, it's just hearsay—and if there's one thing Penelope Bailey doesn't need, it's an army." He took a long swallow of his beer. "But if we don't find out anything more, we'll send a message to Port Raven and see if we can learn where this Zanzibar Brooks spent the last year of his life."

Two more men and a woman approached them in the next hour, none of them with anything to sell except sob stories about how they needed the money. The Iceman was about to leave when a tall, lean man entered the room, looked around, and approached his table.

"You're Mendoza?" he asked.

"Right."

"My name's Quinn. Mind if I sit down?"

"Be my guest."

The man named Quinn seated himself. "Who's he?" he asked, gesturing toward the Kid with his head.

"A friend. Anything you have to say, you can say in front of him."

Quinn smiled. "For what you're paying me, I'll say it in front of everyone."

"You don't know what I'm paying you."

"If it's less than five thousand credits, we've got nothing to talk about."

The Iceman stared at him, appraising him carefully. "What do you think you know that's worth five thousand credits?"

Quinn leaned back on his chair and smiled confidently. "I know where you can find the Prophet." He paused. "Are we in business, or do I walk?"

"We're in business," said the Iceman.

"I haven't seen any money yet."

The Iceman pulled out his roll and counted out five thousand credits, then laid it on the table in front of him.

"Start talking," he said.

"She's on Mozart."

"Mozart? I never heard of it."

"There's a star in the Terrazane sector called Symphony," said Quinn. "They named all the planets after composers, even the ones that weren't habitable. Beethoven and Sondheim are gas giants. Mozart is the third planet out from the star."

"What makes you think she's on Mozart?" asked the Iceman.

"Because I've seen her," said Quinn.

"What does she look like?"

"Blonde, medium height, late twenties, rather pretty actually."

The Iceman shoved the pile of notes over to Quinn.

"What else can you tell me about her?"

"She's one very strange lady, I can tell you that."

The Iceman laid his roll of notes on the table. "Keep talking."

"I work on a cargo ship," said Quinn. "Two weeks ago we developed engine trouble near the Symphony system and went into orbit around Mozart while we made repairs. Some of us got to spend a day on the planet."

"And?"

"It's not much of a world, just an agricultural colony that supplies food to half a dozen nearby mining worlds. But she rules it as if she were some kind of goddess. I mean, her word is *law,* and God help anyone who disobeys her, who even *thinks* of disobeying her." He paused. "She must be some kind of mutant or something, because she seems to know what they're thinking even before they do. They've tried to kill her a couple of times, and even though she doesn't have any bodyguards, they've never gotten close to her. I mean, hell, I saw her myself, plain as day, walking through town like she didn't have a care in the world. She never even asked what we were doing there; it was like she already knew."

"How long has she been there?" asked the Iceman.

Quinn shrugged. "Maybe four or five months."

"Why?"

"Why what?"

"Why is she on Mozart? What's her purpose there?"

"That'll be another five thousand."

The Iceman counted off the amount, and Quinn grabbed the money greedily.

"She plans to set up her own empire in the Inner Frontier," said Quinn.

"She told you that?"

"No, but she told someone on Mozart that I spoke to."

"You're sure?"

"I got no reason to lie to you."

"How does she plan to go about it?"

"They say she's pretty tight with a bunch of mercenaries," replied Quinn. "Maybe she plans to use them and pick up one colony world after another."

"Do you know anything else about her?" asked the Iceman.

"That's it."

"Well, you've been most helpful, Mr. Quinn. Let me buy you a drink before you leave."

"You've done enough for me already," said Quinn, smiling and holding up the wad of money.

"It's no problem."

"I really have to be going."

"But I insist," said the Iceman.

"I told you, I have to—"

Suddenly Quinn was looking into the barrel of the Kid's sonic pistol.

"Try to be a little more gracious, Mr. Quinn," said the Iceman, getting to his feet. "I'll be right back with your drink."

He walked over to the bar, whispered something to the obese bartender, then returned a moment later with a drink.

"Here you are, Mr. Quinn," he said pleasantly, placing the drink down on the table in front of Quinn.

"If you think you can poison me right here in front of everyone, you should know that I have friends," said Quinn.

"How very comforting," said the Iceman. "Now, drink up."

Quinn looked at the Kid's pistol once more, and then, very slowly, he lifted the glass up to his lips.

"Now, swallow it," said the Iceman sternly.

Quinn closed his eyes, took a deep breath, and downed the drink in a single gulp. Then he leaned back, half expecting to die in hideous agony. When nothing happened, he blinked once, then leaned forward, seemed about to say something, and then became almost rigid.

"It's all right, Mr. Quinn," said the Iceman. "You can hear and understand every word I'm saying. Let me assure you that you have not been poisoned, nor do I intend to rob you. I just want to repeat a couple of my questions." He paused. "What is the Prophet's purpose on Mozart?"

"I don't know," murmured Quinn, his words slurred slightly.

"And no one on Mozart told you that she planned to set up her own empire, did they?"

"No."

"But you did see her there?"

"Yes."

"Thank you very much, Mr. Quinn," said the Iceman. He leaned over and took half of his money back. "You earned the first five thousand credits . . . but you really shouldn't be so greedy. I didn't get to be a rich man by paying people to lie to me." He got to his feet and motioned the Kid to do the same.

"We're going to leave now, Mr. Quinn," he continued. "Your muscles will respond to your commands in about ten minutes, and you'll suffer no side effects from the drug I had placed in your drink. It's a powder that encourages you to tell the truth, with just enough of a narcotic added so that you should enjoy the next couple of minutes immensely." He gave the motionless man a friendly pat on the shoulder, and suddenly his voice became low and ominous. "I would strongly suggest that you enjoy your five thousand credits, and that you make no attempt to follow us when you are once more capable of movement."

Then he and the Kid walked back through the labyrinthian corridor and out the main entrance of the House of Usher.

"What do we do now?" asked the Kid as they began walking down Nightmare Alley.

"Now?" repeated the Iceman. "Now we follow our lead as far as we can. We try to learn a little more about Mozart, and we try to find some more people who have been there and seen the Prophet. Then we try to find out what she's done that has alerted the Anointed One to her presence and made him decide that she presents a greater threat to him than the Democracy does."

"*If* she does," the Kid corrected him.

"Oh, she does, all right," said the Iceman with absolute conviction. "I'm just surprised that he's figured it out."

"And once we do all that," said the Kid, "*then* we go to Mozart?"

"One of us does," answered the Iceman.

13

The Iceman remained on Confucius IV for another day, but could learn nothing further about the Prophet. However, the Silicon Kid managed to learn a little something about the Iceman.

They were sitting in the lobby of their pagoda-like hotel, having breakfast prior to going to the spaceport, when Quinn entered the building, walked across the lobby, and confronted them.

"I see you're feeling better," said the Iceman pleasantly.

"You son of a bitch!" snarled Quinn, attracting considerable attention from the other diners. "You doped me up and took my money!"

"You sold information you didn't have," answered the Iceman. "That made it *my* money."

"It's mine, and I'm here to take it back! If I have to kill you for it, I will!"

The Kid tensed, but the Iceman leaned over and laid a restraining hand on his shoulder.

"The man means business," he said. "We'd better give him what he wants."

"But—" began the Kid.

"It's just money," said the Iceman. "It's not worth dying for."

He reached into the pocket where he kept his roll of bills while Quinn watched him intently. Then he calmly pulled out a small pistol and fired it, point-blank, between Quinn's eyes. Two women shrieked and a waiter dropped his tray. The tall man was dead before he hit the ground.

"I told you it wasn't worth dying for," said the Iceman to the corpse.

"You killed him!" said the Kid.

"I sure as hell hope so."

"You didn't even give him a chance."

"You think this is some kind of a game?" said the Iceman irritably. "We don't play by any rules out here." He paused. "The man came here to rob me or kill me. Maybe you think I should have waited for him to draw his weapon?"

The Kid made no reply, and the Iceman got to his feet as the manager and two security guards approached him.

"Everyone in the restaurant was a witness," said the Iceman. "He threatened to kill me."

"He threatened to kill you if you didn't give him your money," said a man at the next table.

"Same thing," said the Iceman. "I didn't come here to be robbed at gunpoint."

"His gun's still in its holster," noted the manager.

The Iceman shrugged. "He was a lousy robber."

"We've got the whole thing on holotape," said one of the security guards. "If it happened the way you said, you don't have any problem."

"I never did," replied the Iceman, and somehow the Kid knew that he was right.

Two policemen entered the hotel a moment later and walked over to the crowd that was clustered around Quinn's body, then listened as the Iceman repeated his story.

"Sounds good to me," said one of them. "You want to come down to headquarters and make a statement?"

"I'll make it right here," said the Iceman. "The man was a fool. He paid for his foolishness."

"That wasn't the kind of statement I had in mind," said the officer with a smile.

"It's the only one I care to make," replied the Iceman. "Can you check the holotape this morning? My associate and I plan to leave Confucius this afternoon."

The officer stared at him intently. "You're Carlos Mendoza, aren't you?"

"Yes."

The officer nodded. "I thought so," he said. "If you say it was self-defense, that's good enough for me. You're free on your own recognizance, and we'll view the tape before noon. If it supports your story, you'll be free to leave on schedule."

"Fair enough," said the Iceman.

The holotape verified the Iceman's account of the incident, and they took off in early afternoon.

"Now I know why they call you the Iceman," remarked the Kid as they left Confucius far behind them.

"Oh?"

"You're as cold and emotionless as you say Penelope Bailey is," said the Kid. "I'm not saying that's a bad way to be," he added hastily. "Out here it's probably a survival trait." He paused. "You must have been one hell of a dangerous man when you were younger."

"I'm more dangerous now."

The Kid stared at him for a long moment, then shrugged. "If you say so." He paused. "By the way, a lot of people on Confucius seemed to know you."

"I've done business there before."

"They all called you Mendoza rather than the Iceman," continued the Kid. "Why?"

"Nicknames come and go, but I've been Carlos Mendoza all my life."

" 'The Iceman' fits you better."

"Thank you . . . I think," replied the Iceman with an amused smile.

"What other names have you had over the years?"

"They're not important."

They fell silent for the next few minutes. Then the Kid walked to the galley and made himself some dinner. When he returned to his seat, he found that the Iceman was studying the navigational computer's holographic representation of the Terrazane sector.

"Looking for Mozart?" asked the Kid.

"I've found it," said the Iceman, indicating a star that was blinking a bright yellow. "This is Symphony. Mozart is the third planet circling it."

"How far away is it?"

"From here?" said the Iceman. "At full speed, we can make it there in a little over one Standard day."

"What do I do once I get there?" asked the Kid.

"Eventually you'll try to get close enough to Penelope Bailey to find out what her plans are. As for what you'll do immediately, I don't know yet. That's why we're heading for Aristotle."

"Aristotle?"

"It's a university planet on the edge of the Democracy. We'll pay a fee and tie into their computer, and find out what we can about Mozart."

"Why don't we just tie into the Master Computer on Deluros VIII?" asked the Kid.

"Because she's more likely to have someone monitoring the Master Computer than the one on Aristotle," replied the Iceman.

"What makes you think so?" persisted the Kid. "After all, if she's as bright as you say ..."

"I never said she was bright. I said she was precognitive."

"Whatever," said the Kid. "Why won't she be monitoring the computer on Aristotle?"

The Iceman leaned back and switched off the holographic display. "She's the most powerful and dangerous being alive, but she's not without her limitations," he said at last. "She spent her childhood on the run until she was eight years old, and she spent the next sixteen or seventeen years in a twenty-by-twenty cell. How much of the galaxy can she have seen? Deluros VIII is the capital world of the race of Man, so of course she knows about it—but I'll bet she's never even heard of Aristotle."

"You'd better be right," said the Kid. "You may be making the bet, but I'm the one who has to pay if you're wrong."

"I'm not wrong," said the Iceman. "She has powers beyond anyone's comprehension, but she's not all-knowing." He paused. "Anyway, once we learn a little more about Mozart, we'll have a better idea what identity you should assume there."

"Why don't I just show up as a gun for hire?" suggested the Kid.

The Iceman chuckled.

"What's so funny?" demanded the Kid.

"Nobody ever needed a hired gun less than Penelope Bailey," said the Iceman. "Besides, even if she did, she'd want references—and since I'm the only reference you've got, you wouldn't make it to noon."

"I could say I worked for the Gravedancer."

"Lomax *is* a hired gun. He doesn't hire them himself."

The Kid shrugged. "It was just a suggestion."

"If you believe even half of what I've told you about her, it was a stupid suggestion," answered the Iceman. "If you want to live through this, you'd better start using your brain."

"All right," said the Kid irritably. "You don't have to bite my head off."

"Your head is all you've got," said the Iceman. "My advice to you is that you remember that, and forget about your silicon-enhanced physical abilities."

"Some of those abilities may prove damned useful on Mozart."

"Like what?"

"Like being able to see in the dark."

"She doesn't have to see; she'll know where you are and where you're going to be thirty seconds and thirty minutes from now."

"If I'm so stupid and so useless, why are you sending me in at all?" demanded the Kid.

"I'd go myself if I could, but I can't hide this limp, and besides, she'd know who I was anyway." He paused. "You're going in because you're the only piece I've got to play."

"Thanks for building my confidence," said the Kid sardonically.

"Just see that you don't get overconfident," responded the Iceman. "No matter how I've prepared you, if you live long enough to meet her, what you're going to see is a very normal-looking young woman, and you're going to think I've exaggerated the threat she poses." He paused for a moment. "Just remember: better men than you have tried to stop her, and every last one of them is dead."

"Then why am I going in at all?"

"You're not going there to hurt her, or even threaten her," answered the Iceman. "You're just trying to get some information. If she can't see far enough ahead, if she doesn't know what you plan to do with it, you just might come out of this in one piece."

The Iceman stood up, stretched his arms (as much as he *could* stretch them in the cramped confines of the cockpit), and turned to the Kid. "I'm going to grab some sleep before we reach Aristotle," he announced. "You might consider doing the same."

The Kid nodded and went to his own bunk. He was sure that he would have a difficult time falling asleep, but after what seemed only a moment to him the Iceman was shaking him by the shoulder.

"What's the matter?" he said groggily, sitting up abruptly, and inadvertently banging his head against a bulkhead. "Am I in the wrong bunk?"

The Iceman smiled. "There are only two."

"Then what's wrong?"

"Nothing. You've been asleep for eleven hours." He paused. "We're in orbit around Aristotle."

"You're kidding!" said the Kid, getting stiffly to his feet.

"Check the ship's chronometer if you don't believe me," said the Iceman. "I already made us some breakfast."

"You never miss a meal, do you?"

"Not if I can help it."

The Kid joined the Iceman in the galley, which was almost as claustrophobic as the cockpit. "Did you ever consider getting a bigger ship?" he asked as he picked up his coffee mug and took a swallow.

"I suppose if I had thought about it, I would have," admitted the Iceman. "I had never planned to leave Last Chance again."

"Not much of a world, if you ask me."

"I didn't."

"A man like you, with the money you've made, you ought to be living next to your friend on Sweetwater."

"It's a matter of taste," answered the Iceman. "I like the Inner Frontier."

"Sweetwater is on the Frontier."

"But it's not really a Frontier world," said the Iceman. "It's a haven for retired billionaires. Last Chance suits me just fine."

"I kind of liked Confucius, myself," said the Kid. "Especially Nightmare Alley."

"You're young yet."

The ship's computer beeped twice.

"Yes?" said the Iceman.

"I have established a link to the geopolitical computer on Aristotle," announced the computer.

"Good," said the Iceman. "Extract whatever information it has on a planet called Mozart."

"Star system?" asked the computer.

"Symphony, in the Terrazane sector."

"Working . . . extracted."

"All right," said the Iceman. "Now see if it's got any data on a human known as the Prophet."

"Working . . . negative."

"All right," said the Iceman. "Break the connection and have the connect fee billed to my account on Binder X."

"Working . . . done . . . connection broken," said the computer.

"Now give me a hard copy of what you extracted."

A moment later the computer produced a single sheet of paper.

"That's everything?" asked the Iceman, frowning.

"Yes."

"Deactivate."

He picked up the sheet and read it, then looked at the Kid. "There's not much information here to go on," he announced.

"So I gather," replied the Kid. "What *do* we have?"

The Iceman looked down at the sheet again. "Mozart is an oxygen world, ninety-six percent Standard gravity, population 27,342 as of the last census." He paused. "The population breaks down this way: sixty-three percent agricultural; twenty-two percent in the export business, and of course what they're exporting are agricultural products; the rest in miscellaneous businesses. No standing army, no navy. The planet is divided into six states, with a central governing body that's elected every three years. Only one spaceport, no tourist industry."

"So I show up as a farm worker looking for a job?" asked the Kid.

The Iceman shook his head. "You get stuck on a farm, you might never get off it."

"I could go to one of their towns and hire on at some store, I suppose."

"Too obvious," answered the Iceman after some consideration. "I mean, who the hell goes to an agricultural world to work as a clerk, or even a store manager?"

"Then what?"

The Iceman stared at him for a long moment. "You're the Silicon Kid," he said. "Go there as a specialist, selling your skills." He paused, waiting for the full scenario to come to him, and then spoke again. "You travel the Inner Frontier, creating whatever chips are needed. A farmer with a predator problem needs to see in the dark to protect his stock; an exporter needs to store a dozen alien languages in his head; a bartender wants to be able to mix drinks faster. You can produce the chips they need. I think it should work."

"I'm good," said the Kid, "but I'm no miracle man—and no surgeon. Even if I make the chips, I can't implant most of them."

"That's not your job," said the Iceman, shrugging it off. "Your job is just to create the chips. It's up to the buyers to get 'em implanted."

"On a planet with a population of only twenty-seven thousand Men, there might not be a doctor who can do it."

"All the better," said the Iceman. "It'll give you a reason to hang around until one can be sent for. They're not going to let you leave until they know your product works."

"What kind of chip can I sell Penelope Bailey?" asked the Kid.

"She doesn't need one."

"Too bad," said the Kid. "It would have been a great way to make her notice me."

"You're just going there to get information," said the Iceman. "If you're very lucky, she won't notice you at all."

"You don't make her sound like the type who confides in her lieutenants," said the Kid. "If I don't make personal contact with her, how am I going to find anything out?"

"I'd be surprised if she *has* any lieutenants," replied the Iceman. "As for gathering information, keep your eyes and ears open."

"You mean like, see if they're importing arms and ammunition?"

The Iceman shook his head. "She doesn't need that."

"Then what?"

"I wish I could tell you," said the Iceman. "It'll probably be something very ordinary, until you remember that a very extraordinary woman is behind it."

"Give me an example."

"See if she's ordered half a dozen books about Deluros VIII; it could mean she plans to go there next. Find out if she's ordered a Lodin language tape; she could be planning an alliance with the Lodinites. Don't bother with what she's doing now; she's seen the present so many times in so many of its manifestations it's almost as if she's walking through a play. Whatever she's saying and doing now is old news to her; she's looking days or weeks ahead."

"That's not a hell of a lot to go on," said the Kid.

The Iceman smiled grimly. "Were you under the delusion that this was going to be easy?"

"No, but—"

"Just remember that you're *only* there for information—and if it's too difficult to get, if you have to rob or kill someone to obtain it, forget it, because she'll see what you're going to do before you even think of it. Do you understand what I'm saying to you?"

"Yes."

"Good—because your life depends on it." The Iceman paused for a moment. "Your life, and maybe forty trillion others," he amended.

PART 3

———
———
———
———
———
———
———
———
———
———
———

The
Silicon
Kid's
Book

14

Mozart's spaceport was just beyond the city limits of Minuet, a town that supplied the surrounding agricultural community with the basics: a grocery store, a very small medical clinic, a trio of seed stores, a pair of restaurants, some small hotels, and a theater that housed live entertainment four or five days a year.

Just past the spaceport were huge silos where mutated corn and wheat were dried out and stored until they could be shipped, and enormous pens that held genetically altered cattle that topped four thousand pounds at maturity.

The Kid landed, made arrangements to store the Iceman's ship in a hangar, and then entered the small spaceport, where a slidewalk took him directly to a customs booth. He entered it, sat down, and faced a computer with a glowing red sensor.

"Name?" said a mechanical voice.

"Neil Cayman," he replied, then added, "also known as the Silicon Kid."

"Display your passport to the sensor, please."

He held his passport up.

"Are you bringing any foodstuffs or animals from off-planet?"

"No."

"Please state the nature of your business on Mozart."

"I am a salesman, specializing in custom-tailoring computer chips for surgical implantation."

"Do you possess cash or a line of credit totaling at least two thousand credits or its equivalent?"

The Kid held up the money the Iceman had given him, and the sensor scanned the denominations.

"No visa is required for your trip to Mozart. Please enjoy your stay, Neil Cayman." There was a pause. "I can find no reference to your alias," continued the computer. "Would you like it appended to your passport?"

"Yes, please."

"Please hold up your passport again."

He did so, and a very thin laser beam shot out and burned a tiny notation onto the titanium card, just beneath his holograph and legal name.

"I have some questions," said the Kid, putting the passport back into his pocket.

"I am programmed to answer most questions dealing with Mozart," replied the computer. "Should the nature of your question require a subjective answer, I will direct you to the proper planetary authority who *can* answer you."

"That's very accommodating of you," said the Kid wryly.

"I exist to serve."

"I'll need a place to stay while I'm here. Can you recommend a hotel in Minuet?"

The computer's screen suddenly came to life. "These five establishments currently have rooms or suites available," it said, flashing a listing.

"Can you make a reservation for me?"

"Yes."

"Fine," said the Kid, studying the list. "I'd like a room at the Manor House."

"For how many nights will you require your room?"

"I don't know," answered the Kid. "Can you make it open?"

"Yes. Ground floor or second floor?"

"Second floor."

"Room 207 has been reserved in your name."

"I'll also need a vehicle."

The screen changed. "Here is a list of those vehicles available for rental at the spaceport, plus their daily charges."

The Kid selected one.

"One more thing," said the Kid. "I'd like to know if any business on the planet specializes in implanted biochips."

"No."

"Good. Can I place an advertisement in every planetary newspaper or newstape to the effect that I have just arrived and that that is my specialty, and that I can be contacted at the Manor House?"

"Working . . ." said the computer, buzzing quietly. "There are three planetary newstapes, Mr. Cayman, two weekly and one daily. Each has requested that you supply an exact wording for your advertisement."

"I see," said the Kid. He paused for a moment. "I assume there's a personal computer with a planetary tie-in in my room at the Manor House."

"That is correct."

"If you can have the electronic addresses of the three newstape advertising departments waiting for me on my computer, I'll create the ads when I get there."

There was a brief humming. "It has been done."

"Oh, one more thing," said the Kid. "I'd like a listing of churches on the planet."

There was an immediate listing of fourteen churches. All were sects that were known to him; none seemed likely to be connected to the Anointed One or Penelope Bailey.

"Thank you."

The Kid got up and left the booth, walked to the vehicle rental area, signed for the groundcar he had selected, brought up a map that included the spaceport and Minuet on the instrument panel's viewscreen, and began driving toward the town, passing what seemed like two or three miles of cattle feedlots along the way.

Minuet was a small town, and as he reached the commercial district, he realized that the computer had been somewhat optimistic in its use of the word "hotel." The Manor House, like its fellow hostelries, was a refurbished structure that had been built some two centuries earlier and had been a very impressive mansion before it had been remodeled and turned into a rooming house. Now it catered to visiting salesmen, most of whom dealt in mutated seeds and fertilizers that had been created to work on worlds similar to this one.

He left the groundcar in a lot behind the house, checked in at the desk, registered his voiceprint, waited until the lock on the door to Room 207 was coded to it, and allowed the airlift to gently transport him to the second level of the boardinghouse.

The room itself was a little more spartan than the one he had stayed in on Olympus. It consisted of a bed, two chairs, a computer station in the corner, and a bathroom with a Dryshower and a chemical toilet. He pulled the addresses of the newstape offices from the computer, wrote a brief ad, and sent it off to each of them. He then ordered electronic editions of the three newstapes, scanned them as they appeared on his computer, and was not surprised to find no mention of the Prophet in any of them. He left the room after about an hour, descended to the ground level, and walked across the street to a small restaurant, where he ordered lunch.

When he returned to his room, there was already one response to his advertisement, from a silo manager who had breathed in one preservative too many and wanted a chip to warn him when the chemical content in the air reached a certain level. He asked the man to send him the formulas for those preservatives that were being used, and promised to get back to him within three days. Then, with nothing further to do, and not wishing to spend the afternoon actually creating the chip, he decided to lie down and take a nap until dinnertime.

When he awoke he ate a dinner of mutated soya products in the same restaurant where he had had lunch, then walked out onto the street just as the sun was going down. It was cool and dry, with a very mild breeze coming from the west, and he found it very refreshing.

He looked up and down the street, unwilling to go back to his room right away. Most of the town was already closed down for the night, and he found that if he wished to remain away from his hotel, his choice was limited to a holo theater, a tavern, and a casino. He didn't like holos, and he knew just enough about gambling to know he wasn't much good at it, so he wandered over to the tavern.

It was rather small, especially for the only tavern in the town. As soon as he entered it he encountered a purple-and-gold avian that was chained to its perch atop a metal stand. It stared at him, screeched once, and then concentrated on preening itself, paying him no further attention. The Kid gave it a wide berth—it was relatively small, no more than three pounds, but it had a wicked-looking beak—and walked up to the bar, where he ordered a beer. The bartender nodded, filled a glass, and slid it over to him. The Kid picked it up and carried it over to an empty table near the back of the room.

A few moments later a tall man, dark of skin and sporting two gold teeth that gleamed whenever he spoke or smiled, walked over to him, a beer in his hand.

"Mind if I join you?" he asked. "All the other tables seem to be full."

"Be my guest," said the Kid.

"Thanks," said the man. He extended his hand. "My name's James Mboya."

"Neil Cayman," said the Kid, taking his hand.

"You're new here, aren't you?"

The Kid nodded. "Just got in today."

"What are you selling?"

"What makes you think I'm selling anything?"

Mboya laughed. "Because nobody comes to a farming world for pleasure."

"Doesn't anyone ever come here to buy instead of sell?"

Mboya shook his head. "All our beef and produce are contracted for the next decade. We supply a hell of a lot of worlds." He paused. "I could sell you some gold, if you want." He grinned, displaying his two gold teeth. "They're removable. I hock 'em whenever I need some money, then buy 'em back when I'm flush."

The Kid sipped his beer. "Chips," he said at last.

"I beg your pardon?"

"Computer chips. That's what I sell."

"What kind?"

"Whatever kind you want me to create for you."

"Something that would make me feel ten years younger when I wake up in the morning might be nice," said Mboya with a smile.

"It could be done," said the Kid.

"Really?"

"You wouldn't *be* any younger, but I could create a chip that would mask any aches and pains you had."

Mboya snapped his fingers. "Just like that?" he asked, still smiling.

"No," said the Kid. "I'd have to speak to your doctor, find out what's ailing you, which muscles are degenerating, learn your whole medical history. *Then* I could make it." The Kid paused. "*He'd* have to implant it, though; I'm just a technician, not a surgeon."

"How long do you plan to be on Mozart?" asked Mboya. "If I can put the money together, you just might have yourself a client."

The Kid shrugged. "It depends on how much business I can do

here," he said, taking another sip of his beer. "I've placed some ads. Now it's just a matter of waiting."

"Maybe I can show you around while you're here," offered Mboya. "Not that there's all that much to see."

"Well, there's one thing I'd like to see," answered the Kid after some thought.

"Oh? What is that?"

"While I was on a nearby world, I heard that you've got someone here called the Prophet, someone who can see the future." He paused. "I'd like to meet her."

"Why?"

The Kid smiled. "I'd sure like some investment advice. Maybe I could trade a couple of custom-made chips for it."

"Well, I see her from time to time," answered Mboya. "I can pass the word and see if she's interested." He paused. "No reason why she shouldn't be," he added thoughtfully. "I mean, just knowing you're going to wake up with a hangover doesn't make the hangover go away."

"I'd appreciate that," said the Kid. He noticed that Mboya had finished his beer. "Let me buy the next round."

"Thanks," said Mboya. "Much appreciated."

The Kid signaled the bartender to bring two beers over to the table. "Other than frequenting the casino down the block, what do people do for fun around here?"

"This is an agricultural world," replied Mboya with a laugh. "They talk about planting, fertilizer, and the weather. Mostly the weather. Once in a long while they might have a cattle show. That's about it."

"Not exactly thrilling," said the Kid wryly.

"If you want thrills, you should go to a world like Calliope, or maybe Confucius—not a farm world."

"Have you ever been to them?"

"Once or twice," said Mboya.

"What the hell kind of business can a farmer possibly have on Confucius?" asked the Kid as the bartender arrived with their beers.

Mboya paused and studied the Kid. "I didn't say I was a farmer."

"No, I suppose you didn't," said the Kid. "What *do* you do?"

Mboya shrugged expansively. "Oh, a little of this, a little of that. A few deals here, a few there."

"How long have you been on Mozart?"

"A few months. It's a pleasant enough world. A little on the dull side, as you've already noticed, but the climate's nice, the people are friendly, and your money goes a long way here." He paused. "It's no worse than most worlds, and probably better than a lot of them."

"Where are you from originally?" asked the Kid, picking up his new beer and taking a swallow.

"Back in the Democracy," said Mboya with an expression of contempt. "A little world named Far London." He paused. "I decided that a man with my talents could go a lot further on the Inner Frontier."

"What *are* your talents?"

"You'll laugh."

"No, I won't," said the Kid.

Mboya shrugged. "Right at the moment, I'm in pest control."

"Pest control?" repeated the Kid, surprised.

"You have a pest problem, you send for me and I cure it."

"Well, at least I understand why you're on an agricultural world," said the Kid. "They must have a lot of work for you here."

"I keep busy," answered Mboya, finishing off his beer and putting the empty glass back on the table.

"Sounds like dull work, if you don't mind my saying so," said the Kid.

"I rather enjoy it," replied Mboya.

"To each his own."

"True," agreed Mboya. "As for myself, I'd go crazy spending all my time creating computer chips."

"So would I," answered the Kid. "That's why I was looking for a little action."

"If you don't like gambling, you're out of luck in Minuet," said Mboya.

"It occurs to me that the Prophet could break the bank if she's all she's supposed to be," said the Kid.

"I doubt they'd allow her to play," responded Mboya.

"She's that good?"

"If you owned the casino, would you take the chance that she might be?" asked Mboya.

"I wonder what the hell someone like her is doing out here on a world like this in the first place," said the Kid.

"You seem very interested in her," observed Mboya.

"She sounds like a very interesting person," answered the Kid. "And I really *could* use some investment advice."

"What, exactly, have you heard about her?"

"Just that she's supposed to be able to foresee the future," answered the Kid.

"Nothing more?"

"Well, I heard some rumors that she used to be the Oracle, but I don't believe it." The Kid watched Mboya to see if there was any reaction. There wasn't. "Hell, everyone knows that the Iceman killed the Oracle a few years back."

"The Iceman!" said Mboya. "Now, *there's* a name to conjure with!"

"You've heard of him?"

"Who hasn't?" replied Mboya. "He's a legend out here." He paused. "I'd like to meet him someday—if he's still alive, that is."

The Kid looked at the empty glasses. "Care for another round?" he asked.

"No," said Mboya. "I think I'm going to go try my luck at the roulette table down the street."

"I never much liked roulette," said the Kid. "Too big a percentage for the house."

"I don't like it all that much myself," said Mboya. Suddenly he grinned. "But as the old saying goes, it's the only game in town. In this case, literally."

"Good luck," said the Kid.

"Perhaps you'd care to come along?" suggested Mboya, getting to his feet. "They've also got blackjack, poker, and *jabob*."

"I'll probably be along later," said the Kid. "I think I'll have another beer first. I had a long nap this afternoon; I'm good for hours yet."

"Well, thank you for the beer, Mr. Cayman," said Mboya. "I hope you'll let me return the favor if you show up at the casino before I leave."

"It's a deal," said the Kid.

Mboya grinned. "That's always assuming I haven't gone broke in the interim."

"One of those gold teeth ought to buy the best bottle in the house," said the Kid.

Mboya laughed and walked out into the night, and the Kid picked up his glass and walked over to the bar.

"I'll have another," he said.

"Coming right up," said the bartender, bringing him a fresh glass.

"Interesting guy, that Mboya," said the Kid. "Does he come here often?"

"Oh, he comes by every now and then, when his boss sends him," answered the bartender. "But I've never heard him called Mboya before."

"That's not his real name?" asked the Kid.

The bartender shrugged. "For all I know it is—but out here on the Frontier they call him the Black Death."

"The Black Death?" repeated the Kid.

"The way you two were getting on, I thought you knew him."

The Kid shook his head. "He just walked up and introduced himself. Told me he was in pest control."

The bartender chuckled. "Well, in a way, I suppose he is."

"In what way?"

"He's the Prophet's bodyguard."

15

The Kid nursed his next beer for half an hour, then wandered over to the casino.

It was a large room, far larger than the Iceman's on Last Chance. There were half a dozen blackjack tables, four poker tables, a pair of roulette wheels, a craps table, a billiard table, two *jabob* games, and another alien game that he had never seen before.

The casino was relatively empty when the Kid arrived. There were perhaps fifteen men and women playing the various games, and not a single alien to be seen. The Kid immediately spotted Mboya, the solitary player at one of the roulette wheels, and walked over to him.

"Hello, Neil," said Mboya with a friendly smile. "Glad you decided to come on over."

"There was nothing else to do," said the Kid with a shrug. "By the way, do I call you Mr. Mboya or Mr. Death?"

Mboya laughed. "James will do."

"But you *are* the Black Death?" persisted the Kid.

"Some people call me that." Mboya studied the table, then placed a pair of chips on Odd and another on Red.

"I see you like to play it safe," noted the Kid.

"The odds are thirty-five to one that you'll lose if you bet on a number," answered Mboya. "I don't really expect to win when I come here, but I'd like my money to last long enough for me to enjoy myself for a couple of hours."

"Why are you here at all?" asked the Kid.

"I like to gamble. Where *should* I be?"

"Talking to me. That was your assignment, wasn't it?"

"I *am* talking to you," said Mboya easily. "No reason why I shouldn't enjoy myself while I'm doing it."

"Does she send you out to talk to every newcomer to Mozart?" asked the Kid.

"No," said Mboya as the wheel started spinning. "Just the ones she's curious about."

"Why is she curious about me?"

Mboya shrugged. "Who knows what makes her curious, or why she does anything she does?" He cursed beneath his breath as the number came up Even and Black. "Damn! You wouldn't think anyone could lose this consistently! I bet Black four times in a row and it comes up Red all four times . . . so I finally bet Red, and it comes up Black. If I didn't know better, I'd say the wheel was rigged."

"What makes you think it isn't?" asked the Kid.

"Because if it was, no man having anything to do with this casino would be alive tomorrow morning," answered Mboya seriously. "And they know it." He stared at the table again, trying to decide which number to bet, then finally shrugged and straightened up. "I've had enough of this game. It's time to find a slower way to lose my money." He spotted the empty pool table. "You ever shoot any pool, Neil?"

"Once in a while."

"Good," said Mboya, walking to the table and studying its green felt surface. "Care to play for a small stake, just to make it interesting?"

"It wouldn't be fair," said the Kid.

"I'm not a hustler," Mboya assured him.

"I know. It wouldn't be fair, because you can't win."

Mboya grinned. "Well, now, I wouldn't necessarily say *that*, either."

"It's the truth," said the Kid.

"I thought you only played once in a while."

"That's right."

"Then why should I believe you?"

"Believe whatever you want." Suddenly the Kid shrugged and smiled. "One hundred credits a game?"

"Sounds good to me," said Mboya, selecting a cue and starting to chalk the tip of it.

"Just remember I warned you," said the Kid, picking his cue

and walking back to the table.

"I admire your confidence," said Mboya. "Rack 'em."

The Kid's confidence turned out to be well placed, as he had known it would be. The chips that were tied into his eyes showed him every tiny irregularity in the table's surface; the chips in his shoulders allowed him to make every shot with the same sure stroke; the chip he'd had implanted on Sweetwater allowed him to lean far over the table without any discomfort or loss of balance. He easily beat Mboya three games in a row, and was about to rack the balls for a fourth game when the Black Death called it quits and pulled three hundred-credit notes out of his wallet.

"You ought to quit the chip business and turn pool shark," he said ruefully as he laid the money on the table.

"Maybe someday I will," answered the Kid, picking it up and stuffing it into his wallet.

Mboya signaled to a lone waiter, who was wandering around the casino taking orders.

"A pair of beers, please," he said when the waiter approached them. He wiped his brow and turned to the Kid. "Let's have a seat. Losing at roulette and pool is thirsty work."

"You never had a chance," said the Kid, following him to an unoccupied card table.

"I knew that after about the fifth shot," Mboya agreed with a wry smile as he sat down opposite the Kid. "I don't know where you learned to play, and your style is unorthodox as all hell—but somebody sure as hell taught you well."

It was the Kid's turn to smile. "I doubt that I've played half a dozen times in my life."

"I don't believe it!" said Mboya adamantly.

"I have no reason to lie to you," said the Kid. "I didn't lie about your chances, either: I told you on the front end that I was going to win."

"So sue me," said Mboya. "I didn't know you'd be that good."

"There's a lot about me you don't know," replied the Kid. He paused. "That neither you nor your boss knows."

"I don't suppose you'd care to confide in me," suggested Mboya with a smile.

The Kid shook his head. "Anything she wants to know, she can ask me directly."

"That's not her style, Neil."

"They she'll have to change it," said the Kid firmly.

Mboya seemed amused. "She doesn't change for other people; they change for her."

"Why?"

"Because she's the Prophet." He paused. "Why are you so interested in meeting her?"

"I told you."

"I know what you told me," said Mboya. "I just thought you might prefer to tell me the truth."

"Are you calling me a liar?" said the Kid.

"Not at all," answered Mboya calmly. "If I called you a liar, you'd probably take offense, and then I'd have to kill you—and you seem like a nice enough young man."

"I might be a lot harder to kill than you think," said the Kid.

"That's possible," admitted Mboya. "A lot of men I've killed were harder to kill than I had thought they would be—but they're all dead, just the same." He paused. "Maybe we ought to change the subject, before I start getting curious about just how hard you'd be to kill."

"Suits me," said the Kid. "I've got no quarrel with you. You're just the hired help." He paused. "Of course, you did lie to me over at the tavern."

"Why would I lie to you?"

"You said you were in pest control."

"I am," answered Mboya easily. "That's why I'm here: to see just how much of a pest you intend to be, and how much controlling you'll need."

"I told you," said the Kid. "I sell computer chips."

"I know what you told me," said Mboya. "I didn't believe you then, and I don't believe you now."

"Order a chip from me and you'll see you were wrong." The Kid smiled. "If nothing else, it'll improve your pool game."

The waiter finally arrived with their beers, and Mboya tossed a couple of coins on his tray.

"They make a lot of good things on Mozart," said Mboya, grimacing as he emptied the container into his glass, "but beer, alas, isn't one of them."

"So order an import."

"As long as I'm here, I feel I ought to support the local industries."

The Kid stared at him curiously. "You're a strange kind of killer."

"Well, if it comes to that, you're a strange kind of traveling salesman," replied Mboya.

The Kid stared at him. "I was minding my own business," he said defensively. "*You* sought *me* out."

"That's my job."

"So you said," replied the Kid. "I'd just like to know why she's curious about me."

Mboya grinned. "Mine is not to reason why."

"Yours is just to protect her with your life, right?"

"Wrong."

"The bartender at the tavern said you were her bodyguard," said the Kid.

Mboya shook his head. "She doesn't need a bodyguard. I'm just her eyes and ears when she's occupied with other matters—which is most of the time."

"What's she like?"

"Different."

"In what way?"

"*I'm* supposed to be asking the questions," said Mboya.

"I don't have to answer them."

"No," agreed Mboya. "But you'd make my job much easier if you would."

The Kid finally took a long swallow of his beer, then stared at Mboya. "Why do I care if your job's easy or hard?"

"Because when I get frustrated in my work, I get ill-tempered," said Mboya. "Believe me, you wouldn't like me when I'm ill-tempered."

"I don't think I like you all that much right now," answered the Kid.

Mboya studied him carefully. "Do you know something else you're not telling me, Neil?"

"Like what?"

"I don't know. But most people don't talk to me like that unless they think they've got some kind of an edge."

"What I know is *my* business," answered the Kid. "And you can stop calling me Neil."

"I thought it was your name."

"It used to be. Nowadays I'm the Silicon Kid."

"Never heard of you," said Mboya.

"You will," said the Kid. "That's a promise."

"So you think you can make your reputation by taking out

the Prophet, is that it?" asked Mboya, obviously amused by the thought. "Take my advice, Kid, and forget about her. Go after the Gravedancer, or maybe Lizard Malloy. Who knows? If you get lucky, or you catch them on a bad day, you just might live through it."

"I didn't come to Mozart to kill anyone," replied the Kid. "I'm just here to sell computer chips."

"Ah, I understand now!" said Mboya with an amused grin. "We're all going to hear about you because you're going to become the galaxy's most famous traveling salesman."

"You're going to hear of me because there's always going to be someone like you who doesn't take me seriously," said the Kid. "And that's a mistake."

"Well, I'll certainly take that under advisement," said Mboya. He paused and stared at the Kid. "By the way, where's all the silicon that makes you the Silicon Kid?"

"It's in place," said the Kid.

"That's right," said Mboya. "You specialize in implants, don't you?"

"Yes."

"Well, you'll have to pardon me if I don't faint dead away with terror," said Mboya.

"I pardon you," said the Kid seriously.

Mboya placed his glass on the table. "You're an interesting young man," he continued. "I bear you no ill will, and I wish you a long and happy life."

"Thanks. I plan to enjoy it."

"Then take my advice and don't go looking for—" Suddenly Mboya froze, his eyes on the doorway.

"Is something wrong?" asked the Kid, turning to see what Mboya was staring at.

Three men, all dressed in nondescript outfits, their pockets bulging with weapons, had entered the casino, but instead of walking to the tables, they fanned out across the front of the room, staring at Mboya.

"Time for me to go to work," said Mboya wryly.

He got up and walked halfway across the room, stopping about twenty feet from the newcomers.

"I thought I told you you weren't welcome here," he said, facing the man in the center.

"I know what you told me," replied the man.

"Nothing's changed since last week. You're still not welcome on Mozart."

"Oh, something's changed, all right," said the man. He grinned. "This time I'm not alone."

"Nothing's changed," repeated Mboya. "I think the three of you had better turn around and go right back to the spaceport."

"Not a chance," said the man.

"Well, I can't *make* you behave sensibly," said Mboya with a shrug. "I can only suggest it."

"You know what we're here for," continued the man. "Where is she?"

"Where is who?"

"No games now," said the man. "We've come for the Prophet."

"The Prophet?" repeated Mboya. "Never heard of her."

"If we have to kill you to get to her, we will."

"What's all this talk of killing?" asked Mboya pleasantly. "This is a peaceful little world."

The man laughed. "If it's such a peaceful world, what are *you* doing here?"

"Keeping the peace," said Mboya.

"I'm going to ask you just once more," said the man. "Where is she?"

"None of your business," said Mboya. "Now I've got a question for you."

"Yeah?"

"Can you count to five? Because that's how many seconds you've got to get out of here."

The man glared at him for the briefest of instants, then he and his two cohorts all reached for their weapons. Mboya's own sonic pistol appeared in his hand as if by magic, and two of the men were dead before they could draw their weapons. Mboya crouched as he pivoted toward the third man, only to find that he was already wounded, his left arm smoldering from the blast of a laser beam. The man got off a quick, inaccurate shot at Mboya, who killed him a second later.

"Somebody go for the police!" ordered Mboya as the patrons, most of whom had hit the floor, began getting to their feet. Two men immediately left the building.

"I suppose I should thank you," continued Mboya as he turned to the Kid, whose laser pistol was still in his hand, "but it was stupid to get involved. Why the hell did you do it?"

"I wanted to see if I was faster than you," said the Kid. "I am."

"You shot a man you never saw before just to see if you were faster than me?" repeated Mboya incredulously.

"That's right."

"Some people might call that attempted murder."

"If they arrest me, they'll certainly have to arrest you, too," said the Kid. "Do you think they're going to?"

Mboya stared at him for a long moment. "You're a dangerous young man, you know that?"

"I know that."

"How many men have you killed?"

"None yet," admitted the Kid. "But I have a feeling I'm going to enjoy it when I finally get around to it."

"I'll just bet you are," said Mboya. He paused. "You'd better get your ass back to the hotel. I'll take care of the authorities."

The Kid nodded and walked around the bodies. When he got to the doorway, he turned back to Mboya.

"I *was* faster than you," he said.

"But you didn't kill him," Mboya pointed out. "You missed."

"I'm still adjusting to the chips. I'll aim better next time."

"If it had been me instead of him, you wouldn't have lived to have a next time," said Mboya. "You took him by surprise. He was looking at me when you shot him." He paused. "Now that I know what you can do, you'll never take *me* by surprise."

"I don't want to. If I ever take you, it'll be in a fair fight."

"Well, that's comforting to know," said Mboya wryly.

The Kid remained in the doorway. "Do you think she'll meet with me now?" he asked at last.

"I don't know."

"Remind her that they were out to kill her."

"I don't *have* to remind her," answered Mboya. "That's why I left the restaurant and came here. She knew they were going to show up."

"Remind her, anyway," said the Kid. "I still want some investment advice."

"Sure you do," said Mboya.

The Kid heard a commotion about a block away. The police were accompanying the two gamblers, and he decided that he might as well follow Mboya's instructions and return to his hotel. Remaining here wouldn't get him any closer to the Prophet, and the resultant publicity might cost him enough customers so that he would no longer have an excuse for spending two or three weeks on the planet.

"I'm staying at the Manor House," he said to Mboya.

"I know."

"I'll be waiting to hear from you."

"Don't hold your breath," said Mboya.

The Kid stepped outside, waited until the policemen and gamblers had passed him and entered the casino, and then walked back to his hotel.

It had been an interesting night. He had made contact with a man who worked for the Prophet, and he had seen a shootout. In fact, he had participated in it, and the adrenaline his body had produced wasn't totally dissipated yet. It was a hell of a feeling, that sense of excitement, and he knew that he had found his future vocation, once this business with Penelope Bailey was over. As he took the airlift to his room and sprawled, fully dressed, on his bed, he promised himself that those minstrels who wandered from world to world, singing songs of Santiago and Billybuck Dancer and the Iceman, would someday sing songs about the Silicon Kid as well.

16

The Kid was having breakfast across the street when Mboya entered the restaurant and walked over to his table.

"She'll see you," he said.

"When?" asked the Kid.

"Now."

"Just wait until I finish my breakfast and I'll be right with you."

"You're finished," said Mboya. "You don't keep the Prophet waiting."

"*I* do," said the Kid, taking another mouthful and chewing it thoughtfully.

"If you're doing this to impress her, you're wasting your time," said Mboya. "You're less than an insect to her."

"*You* may be less than an insect," said the Kid. "I'm not."

"What makes you think so?" asked Mboya contemptuously.

"Because you don't invite insects for interviews," said the Kid. He spent a few more minutes finishing his meal while Mboya watched him, then drank his coffee, left a pair of New Stalin rubles on the table, and finally got to his feet. "All right. Let's go."

He followed Mboya to a groundcar, and a moment later they were speeding south, out of the city. They passed a number of farms, then came to still another farm, no different in any respect from the last dozen, and pulled up to a geodesic dome that overlooked a small pond.

"No guards," noted the Kid.

"She doesn't need any."

141

"Not even you?"

"Not even me," said Mboya.

"Well, let's go on in."

"She wants to see you alone," said Mboya. "I'll be waiting for you out here."

"What room is she in?" asked the Kid, getting out of the landcar.

"How should I know?"

The Kid shrugged, let the slidewalk take him from the car to the front entrance, and waited for the door to open. There were no cameras, no retina identification scanners, no signs of any security system. The door slid into the wall after a moment, and he walked into a circular foyer.

"I am here," said a feminine voice, and he followed it into a large room that possessed a window wall overlooking the pond.

Seated on an exotic chair carved from some alien hardwood was Penelope Bailey. She was blonde, slender, dressed in a loose white gown. The Kid decided that she *should* have been rather pretty, but somehow she seemed to possess no sexuality and precious little humanity. There was something about her eyes, something he couldn't quite put his finger on; even when she looked at him, she seemed to be focusing on something beyond him, something that only she could see.

"Welcome, Mr. Cayman," she said, and even her voice seemed remote, as if her mind were elsewhere and the rest of her was going through some preordained performance.

"Good morning, Prophet," replied the Kid.

"Please be seated."

"Where?"

"Wherever you choose."

"Thank you," said the Kid, sitting down on a couch covered in a metallic fabric that continually changed colors as the sun shone in on it.

Suddenly Penelope shifted her position and raised her right arm above her head for just an instant.

"Is something wrong?" asked the Kid.

"No."

"You seem uncomfortable," he noted.

"You are very transparent, Mr. Cayman," she said with an almost alien smile.

"I don't think I understand what you're saying."

"You know why I changed my position, so why pretend that you do not?"

"I have no idea why you moved the way you did," answered the Kid.

She shook her head, still smiling, her eyes still focused on some unimaginably distant point. "You come to ask for my advice, Mr. Cayman, and yet you refuse to be honest with me."

"I *am* being truthful with you."

"No, Mr. Cayman." She arose and walked over to the window. "You were sent to Mozart to find me, and I know that you were not sent by that bizarre criminal who calls himself the Anointed One." She paused. "That means whoever sent you knew me many years ago, before I became the Prophet. Only two such men are still living, and one of them is retired." She turned to him, her eyes staring into his, but focusing beyond them. "You were sent by Carlos Mendoza, who is known as the Iceman, and since he would not send you here without telling you who and what I am, you know that when I make sudden movements or commit acts that seem incomprehensible to you, as many of them must, I am controlling or manipulating various futures."

The Kid stared at her without answering for a long moment. "You're as good as he said you were," he replied at last.

"I take that as high praise," she said. "He is the one man who has ever stood against me, the one man in the whole of creation whom I have ever feared."

"Are you still afraid of him?" asked the Kid.

She shook her head. "No, I am not."

"You haven't got much reason to be," said the Kid. "He's a fat old man with a limp."

"A limp *I* gave him twenty years ago," she said, staring off into the distance.

"Why didn't you kill him then?"

"I was very young," replied Penelope. "I thought he would die of his wounds, and I wanted him to suffer."

The Kid was about to make a comment when she held up a hand.

"What is it?" he said.

"Watch," she said, indicating the far side of the pond.

"What am I supposed to be looking at?" he asked, staring out through the window.

"There is a small animal atop its burrow, is there not?" she asked, still looking into his eyes.

"Yes," he said. "Kind of a muddy red in color."

"Watch closely," she said.

A few seconds later an avian swooped down, grabbed the animal in its claws, and flew off with it.

"You knew that was going to happen."

"I know *everything* that is going to happen," she said. "I am the Prophet."

"Could you have saved the rodent?"

"Certainly," she said. "There are an infinite number of futures. In some of them, the rodent spotted the avian in time to retreat to its burrow. In others, the avian was distracted and did not see the rodent."

"How could you have changed what happened?" asked the Kid.

She smiled again, but did not answer him.

"Would you care for something cool to drink, Mr. Cayman?" she asked after a moment. "It promises to be a warm day."

"Why don't you make it cooler?" suggested the Kid.

"The house is climate-controlled," she replied. "And I have more important things to do."

"In that case," said the Kid, "I'll have some water."

"Follow me, please," she said, walking down a gleaming white corridor to the kitchen.

"Don't you have any servants?" asked the Kid as he looked around the gadget-filled room.

"Millions of them," she replied, holding a glass under a tap. "Cold," she whispered, and the water poured out. When the glass was filled she said, "Stop," the flow of water ceased, and she handed the glass to the Kid.

"Thank you," he said, draining the glass with a single swallow.

"You are welcome, Mr. Cayman," she said. "Come sit outside with me, beneath the shade trees."

"Are you sure you want to go out?" he asked. "As you pointed out, the house is climate-controlled."

"I had an unpleasant experience, which I am certain you were told about," she replied, leading him out to a shaded patio. "I don't like feeling confined."

The Kid recalled the dust and asteroids circling Alpha Crepello. "No, I guess you don't."

He sat down on a wooden bench and she seated herself on an indentical bench about ten feet away from him, then stood up instantly.

"What's the matter?" asked the Kid.

"Nothing is wrong, Mr. Cayman."

"Then why—"

She smiled. "There is an event—its nature need not concern you—that must come to pass on a world called Cherokee. The past is fixed and immutable, Mr. Cayman, but there are literally an infinite number of futures. In every future in which I remained seated, it did *not* come to pass. In a handful of those in which I stood up, it may yet happen."

"But how can standing up on Mozart effect something light-years away?" asked the Kid.

"I neither know nor question the why of it; I only know the truth of it." She paused. "Now shall we get down to business, Mr. Cayman?"

"That's what I'm here for."

She stared at him, and for just a moment her eyes focused. He decided uneasily that he preferred her to stare off into what he imagined was the future.

"You must excuse me, Mr. Cayman, but I'm not at all sure what you're here for."

"I thought you knew everything," said the Kid.

"I know the plethora of futures that will be," she replied. "I do not know everything that was."

"That doesn't make any sense."

"It makes sense to *me*," she said. "Now perhaps you will be kind enough to tell me why you have come to Mozart."

"If you know the future, you already know what I am going to say."

"You *might* say any of a hundred things," replied Penelope. "You are quite a liar, you know, and a bit of an egomaniac as well. I wish to hear whatever it is that you *will* say."

"How will you know if I'm lying?" asked the Kid.

"Because I already know most of the answer to any question I ask."

"Then why ask at all?"

"To determine how trustworthy you are, Mr. Cayman."

"Why do you care?"

"All in good time, Mr. Cayman," said Penelope, staring off into time and space again. "Please answer my question now."

"I've come to Mozart to sell computer chips," said the Kid.

"That is the fact of it," she said serenely, "but not the truth of it."

"All right," he said with a shrug. "I was sent here by the Iceman."

"I know."

"That's it, then."

"Why did he send you?"

"He doesn't think anything can kill you, so when he heard about Hades blowing up, he figured you had escaped before it happened."

"And does the Democracy agree with him?"

"No." The Kid paused. "He thinks they're fools."

"He is correct."

"Anyway, he wants to know what you plan to do."

"Of course."

"Not your immediate plans," continued the Kid, "but your long-term plans."

"I plan to survive in a universe that has proven itself hostile to me at every opportunity," answered Penelope without emotion.

"Well, from what I've seen, survival seems to be the least of your problems—assuming you have any problems at all."

"I am just flesh and blood, Mr. Cayman," she replied. "Someday I will die, just as any other human being dies." Suddenly she smiled in amusement. "It will not be at your hands, Mr. Cayman. If you pull out your laser weapon and attempt to fire it, as you are considering doing, it will misfire and explode in your hand."

"I wasn't considering any such thing," lied the Kid.

"You have been warned, Mr. Cayman," she said. "Your fate is in your hands."

The Kid withdrew his pistol and studied it. "It was working just fine last night," he said.

"In a million futures, it will function correctly this morning," said Penelope. "I will not allow any of those futures to come to pass."

The Kid stared at his pistol for a moment, then shrugged and replaced it in its holster.

"Now I've got a question for you," he said.

"About investments?" she asked in a mocking tone.

"No."

"Ask your question, Mr. Cayman."

"Why haven't you made yourself ruler of the whole damned galaxy? It doesn't seem to me that anyone's got the power to stop you."

"Perhaps someday I shall," she replied. "I have other, more pressing things to do first."

"Such as?"

"You wouldn't understand."

"Try me."

She stared at him, and a contemptuous smile crossed her face. "If you could see what I see, if you tried to make sense of it and bring order to it, it would drive you quite mad. Even as we speak, a starship on its way to Antarres must malfunction, a miner on Nelson 5 must dig a mile to the west of his camp, a politician on New Rhodesia must accept a bribe, a chrystalline alien on Atria must receive a subspace message from far Orion. There are a thousand events that must transpire, each in its exact order; a million futures must vanish every nanosecond; and you ask me to explain all this to you? Poor little human, who seeks only a full belly and a fat wallet, who dreams of heroic deeds and grateful maidens, and who is doomed only to become a speck of dust in a galaxy already overflowing with dust." She paused. "No, Mr. Cayman, I do not think you could comprehend my goals or my explanations."

The Kid stared at her for a moment. "Whatever your goals are, you need a better lieutenant than James Mboya," he said.

"You have a candidate in mind to replace the Black Death?" she asked, and he got the distinct impression that she was laughing at him.

"You're looking at him," he said.

"I thought you worked for the Iceman."

"I work for winners," said the Kid. "You're a winner."

"I am very happy with the Black Death's services," replied Penelope.

"I'm better than he is."

"In what way?"

"I'm quicker, stronger, faster," said the Kid. "And I can make you just as quick and strong."

"With your chips?" she suggested.

"That's right," said the Kid. "You fire Mboya and take me on and, as much as you are, I can make you more."

"You can make me even less human than I am?" she asked

mockingly. "That's an interesting proposition, Mr. Cayman."

"You don't even have to fire him," said the Kid. "I can kill him as soon as I leave the house. He's waiting outside for me."

"But I don't want you to kill him, Mr. Cayman," she said. "Nor do I want your chips." She stared at him, and once again her eyes seemed to focus on the here and now. "I never wanted to be the Prophet, Mr. Cayman. What seems a gift to you has often seemed a curse to me. I wanted to be like every other human being, and I have been harassed and chased and imprisoned for most of my life because I was different. And now you offer to make me even *more* different? You'll have to do better than that."

"If you want to be like everyone else, why not just take a new identity and move out to the Spiral Arm or the Outer Frontier?" asked the Kid.

"Because I *am* different," replied Penelope. "I didn't wish to be, but I cannot deny the fact of it. Wherever I go, they will seek me out; wherever I hide, they will find me. Fate has been very cruel to me, Mr. Cayman; now that my powers are mature, I plan to defend myself as best I can."

"You can defend yourself by hiding."

"I can defend myself by making sure that no one alive or yet to be born can ever harm me again," she said. "I will do whatever must be done to protect myself."

"Including blowing up planets?" asked the Kid.

"An eye for an eye, Mr. Cayman—and there were a lot of eyes on Hades. What happened there was justice on a grand scale." She paused. "You might consider that before opposing me."

"I'm not trying to oppose you," said the Kid. "I'm trying to *join* you."

"If I allow you to serve me, I must have your complete obedience," she said.

"You'll have it."

"You will be well paid, but you will also be asked to do many things that you may find unpalatable."

"You just pay me the money, and let me worry about the rest of it," said the Kid.

"One of the first things I will have you do is betray Carlos Mendoza."

"I kind of thought you might," said the Kid with a grin.

"That doesn't bother you?"

"No."

"Even though he is your friend?"

"He's on the wrong side of the fence," said the Kid. "There's no way he can win. If I don't deliver him to you, someone else will—so I might as well get paid for it."

Penelope stared thoughtfully at him. "You seem like a very practical young man, Neil Cayman," she said. "I think you may prove useful to me in ways you do not even comprehend."

"Then I'm hired?"

"You are hired."

"We haven't talked about money yet," he noted.

"You will find that I am more than generous," answered Penelope. "And if you are loyal, you will wield such power as you have heretofore only dreamed about."

"Sounds good to me," said the Kid. "And by the way, I'm not Neil Cayman any longer."

"Oh?"

"Everyone out here on the Frontier seems to choose a new name for themselves. I'm the Silicon Kid."

She smiled. "That is a very impressive and descriptive name. It will suffice for the time being."

"You've got another one planned for me?" he asked.

"Perhaps."

"I don't suppose you'd care to tell me what it is?"

"When the time comes," said Penelope. She got to her feet. "And now our interview is over. The Black Death will take you back to your hotel. I know that you wish to pit your skills against his." She paused. "From this day forth, you are not to fight with *anyone* except on my express orders. Is that clear?"

"It's clear," he said reluctantly.

"Good. You will hear from me when I need you."

"You can see the future," said the Kid as she ushered him through the house. "So why not tell me now when you'll need me?"

"Because *I* do not exist to serve *you*, Mr. Cayman."

He walked out the front door and climbed into Mboya's groundcar. Penelope watched them pull away, then walked to her bedroom and emerged, a moment later, with a small rag doll. She clutched it lovingly to her bosom and continued to stare blindly into time and space, occasionally making a gesture or striking a pose that would help bring the particular future she envisioned into being.

17

Mboya was waiting for the Silicon Kid in the groundcar as the slidewalk took him away from the Prophet's domicile. He climbed in, still assimilating what he had heard, and a moment later Mboya was driving him back toward Minuet. "So how did it go?"

"I'm working for her," answered the Kid.

A humorless smile crossed Mboya's face. "Remind me never to turn my back on you."

"What is that supposed to mean?" demanded the Kid.

"I know why you came here and who sent you," said Mboya. "You sold him out, Judas."

"I plan to get a hell of a lot more than thirty pieces of silver," said the Kid. "Besides, he hasn't got a chance. You know that."

"That doesn't make any difference," replied Mboya. "When you make a commitment, you're supposed to keep it."

"Why don't you let *me* worry about that?" said the Kid angrily.

"What if you decide the Anointed One is more powerful than the Prophet?" said Mboya. "You going to change sides again?"

"He'd have to be something awfully special to be more powerful than *her*."

"Maybe he is. He's supposed to have more than a hundred million followers who all but worship him."

"He's just a man," said the Kid. "She's something . . . well, *more*."

Mboya drove in silence for a few moments, passing the same farms they had driven by on the way out. As they reached Minuet, he spoke again. "I hope you have to go up against him."

150

"The Anointed One?" asked the Kid.

Mboya shook his head. "The Iceman."

"He's a fat old man," said the Kid. "I can take him."

"A lot of people have thought they could take him," said Mboya. "But he's still here. Even the Prophet couldn't kill him."

"He won't pose any problem at all," said the Kid. "Hell, he still thinks I'm on his side."

Mboya smiled. "Kid, he *never* thought you were on his side."

"How the hell do *you* know what he thinks?" demanded the Kid. "You've never even met him."

"He's lived seventy-odd years on the Inner Frontier," answered Mboya easily. "You don't get that old out here by being stupid."

"Are you saying *I'm* stupid?" asked the Kid heatedly.

"If you think you can fool the Iceman or take him out, you are," responded Mboya. "Even if he didn't know *you,* he knows *her.* He knows what she can do, how she can influence people and events."

"So who's going to kill him? You?"

"When the time comes," answered Mboya.

"What makes you better able to than me?"

"I respect him," said Mboya. "I won't make any careless or foolish mistakes."

"And you think I will?"

"It's a possibility." Mboya paused. "You know that he's gone up against the Prophet twice and lived to tell about it, and yet you keep describing him as a fat old man who poses no threat to you."

"That's right."

"You still don't see it, do you?"

"See what?" asked the Kid irritably.

"You don't think he survived his meetings with the Prophet because he was *faster* than you, do you? What difference do physical attributes make when she knows what you're going to do before you yourself do?" Mboya paused again. "He survived because of his brain, not because of his gun. And he'll beat you the same way."

"I've heard enough of this crap!" said the Kid. "I can take him *and* you together without drawing a deep breath—and don't you forget it!"

"Can you take the Gravedancer, too?" asked Mboya.

"What do you know about him?"

"I've researched you thoroughly, Kid. I know every place you've been since you left Greycloud, and who you've been with."

"Bully for you," said the Kid sullenly.

"By the way, that wasn't a rhetorical question. *Can* you take the Gravedancer?"

"Why?"

"Because he's working for the Anointed One now," answered Mboya. "That means sooner or later one of us is going to have to go up against him."

"I can take *anybody*," said the Kid confidently.

"Once you learn to shoot straight," said Mboya sardonically.

"Anybody," repeated the Kid.

"Even men who know your secret?"

"What the hell is *that* supposed to mean?"

"Just that the Iceman and the Gravedancer both know that whatever you are, you owe it to those implanted chips. If they know they're going to go up against you, don't you think they'll find some way to negate them?"

"There's no way it can be done," answered the Kid. "These are biochips. I'm their energy source. There's no field you can create that can make them stop functioning."

"I don't know about that," said Mboya.

"I do."

"Maybe . . . but just about the time you tell a man he can't do something—whether it's climb down from the trees, or cross an ocean, or fly a starship, or negate a biochip—he usually finds a way to do just that. We're a very successful race of lawbreakers: we've broken all the laws of gravity, and Einstein, and—"

"Spare me the lecture," said the Kid. "These chips will keep functioning until I'm dead."

"Well, I wish them a long and happy life," said Mboya, pulling up to the Kid's hotel.

"You know," said the Kid as he got out of the groundcar and turned to face Mboya, "before you worry about the Iceman or the Gravedancer, you've got a bigger problem."

"Oh?"

"You're going to have to face *me*."

"Why?" asked Mboya.

"She can't have two enforcers," said the Kid. "I'm going to have to prove to her that I'm the best. There's only one way to do that."

"We can do it right here and now, if you're dead set on it," said Mboya with no show of fear or surprise.

The Kid shook his head. "I'll choose the place and time."

"What makes you think I'll let you?"

The Kid grinned. "Because you're an honorable man."

He turned on his heel and walked into the lobby of the Manor House. He picked up a newstape, took it to his room, watched with disinterest as its headlines flashed by, and then walked over to a mirror, where he studied himself moodily.

His clothes were flashy and stylish, but he decided they needed to make more of a statement, become an identifiable trademark. It was true that the Iceman dressed for comfort, but Lomax always wore black, and the holos he had seen of Father Christmas always showed him in a modified red and white Santa Claus outfit, with a pair of sonic pistols suspended from a shining black patent-leather belt.

But what kind of outfit would instantly label him as the Silicon Kid? A shirt with chips sewn into it? He shook his head; too garish. Something with his "S.K." initials monogrammed onto it? He quickly rejected the notion as amateurish. Then what?

He could simply dress as he had been dressing, but what was the use of being the Silicon Kid if people didn't know it? That was the problem with the Iceman and Mboya: they had the credentials, but they lacked a certain style. And if he was going to be the Prophet's right-hand man—at least until he figured out how to get rid of her—he wanted people to know him the instant he landed on a planet, the moment he entered a town or a room.

Perhaps some weapon that was uniquely his own? After all, with his implants, he could handle any weapon with such speed and dexterity that no one alive could match him, so why be limited to laser, sonic, or projectile weapons?

The more he thought about it, the more he liked the idea. He would create a weapon of a type that no one else possessed, one that would forever be his trademark. And if it was one that could kill the Prophet when the proper time came, so much the better.

Excited, he walked over to the computer on his desk, activated it, and had it tie into tiny Minuet library, accessing information on the various types of weapons currently in use. He found nothing very useful there, and was considering accessing a larger library on a nearby world when the computer's screen went blank.

"What's wrong?" he demanded.

"I have an incoming message," answered the computer in a mechanical voice.

"All right, let's see it."

It was from a young woman who had lost the use of her left arm in an accident, and wondered if he could create a chip that would restore the arm to its former state.

"Tell her that if the nerves have been damaged, she'd be better off with a prosthetic arm. If it's something else, have her doctor forward her records to me."

"Working . . ." said the computer.

"Wait a minute!" he said suddenly.

"Operation suspended."

He'd already made contact with the Prophet, so why bother with the façade?

"Just tell her that I'm sorry, but I can't help her."

"Working . . . done."

"Deactivate."

The computer went dead, and an instant later the vidphone came to life.

"Yeah?" said the Kid, activating it.

The holographic image of Penelope Bailey hovered above the machine.

"I see my two guard dogs have been growling at one another," she said in amused tones.

"I thought he was enough of a man not to go running to you for help," said the Kid contemptuously.

"He is in my employ, as are you," she said serenely. "My employees have no secrets from me."

"Send him on his way," said the Kid.

"Why?"

"You don't need him. You've got *me* now."

"Poor, futile little Man, thrashing about in the darkness, dreaming of triumph and glory," said Penelope. "How can you have any idea what I need?"

"You didn't hire him for his personality," answered the Kid. "You hired him because he's the Black Death." He paused. "Well, you've got someone better working for you now."

"Better at what?" she asked with a smile. "Do you really think I need *you* to do my killing for me?"

"You didn't seem to have any objection to letting him do it last night," noted the Kid.

"He merely saved me the bother of dispatching three unpleasant individuals. I was never in any physical danger from them."

"Come on, lady," he said. "If you don't need killers, what are men like Mboya and me doing on your payroll?"

"Great forces have been set in motion," she answered, "forces far beyond your ability to fathom. Each of you has a role to play, and each of you will play it."

"What role?"

"You will learn your destiny in the fullness of time."

"Have I *got* a destiny?"

"Most assuredly," she replied. "That is why I let you live."

"What were you going to do—have Mboya gun me down on the way out if you decided you didn't want to hire me?"

"You still don't understand what you are dealing with, do you?" she said. "In a million times a million futures, you will live out the day, Neil Cayman. But you are a very high-strung young man, and in a tiny handful of the futures I can foresee, you will die of a sudden cerebral hemorrhage. And in *one* future, you will have an intimation of your death. That future will occur when I do *this*." And with that, she walked to her window wall and placed both hands against it, fingers splayed wide, as she looked out on her pond.

The Kid felt a sudden pain flash through his head. He yelled incoherently, then dropped to one knee. The pain became worse, more intense than any he had ever known, and he curled into a fetal ball, his fists pressed against his temples.

And then, suddenly, the pain was gone. It took him a full minute to regain his feet and focus his eyes, and he saw Penelope's image smiling at him from a few inches over the vidphone.

"Do you begin to comprehend?" she asked serenely.

"How the hell did you do that from thirty miles away?" he muttered.

"You have seen what I did to Hades, and yet you wonder at my abilities? Perhaps the Black Death was correct; perhaps you are not bright enough to be useful to me."

"He told you that?" demanded the Kid.

"Certainly," she replied. "He has no secrets from me."

"Well, if I'm too dumb to work for you, maybe I'll just go back to the Iceman!" he snapped.

For just the merest fraction of a second he thought he finally detected an emotion on her face—terror, perhaps, or hatred, or possibly simply contempt—but then it vanished and she focused her gaze on him again.

"That would not be very wise, Neil Cayman," she said. "You would be dead before you left the planet." She paused. "You have given your allegiance to me. Only I can return it to you; you may not take it back." She smiled an emotionless smile. "Or perhaps you would like another demonstration of my power."

"No," he said. "You win." *For the moment,* he added mentally.

"You are high-spirited, just like a young animal," she said. "I do not hold that against you. In fact, I find it admirable. But like any other young animal, you must be trained. Your spirit must be directed. *Then* you will begin to earn your keep."

"I'm no animal," said the Kid.

"You are *all* animals," she said, and broke the connection.

18

The Kid spent the next five days lounging around the Manor House, eating, sleeping, watching holos, doing a little drinking and a little gambling, trying unsuccessfully to keep from being bored. He accepted a couple of assignments to create biochips, just to alleviate the boredom.

He impatiently awaited a summons from Penelope Bailey, and couldn't figure out why she had hired him only to let him rot in a tiny hotel on a nondescript planet. Then, on the fifth evening after his meeting with her, he happened to catch a newscast on the holo set and realized that she had been far from inactive.

According to the report, more than eighty temples on some thirty different worlds, each belonging to the followers of Moses Mohammed Christ, known as the Anointed One, had burned due to unknown causes, killing almost 200,000 men and women and injuring twice that many. Foul play was suspected, of course, but to date not a single instance of arson had been uncovered at any of the sites.

And why should they have found any evidence of arson? thought the Kid with a grim smile. You want this temple burned to the ground? Hold your hand thus and so, and the wind will blow the flame from a candle up against the window coverings. You want that temple consumed by fire? Move eight feet to the right, and a man with a lit cigar in his hand will have a heart attack, and the rug will catch fire an instant later. Stand on one leg and lightning will strike another temple.

It was power beyond imagining—and yet she needed him, needed Mboya, needed still others whose names he didn't know and whose functions he could only guess at. She was power incarnate, but she was not all-powerful; the inhabitants of Hades had kept her imprisoned for almost seventeen years. She needed help—*his* help—although he couldn't yet imagine why. And she could be defeated, or at least fought to a draw. The Iceman had proven that, and he was certainly more than equal to anything that the Iceman might have done.

He checked the news the next morning—twelve more temples had been added to the total—and went out for breakfast. He waited for a pair of trucks to pass by, then crossed the street and entered the small restaurant where he had been having most of his meals. To his surprise, Mboya, who usually slept quite late after a night at the casino's gaming tables, was sitting alone at the back of the nearly empty establishment, drinking a cup of coffee.

"Good morning," he said when he saw the Kid.

"Morning," replied the Kid.

"Come join me," said Mboya.

The Kid looked around the restaurant for a moment, then shrugged and walked past half a dozen empty tables. He sat down opposite Mboya and ordered coffee and a roll.

"I haven't seen you for a couple of days," said Mboya.

"I've been around," answered the Kid. "Working on chips, mostly."

"Why bother? You're working for *her* now. No need to keep up pretenses."

"I'll stop if she ever gets around to giving me something to do," said the Kid. He gazed out the window. "I grew up on a planet just like this one. There's nothing to do here."

"Have you practiced your marksmanship lately?" asked Mboya with a grin.

"I don't need to. It's just a matter of adjusting to the implants. I'm used to 'em now."

"Then I assume you'll never miss again?"

"That's right," said the Kid seriously.

"Good," said Mboya. "I'm glad to hear it."

"And I don't need someone taunting me this early in the morning," added the Kid, making no attempt to hide his irritation.

"I wasn't taunting you," answered Mboya. "I was being sincere."

"Sure you were."

"I was," repeated Mboya. "I'm calling it quits. That means

sooner or later she's going to send you up against the kind of men I've been pacifying for her. Being a lousy shot isn't conducive to your health."

"You're quitting?" repeated the Kid, surprised.

"That's right."

"Aren't you a little young for retirement?"

"I'm not retiring," said Mboya. "I'm just not going to work for *her* any longer."

"Why not?" asked the Kid as his coffee finally arrived.

"Don't you listen to the holo or scan the newstapes?" asked Mboya. "She's just launched an undeclared war on the Anointed One."

The Kid frowned. "Do you know something about him that I don't know?"

"Probably not."

"Then what has that got to do with you quitting?"

"Look," said Mboya. "I'm a gunman. I kill people for a living. I'm not especially proud of it, but I'm not ashamed of it. I live by a code: I've never gone up against a man who didn't have a chance, and most of those I've killed have deserved it."

"So?"

"Don't you understand? *She* can kill half a million men without even leaving her house." He grimaced. "That's not killing anymore, not the way I do it. It's genocide, and I don't want any part of it."

"What's the difference between killing three men or three thousand?" asked the Kid. "They all follow the Anointed One and they all want her dead."

Mboya sighed. "It's difficult to explain."

"Try."

"All right. To me, killing is a profession, and it's got rules to it. You stand close enough to look your opponent in the eye, you always give him a chance to back off, you talk to him, you try to see into his soul and seek out his weaknesses, you risk *your* life to take *his* life. It's a very *personal* thing." He paused. "To her, it's just expediency. Ten men, ten million men, it's all the same—and none of them had a chance. None of them even knew what killed them."

The Kid considered what Mboya had said, then shook his head. "I don't see it," he said. "*You* kill her enemies, *she* kills her enemies. The only difference is the number."

"It's a competition, or at least it should be," said Mboya. "I'm competing against my opponent, sure, but I'm also competing against a standard of excellence I set for myself. I don't really care if the person I'm working for is on the right or the wrong side of the dispute; that doesn't affect me at all. It's the principle and the competition that count." He paused. "But *her*—she's gone beyond all reference points. I'm competing with myself, but she's competing with God, or maybe Nature. No one else can kill that profligately. She doesn't need me, and I don't want any part of what she's doing."

"But she *does* need you, or she wouldn't be paying you," said the Kid.

Mboya shook his head. "She's got you now, and good luck to her. Me, I'm going out to the Quinellus Cluster, where no one has ever heard of the Anointed One *or* the Prophet."

"Soon everyone shall hear of me," said a voice from the doorway, and they both turned to see Penelope Bailey standing there, staring at them.

"I thought you might show up," said Mboya.

"What did you expect?" replied Penelope. "You made a commitment to me, and now you intend to break it."

"You must have known I would, or you wouldn't have hired *him*," said Mboya, jerking his head in the Kid's direction.

"Why I hired him is not your concern," she said.

"True enough," agreed Mboya with a shrug. "My only concern is getting out of this situation." He stared at Penelope. "You can keep whatever money I've got coming."

She shook her head. "I have no need of money," she said. "I hired *you*. You have yet to serve your purpose."

"If you can see the future, you know that I'm leaving and that nothing can change my mind," said Mboya. "If you force me to stay right now, I'll just catch the next ship out of here once you're gone."

"No, you won't," replied Penelope. "You will not leave until I say that you may."

"But *why*? You've got the Kid now. He says he's faster than I am, and for all I know he's right. You don't *need* me."

"I alone know what I need," answered Penelope. "You made a commitment to serve me. I will not release you from that commitment."

"You can kill whole planets without even leaving your house," persisted Mboya. "Why do you need me to kill your enemies off one at a time?"

"I owe you no explanation," said Penelope coldly. "You came to *me* for employment. I gave it to you. Now you will fulfill the terms of our agreement."

"You probably manipulated me into coming, just as you manipulate everything else," said Mboya. "Free will isn't a valid concept when you're involved."

"What *are* you doing here?" asked the Kid, who had been listening to them intently.

"I am here to stop the Black Death from betraying me," answered Penelope.

"If you can see the future, you know I have no intention of betraying you," said Mboya, trying to keep his voice level and reasonable. "I just want to get out of here."

Penelope stared unblinking into his eyes. "I will not permit it," she answered.

"But *why?*" he insisted.

"I told you: you have not yet served your purpose."

"Just what the hell *is* my purpose?"

"To serve me faithfully and obediently."

"For how long?"

"Until I no longer need you," answered Penelope.

"How long will that take?"

Penelope shrugged eloquently. "A day, a week, a month, a year, a lifetime—or perhaps only a moment."

"How will I know?"

"Because I will tell you," she said.

Mboya stared at her long and hard, and finally he nodded. "All right," he said. "But it had better be closer to a day than a lifetime."

"Are you giving me orders now?" she asked, making no attempt to mask her amusement.

"No," he said.

"That was a damned quick change of heart," said the Kid sardonically.

"She's the Prophet," answered Mboya. "If I can't convince her to let me go, what else is there to do?"

"I'm glad you have seen the error of your way," said Penelope. "Now I want both of you to come with me. We have business elsewhere."

Mboya and the Kid got to their feet, left a handful of coins on the table, and followed her out into the street. The sun was higher in the sky now, the morning dew had evaporated, and the air was warming up. There were a handful of vehicles parked in front of the various feed and general stores, but it was totally devoid of pedestrians.

Penelope turned to her left and started walking south, and the Kid and Mboya turned to follow her. After they had gone half a block, she stopped.

"What is it?" asked the Kid.

Penelope turned to him, though once again her eyes were focused far into the future. "The restaurant was the wrong place," she said. "Here, in the street, is where we shall resolve our conflicts."

"I don't understand."

She pointed to Mboya. "That man tried to desert me. He still harbors the hope of leaving the planet once I have returned to my house. Such disobedience cannot be tolerated."

The Kid suddenly felt the muzzle of a sonic pistol jammed against his rib cage.

"Sorry, Kid," said Mboya, "but I want your pistol."

The Kid remained motionless for a moment.

"Give it to him," said Penelope.

"I don't give my weapon to anyone," said the Kid.

"He will kill you if you disobey him," said Penelope. "And then what use will you be to me? Give it to him."

The Kid paused for another moment, then very carefully withdrew his laser pistol and handed it to Mboya.

"Thanks for not being stupid," said Mboya, tucking the pistol into his belt. He looked at Penelope. "I thought we had an agreement."

"You had no intention of keeping it," she said.

"What happens now?" asked Mboya. "Do I die of a stroke or a heart attack? Or do you cause a meteor to fall on my head? I know I can't touch *you*, but whatever happens, I plan to take *him* with me."

"I will do nothing to hinder you," said Penelope. She smiled at him, a smile that terrified him far more than the thought of the various fates awaiting him.

"You're just going to let me go to the spaceport and take my ship out of here?" Mboya said dubiously.

"You will not live to reach the spaceport."

"I thought you just said that you weren't going to kill me."

"I am not," said Penelope. She looked at the Kid. "*He* is."

"What the hell are you talking about?" rasped the Kid. "He's got a gun in my ribs, and you made me give my own weapon away."

"I am the Prophet," she said serenely. "Did you not promise to follow me blindly?"

"Yes, but—"

"Then kill him."

The Kid stared into her expressionless face for a moment. Then he pivoted on his heel and tried to slap the pistol out of Mboya's hand.

Mboya was ready for him and stepped back. The Kid missed and went sprawling on the street.

"Get up," said Penelope.

The Kid got carefully to his feet, staring at the barrel of the sonic pistol that was aimed at him.

"Don't make me do this, Kid," said Mboya, alternating his attention between the Kid and Penelope.

"Now attack," said Penelope.

"You're crazy!" snapped the Kid. "I take one step toward him and I'm a dead man!"

"Would you rather face him—or me?" said Penelope.

The Kid considered her question, then sprang toward Mboya with a howl of animal rage, fully expecting to be dead before he reached him.

Mboya pulled the trigger, and his sonic pistol sputtered once and then went dead. The Kid reached him an instant later, and the two men rolled on the street, scratching, gouging, kneeing, pummeling.

The Kid tried to pull a knife from his boot, but Mboya knocked it loose from his hand, and it flew some twenty feet away. Then, suddenly, they were on their feet again, and the Kid realized that he was up against a superior fighter, a man who knew every martial discipline, whose feet were as deadly as his hands, perhaps moreso.

The Kid swung a roundhouse right at Mboya, who ducked, stepped inside it, gave him two quick blows to the ribs and a spinning kick to the jaw that sent him sprawling.

He was up again instantly, and this time he remembered the

implants. No longer did he try to overpower his heavier antagonist, but concentrated on blocking blows and kicks while striking with lightning-like swiftness. He broke through Mboya's guard three times, but realized that he wasn't doing sufficient damage, that speed alone wouldn't carry the day against Mboya's expertise. He began backing away in the direction of the knife, and a moment later allowed Mboya to land a solid kick to his chest, hurling him backward onto the street.

This time when he got up it was with the knife in his hand. Mboya saw it and went into a defensive posture, but for all his many skills he was no match for the sheer speed with which the Kid wielded his weapon, and within seconds the Kid had slashed him twice on the ribs and once on the side of the neck. Mboya instinctively placed a hand to the neck wound, exposing his torso, and the Kid plunged the knife deep into his belly. He fell to the ground, holding both hands to his newest wound, and groaning.

"Finish the job," said Penelope as the Kid stepped back.

"Why bother?" replied the Kid. "He's not going to cause you any trouble for a long, long time."

"I said, finish the job," said Penelope.

The Kid stared at Mboya, then looked up at Penelope. "Why?"

"Because I told you to, and no other reason is necessary."

"I thought you were keeping him for a purpose."

"He has served it," said Penelope, staring off into the distance. "Finish the job."

The Kid looked at her for another moment, then knelt down next to Mboya, grabbed his hair with his free hand, and slashed his throat. Mboya gurgled once and then died.

"Satisfied?" said the Kid, straightening up.

"Yes," said Penelope. "I am satisfied."

"What was that all about?" asked the Kid, looking up and down the street for signs of the police, but finding none. "Why didn't you kill him yourself?"

"Because this was a necessary part of your education," answered Penelope.

"I didn't learn all that much," said the Kid wryly.

"You learned the most important lesson of all," said Penelope. "You learned that when I tell you to do something, it must be done, even in the face of certain death." She paused. "You also learned that when I tell you to finish a job, you may not disobey me." She smiled at him, her gaze back from the future and trained intently on his face. "Soon you will obey me without hesitation, without thinking. Soon you will be worthy of the tasks I shall give you and the rewards you shall receive. You are progressing very rapidly, Neil Cayman."

"I told you before: that's not my name anymore."

"I know," she replied, "and I shall not use it again. You have proven yourself to me, and you have earned a new name."

"Good," he said. "I'm glad we agree on that."

"Yes, we do," said Penelope, stepping around Mboya's corpse and walking off toward her groundcar. "Follow me, Fido."

The Kid was about to protest. Then he remembered the pain she had visited upon him at the beginning of the week, and he sighed and fell into step behind her.

19

Penelope commanded her front door to slide open, then ushered the Kid inside and led him through the foyer to the large room that overlooked the pond.

The Kid looked around and saw a rag doll lying on the couch.

"Whose is *that*?" he asked, pointing toward it.

"Mine," said Penelope with no show of embarrassment. She picked it up and cuddled it to her breast.

"Aren't you a little old for dolls?"

"I had a kitten once," she replied, tightening her grip on the doll as if afraid that someone would come into the room and take it away from her. "It wouldn't come near me, and whenever I reached out to it, it hissed and spat at me."

"Maybe it was just a spooky kitten," he suggested.

She shook her head. "I bought a puppy three months ago. It ran up to every stranger, wagging its tail—but it would never remain in the same room with me."

"A rag doll's a poor substitute," said the Kid.

"Perhaps," she agreed. "But it has never run from me, and it has never attempted to betray me, and that is more than I can say about any human I've ever known."

"*Any* human?"

She paused, a wistful expression on her face. "There was one, a very long time ago, a woman who fed me and protected me, and whom I loved very much—but even she turned against me in the end." She turned to face the Kid. "It is more difficult than you think to be the Prophet, to know that every member of the race that gave you birth hates and fears you."

"Not without cause," noted the Kid. "You really did a job on them last night."

"Only because the Anointed One has decreed that I must die." She smiled bitterly. "The Anointed One, whom I have never met, never challenged, never opposed. He was well on his way to attacking the Democracy, but then he somehow heard of my powers and has decided to make war on me instead of upon the Navy. The Iceman, who knows he cannot possibly hinder me, nonetheless pays you to spy on me. The Black Death, who knew what happens to those who are disloyal to me, died rather than stay and continue working for me." She paused and sighed. "I always knew he would."

"If you knew he was going to be disloyal, why didn't you get rid of him sooner?"

"As I told you, he had a function to perform."

"To die in Minuet?"

"To provide you with the opportunity to prove your fidelity to me," she said. "It was imperative that you be presented with a situation where you would surely die if you did not trust in my powers and yield to my authority."

"Why?" asked the Kid. "You had Mboya already."

She shook her head. "He was destined to desert me."

"How do you know I won't?"

"Because you are selfish enough and greedy enough and immoral enough to realize that your best interest lies in total fealty to me," she replied.

"I don't know that I especially like that assessment of me," said the Kid.

"The question is not whether you like it," replied Penelope, "but whether it is true." She paused. "You have made only two friends on the Inner Frontier—Felix Lomax and Carlos Mendoza—and yet here you are, working for me and prepared to betray both of them."

"What do you know about the Gravedancer?" demanded the Kid, surprised.

"Do you think I am without my spies and my informants, or that you can keep any secrets from me?" she asked with an amused smile. "Do not try to change the subject, Fido: have you deserted them or not?"

"My name's the Silicon Kid."

"Your name is whatever I choose it to be," answered

Penelope. "Just as your destiny is."

"Speaking of destinies, there are a lot of people who would pay a hell of a lot of money to know what yours is."

She looked out at the pond.

"I know what it *should* be, but there are still too many variables, too many intangibles, in the equation." She turned to stare at him. "That is why you are here."

"What do you expect me to do?" asked the Kid.

"I have many tasks for you," said Penelope. "If you succeed at them, you will be handsomely rewarded. If you fail, you will surely die."

The Kid looked unimpressed. "This is silly," he said. "Why don't you just read the future and tell me what I have to do in order to succeed?"

She shook her head and looked back at the pond. "That presupposes that there is only one future," she answered. "And as I have explained to you before, there are more futures than there are grains of sand on a beach. I cannot yet see them all with equal clarity."

The Kid sat down on a couch and stretched his arms along the top of it. "All right," he said. "Just what is it that you want me to do next?"

She turned to him, but again he got the distinct impression that she was looking past or through him, into the future.

"You will kill Moses Mohammed Christ, who calls himself the Anointed One."

"Just like that?" asked the Kid with a smile. "He's probably better protected than the Secretary of the Democracy—and he's certain to be awfully well hidden."

"I know where he is."

"How many bodyguards has he got?"

She shrugged. "It makes no difference," she said. "His bodyguards, with one exception, will cause you no problems."

"Who's the one who *will* cause me a problem?"

"Felix Lomax."

"The Gravedancer?" said the Kid. "What trouble can he cause? Hell, he still thinks I'm working for him and the Iceman."

"He will know."

"Not unless you tell him, he won't," said the Kid confidently. "Or are you saying that he's a telepath, too?"

"Neither he nor I is a telepath," answered Penelope. "But on the other hand, neither of us is a fool. He will see you there and he will deduce the reason for your presence."

The Kid considered her statement, then shrugged. "Then I'll kill him."

"He will not be as easy to kill as you seem to think," she said.

"I killed Mboya, didn't I?"

"I was there to help you."

"You didn't lift a finger," he said. "I killed him on my own."

"I did not lift a finger?" she repeated with a smile. "Why do you suppose his pistol failed to function?"

"Well, after that," said the Kid uneasily.

"You really believe that, don't you?" she said with a sigh. "You are a fool, Fido."

"I told you not to call me that!" he snapped.

She looked amused. "Do you think to frighten me? Or do you think that I will be as easy to kill as the Black Death was?"

He glared sullenly at her, but said nothing.

"I admire a show of spirit in any young animal, even a young man," she continued. "But if you direct it at me again, I will have to discipline you. There are men out there—many men—who need killing. You must learn to focus your rage." She paused. "You must also learn that being young and strong and fast, and even unafraid, is not enough when you face an opponent such as Felix Lomax."

"Come on," he said, unimpressed. "If I get in trouble, you'll just do whatever you did with Mboya, and that'll be that. Why are you trying to make this seem more dangerous or difficult than it is?"

"You will be hundreds, perhaps thousands, of light-years away from me," she answered. "I cannot control events that precisely from so great a distance. If I could, I wouldn't need you."

"I can do it without you," he said confidently.

"If it was an impossible task, I wouldn't send you," she said. "I detest waste."

"Well, then?"

"I know that you *can* kill the Anointed One. I do not know if you *will* kill him."

"Thanks for your confidence," he said sardonically.

"There are many futures in which you kill him, and in some you kill Felix Lomax as well. But there are an almost equal number of futures in which you lie dead at Lomax's feet."

"None of those are going to come to pass."

"I hope not, but I do not know."

"*I* know," said the Kid. He paused. "Once I take care of the Gravedancer and the Anointed One, maybe I'll go after the Iceman."

She shook her head. "He is the only man that I have ever feared. You cannot kill him."

"He's an old man who lets other people do his fighting for him."

"You will not oppose him, now or ever," she said.

"But I can take him."

"He was responsible for the death of the only person I ever cared for," she said so softly that the Kid had difficulty making out the words. "He is the man who convinced the Democracy to try to kill me." She paused as the memories came flooding back. "He is the reason I remained imprisoned on Hades after I had manipulated events to arrange my escape. Whenever I have been made to suffer—and I have suffered much, believe me—he has been the cause of it."

"All the more reason for me to kill him."

And for the first time since he had known her, the emotionless mask dropped from Penelope's face. She turned away from the window to face him, and her eyes shone with a terrifying hatred.

"He is *mine*!" she whispered.

The Kid left Mozart six hours later. As his ship broke out of orbit, he was still contemplating the almost tangible fury in Penelope's voice, and feeling very relieved that all he had to do was face the best killer and the most powerful fanatic in the galaxy. He did not envy the Iceman.

And far behind him, Penelope Bailey hugged her doll to her bosom and wondered what her life might have been like had she been an ordinary woman. Then she realized that for the first time in many years she was crying. She wiped the tears off her cheeks, put out of her mind all thought of the way things might have been, and went back to sorting out the various futures that confronted her.

PART 4

————
————
————
————
————
————
————
————
————

The
Anointed
One's
Book

20

Felix Lomax awoke with a start when the ship signaled him that he had an incoming message. He sat erect, blinked his eyes very rapidly for a moment, then instructed the screen to activate.

A holograph of Milo Korbekkian, with Mount Olympus clearly visible through the window behind his desk, instantly appeared.

"Good morning, Gravedancer," he said. "It took me a while to track you down."

Lomax shrugged. "The Iceman keeps moving. I missed him on Sweetwater, and again on Confucius IV." He paused. "He's not doing much to cover his trail. I'll catch up with him sooner or later."

"Sooner," said Korbekkian. "I just got word that he's finally returned to Last Chance."

"You're sure?"

"My source claims to have seen him."

"I notice your source didn't feel compelled to go up against him," noted Lomax caustically.

"The Anointed One has given you the commission. No one else in our organization will try to kill him unless you fail."

"I won't fail," said Lomax. "Just have the second half of the money ready to deposit in my account next time you hear from me."

"We have an agreement. We shall not renege on it."

"See to it that you don't."

Lomax broke the connection and directed his navigational computer to lay in a course for Last Chance, far into the Inner Frontier. Then he unstrapped himself from his seat, made his way through the cramped quarters to the lavatory, shaved and took a quick dryshower, and emerged feeling somewhat refreshed. He selected a few mutated fruits from the galley, ordered the computer to brew a pot of coffee, and sat down to eat the skinless oranges and sweetlemons.

It had been a dull two weeks since he had met the Anointed One. He had no intention of finding the Iceman where anyone loyal to his new employer might chance to see them, and so he had purposely gone off on false trails, and had made sure he hit Sweetwater and Confucius long after his prey had gone. He didn't dare raise the Iceman on subspace radio to relay his findings, since he couldn't know whether the men operating the various sending stations were in league with the Anointed One, so he had simply bided his time, waiting for the Iceman to return to his home world.

In the process, he had learned even more about the extent of the Anointed One's empire, enough to conclude that Moses Mohammed Christ did in fact pose a serious threat to all those worlds on the outskirts of the Democracy and possibly to the entire Inner Frontier as well. He may have held his legions together through the religion he had invented, but he was anything but a simple fanatic. His organization was structured along military lines and functioned with clocklike precision. Every man knew his position, knew who he must report to, knew what was expected of him. Their financing was quite sophisticated: the Anointed One floated the bulk of his principal on a four-world circuit during the course of a Galactic Standard day, drawing interest at each bank during that bank's operating hours before transferring it to the next.

They were ready for the unexpected, as well. Take that firebombing or whatever it was of the churches. By the next morning the Anointed One had a list of every damaged building, every lost member of his organization, every police report concerning what might have happened and who might have been responsible. Monies were dispersed, auxiliary plans were brought to bear, and the organization barely missed a beat.

As for the Anointed One himself, Lomax had the feeling that if he were just one whit more cynical or untrusting, he'd have had the perfect temperament for a gunfighter. He had met with him twice now, and he still didn't know if he was dealing with a religious fanatic, a masterful politician, a superior tactician, or a combination of all three.

Lomax finished his meal, got his coffee, and walked back to the cockpit. It was perhaps the most uncomfortable section of the ship, but for some reason he preferred sitting up there. It wasn't as if he couldn't control the ship—and even its weaponry—by voice from his bunk, or couldn't direct the computer to display a hologram of the viewscreen anywhere within the body of the ship . . . but for some reason, he tended to read, nap, and drink in the pilot's chair. It made him feel closer to the action, even though he knew that was a false premise and that, indeed, there was no action to be had.

So he loafed, and read, and slept, and thought, and two days later the computer announced that he had reached his destination and was entering orbit around Last Chance. He requested permission to land, received the necessary coordinates, and touched down some twenty minutes later.

He walked the dusty mile from the spaceport to the End of the Line, then entered it and looked around for the Iceman, who was sitting alone at a table near the doorway, a tall drink in his hand.

Lomax approached him, holding his hands in plain view, just in case the Iceman either hadn't received his message or, more likely, hadn't believed it.

"Good afternoon, Gravedancer," said the Iceman with a smile.

"Good afternoon," replied Lomax. "May I sit down?"

"Of course. Care for something cold to drink?"

"A beer would be nice."

The Iceman signaled to one of the bartenders, who immediately brought over a tall glass of beer.

"Thanks," said Lomax, taking a long swallow. "You know, someday you really ought to consider paving your streets."

"And stop all my customers from arriving with a killing thirst?" chuckled the Iceman. "Don't be silly." The smile vanished. "And don't drop your hands below the top of the table until we're through talking."

"Didn't the Kid reach you?" asked Lomax.

"Yes."

"Then you got my message."

"I did," said the Iceman. "The question is: do I believe it?"

"Well, do you?"

"Probably. But let's talk, anyway."

"Suits me," said Lomax. "Where's the Kid? Did you send him packing?"

"Not quite," replied the Iceman. "He's on a little errand for me." He paused. "Tell me about the Anointed One. Who is he, and why does he want me dead?"

"He's a religious fanatic," answered Lomax. "His organization is established on more than three thousand worlds, and he's got a couple of hundred million wild-eyed zealots believing he's got a direct line to God. They're willing to go up against the Democracy itself if he tells them to."

"What's that got to do with me?"

"Somewhere along the way, he found or manufactured an enemy that he thinks is even more powerful than the Democracy, or at least poses more of a threat. She goes by the name of the Prophet." Lomax paused. "She's some kind of bandit or killer out here on the Frontier, and evidently you've gone up against her before. More to the point, you survived your encounter, which leads him to believe that you're now in league with her."

"A logical conclusion," said the Iceman. "Wrong, but logical." He paused. "All right, you can drop your hands now."

"Logical?" repeated Lomax, frowning. "Are you saying that this woman is so powerful that if you lived, there has to be a reason for it other than your own abilities?"

"I can see where he might think so," answered the Iceman.

"Why has she kept her identity such a secret?" asked Lomax. "I mean, hell, I've heard the Prophet mentioned maybe three times in the past four or five years."

"You've heard of her before," said the Iceman with the trace of a smile. "She's had other names in the past."

"Such as?"

"The Soothsayer and the Oracle."

"You're telling me the Oracle and the Prophet are the same person?"

"That's right."

"How much danger are you in from her?" asked Lomax.

"Probably no more than you are," responded the Iceman. "Which is not to say I'm not in danger. We all are."

"I don't think I understand."

"What I mean is, I doubt that she has singled me out for termination," said the Iceman. "That would be imbuing her with human emotions and human responses that I don't think she possesses any longer, if indeed she ever did." He paused. "But that doesn't mean the entire race isn't in danger. This is a woman capable of destroying entire planets. I don't know what her eventual goals are, but I can't imagine that humanity as a whole is going to be well served by them."

"She really can destroy whole worlds?" asked Lomax dubiously.

"Absolutely. I've seen the results."

"Then old Moses is probably right about her being behind the fires."

"Who's Moses, and what fires are you talking about?"

"Moses is Moses Mohammed Christ, which is what he calls himself when he's not busy being the Anointed One."

"And the fires?"

"A couple of hundred of his temples on worlds all the hell over the galaxy erupted in flames almost simultaneously. The police on the various worlds haven't turned up any clues, but they're sure it's not arson, and the military agrees. As for Moses, he's dead certain it was the Prophet's doing." Lomax looked across the table at the Iceman. "I thought he was crazy—until now."

"She did it, all right," said the Iceman. "She's the only person who *could* have done it."

Lomax finished his beer and signaled for a refill, which arrived almost instantly. "Am I correct in assuming that the Kid's assignment has something to do with the Prophet?"

The Iceman nodded. "I sent him to the world she's living on."

"Then he's probably dead already."

"I doubt it," said the Iceman. "First, I told him just to gather information, and if she can't see a future in which he kills her, she won't feel it necessary to terminate him. Also," added the Iceman with a smile, "that young man's as transparent as glass. Five'll get you ten he's already sold out and joined up with her."

"What use would she have for him?" asked Lomax.

"He's a connection to you and me, and she probably would like to see us both dead: me on general principles, you because you're working for her enemy."

"I thought you were too insignificant for her to bother with," noted Lomax wryly.

"I'm too insignificant for her to waste her time hunting the galaxy for me," answered the Iceman. "But if the Kid can deliver me to her . . . well, that's a different matter."

"Has it occurred to you," suggested Lomax, "that the smartest thing you and I can do is take a vacation to Deluros VIII, or some other world at the center of the Democracy, and just wait there in comfort until the Anointed One and the Prophet kill each other off?"

"He's no match for her."

"No match?" repeated Lomax. "I told you: he's got close to three hundred million followers."

"Three hundred, three hundred million, three billion, it makes no difference," said the Iceman. "If he goes up against her, he's going to lose."

"Just what kind of power does she possess?"

"She's precognitive."

"Then she'll know how to hide where he can't find her," said Lomax. "I'd hardly call that winning."

"You don't understand," continued the Iceman. "She can see every possible permutation, every conceivable future—and when she sees the one she wants, she figures out how to manipulate events so that it comes to pass." He paused and, finally remembering his drink, took a sip from it. "Take those fires the other night. You don't think she had agents on two hundred worlds set them, do you?"

"There was no sign of arson," admitted Lomax.

"Of course there wasn't."

"Then how did she do it?"

"She sat down and stared into the future—into hundreds, maybe millions of futures—and saw that in one of them, someone dropped a lit cigarette, and in another, a meteor made a dead hit on a temple, and in a third, someone left some oil-soaked rags in one of the storerooms, and so on."

"Okay, she saw all that. How did she make it happen?"

"I don't know," said the Iceman. "I wasn't there. But I've seen her do it before. She'll flinch, or strike a pose, or move to a different spot, or—"

"How does that effect events thousands of light-years away?" interrupted Lomax.

"I don't know," repeated the Iceman. "Hell, I doubt if *she* understands how it works. But she knows *that* it works."

"And what if she can't manipulate her way out of a jam?"

"Then she'll wait until she can," answered the Iceman. "She's been captured before—but she's never *stayed* captured. And," he added grimly, "things have not gone very well for those who did the capturing."

"Okay, so no one wants to get near her," said Lomax. "What's to stop the Anointed One from encircling her planet with warships and obliterating it?"

"I don't know," said the Iceman. "Maybe a meteor swarm would wipe them out, maybe every member of the crew would contract some virus, maybe the weapons would malfunction. Or maybe the bombs would explode, and every living thing on the planet would die—except her."

"So how do you defeat someone like that?"

"I've spent a lot of time thinking about it this past week," answered the Iceman.

"And?"

"There might be a way. I'm not sure."

"I think with someone like her, you'd want to be sure."

The Iceman shook his head grimly. "With someone like her, you can *never* be sure. All you can do is hope."

Suddenly there was a shrill yell from the casino, where a miner had just hit his number at the roulette wheel. The man did a little jig, cashed in his chips, and offered to buy drinks for everyone in the house, a relatively inexpensive proposition as there were only six people in the casino and another four in the bar.

"Where was I?" asked the Iceman, turning back to Lomax.

"You were saying you thought you knew how to beat her," replied Lomax.

"Well, it's a possibility, anyway," said the Iceman.

"Care to tell me about it?"

"I'm going to do more than that," said the Iceman. "I'm going to enlist your aid."

"Oh? How?"

"You came here to do a job, right?"

"I came here to tell you what I had learned," Lomax corrected him.

"You came here to kill me for the Anointed One," said the Iceman.

"Well, that's what *he* thinks, anyway."

"I need his help to accomplish my plan," continued the Iceman. "He's not going to give it to *me*, of course, but there's every likelihood that he'll give it to you."

"Why the hell should he?" replied Lomax. "I'm going to have to report that you were gone by the time I got to Last Chance." He paused, then smiled wryly. "Even if he buys it, he's not going to have much use for me." He considered the prospects. "Maybe I'll just keep clear of him and live on the down payment I got for killing you."

"No," said the Iceman. "You're not going to tell him an obvious lie about not finding me, and you're not going to go into hiding. I told you: I need his help."

"So what *am* I going to do?" asked Lomax.

"You're going to earn his trust, and maybe even move up a couple of notches in his organization, to where you can do me even more good."

"And how do you think I'm going to do that?" demanded Lomax.

The Iceman smiled. "You're going to kill me, of course."

21

They were in the Iceman's office, and Lomax, sitting in a corner beneath a number of plaques and awards that had been given to Carlos Mendoza for his fifteen-year period of government service, was examining various hand weapons. Finally he looked up.

"I think it would be easiest with a projectile pistol," he said. "We could just fill it with blanks. They make a hell of a bang, and you could stick some phony blood beneath your tunic in a plastic bag. Just grab your chest when you hear the shots and cut the bag open."

"True," said the Iceman. "But you don't use a projectile weapon. Your trademark is a laser pistol."

"Hard to fake a laser burn, though," answered Lomax. "I can set it for a precise distance, but if you're a foot farther away everyone will see that it didn't reach you, and if you're three inches too close you're going to have a roasted heart."

"How about a sonic gun?" asked the Iceman.

Lomax shook his head. "If I'm going to use a gun that's not my own, the projectile pistol makes more sense."

The Iceman considered that for a moment, then sighed. "Okay," he said. "I suppose we'll just have to go with it."

Lomax got up, walked to a bar opposite the Iceman's desk, and poured himself a drink from the Iceman's private stock. "You really think this will fool her?" he asked after he had downed the drink and poured himself another.

"It was never intended to fool *her*," replied the Iceman, swiveling on his chair to look at Lomax. "If she looks at enough futures, she'll find me in some of them."

"Then why ∴.. ?"

"To fool *him*," answered the Iceman.

"Why bother?"

"Two reasons. First, I don't want the Anointed One wasting his time or his resources hunting me down," said the Iceman. "And second, I want a nice, spectacular killing to help you win his trust." He paused. "Two killings, actually."

"Two?" asked Lomax.

"Unless I miss my guess, our friend Neil Cayman has taken a look at Penelope Bailey and a look at us, and decided that he'll live a lot longer if he joins forces with her."

"It's possible," admitted Lomax.

"And since the one thing she doesn't need is a personal body-guard, the likelihood is that she'll send him out to kill either me or the Anointed One. The Kid isn't exactly a genius, but he's not suicidal, either. If she sends him after me, he'll desert; he knows I can't be touched on Last Chance. But if she sends him after the Anointed One, you can score even more points with your boss by killing him."

"*Can* I kill him?" asked Lomax. "You mentioned that he's got another implant."

"You do this for a living," said the Iceman. "He's just a kid with quick reflexes and delusions of grandeur. I trust you to find a way."

Lomax grimaced. "I have a feeling it won't be quite as easy as you make it sound."

"I'm about to face Penelope Bailey herself," said the Iceman with a wry smile. "You'll forgive me if my heart doesn't bleed for a professional killer who has to face a hotheaded kid who's feeling his hormones."

"Point taken," said Lomax, returning his smile. Suddenly the smile vanished. "Do you know yet how you're going to take her out?"

The Iceman put his feet up on his desk. "I'm working on it," he replied.

"Well, you've gone up against her twice before. Probably you learned something from it."

"Not much," came the answer. "The first time, I just tried to stop her from killing someone I cared for. The second time, I tried to prevent her from escaping from a prison cell on Hades.

I've never actually tried to harm her before."

"Can it be done?"

"I don't know," said the Iceman honestly. "I think I might have been able to do it when she was eight years old. But now?" He shrugged. "I just know that I have to try."

"Do you mind if I ask you a question?"

"Go ahead."

"*Why* do you have to try?" asked Lomax. "I mean, with the Anointed One, we've got a legitimate fanatic who's sworn to overthrow the Democracy and has a couple of hundred million followers who will shoot at anything he tells them to shoot at. But the Prophet—she's never actually caused any harm, and she's hardly got an army at her beck and call. So why not leave her alone?"

"She doesn't need an army," answered the Iceman, lighting a small, thin Antarrean cigar. "All by herself she's more than a match for the Anointed One." The Iceman puffed on his cigar. "I still don't think you realize just what she is: her motivations aren't human, her thought processes aren't human, her powers certainly aren't human, and her goals aren't human."

"What *are* her goals?"

"Whatever they are, they're contrary to ours."

"How can you be sure of that?"

"Someday, if you live through this, fly out to the Alpha Crepello system," said the Iceman.

"And then what?"

"Then try to find the third planet."

"You're telling me she destroyed an entire planet?" said Lomax, finally finishing his second drink and walking back to his chair.

"That's right."

"Why?"

"She was kept prisoner there for sixteen years."

"Then she had some cause, didn't she?"

"To kill everyone on an entire planet?" demanded the Iceman. "What happens if she doesn't like her tax bill next year? There are eleven billion Men on Deluros VIII; believe me when I tell you she can destroy it just as easily as she destroyed Hades."

"Hades?"

"Alpha Crepello III."

"To your knowledge, has she ever killed any human who wasn't trying to kill her?" persisted Lomax.

The Iceman's mind flashed back over the years, to an ever-youthful gunfighter lying dead in the street, and to a small, wiry woman with a pained, puzzled expression on her face as a red blotch spread across her shirt.

"You might say no," answered the Iceman. "I say yes."

"What's the difference?"

"Because when you have the power to save people and you let them die, I call it murder."

"That's debatable."

"That's why I said you might not agree with me." The Iceman paused. "It's academic, anyway. Either you're with me or you're not. And if you're not, then you're with her whether you know it or not."

"You're paying the bills," said Lomax laconically. "Besides, who knows? I might get to take out the Anointed One as an added bonus."

The Iceman shook his head vigorously. "Absolutely not! We need him."

"We do? For what?"

"All in good time," said the Iceman.

"You can trust me," said Lomax.

"I know I can," said the Iceman. "In fact, I can't do what I have to do without you. I'm just not quite sure of all the details yet."

"Once I leave here, how will you be able to let me know what you want me to do?"

"Give me a scramble code for your ship," said the Iceman, putting his cigar out, withdrawing another from a pocket of his tunic, changing his mind, and replacing it. "When I'm ready to move, I'll contact you and give you your instructions."

"That may not be enough," said Lomax. "The Anointed One moves around. We could be on any of fifty planets when you finally decide to get in touch with me. There's every chance I'll be out of sending range." He paused. "Maybe *I* should contact *you*."

The Iceman shrugged. "As you wish."

"You'll be at the End of the Line?"

"I'll be on Last Chance, at any rate," answered the Iceman. He scribbled a number on a piece of paper. "Here's my code. Load it into your ship's computer when you leave."

"Thanks," said Lomax. "One more question."

"Go ahead."

"What if he's so impressed that I was able to kill you that he sends me after the Prophet?"

"He won't."

"How do you know? You've never met him."

"No man reaches his position without having a brain and using it," answered the Iceman. "If you're good enough to kill me, you're too good to waste against Penelope Bailey. You'll be far more valuable to him as a bodyguard."

"Maybe he doesn't know she can read the future," persisted Lomax. "Maybe he thinks she can be killed just like anyone else."

"Then stall."

"He's not the kind of man you can stall."

The Iceman stared at him for a moment. "All right, then—we'll just have to see to it that you're in no condition to go out after Penelope Bailey for a few weeks."

"I don't like the sound of this," said Lomax.

"You won't like the feel of it, either," said the Iceman. "But it's the only way to make sure he doesn't send you after her."

Lomax returned the Iceman's stare. "Let's have it."

"I think I'm going to have to bust you up a little bit in the bar tonight. It'll lend authenticity to your reason for shooting me down."

"How much?" asked Lomax suspiciously.

"Not too much. Maybe an arm or a leg, just enough to keep you from being able to go after Penelope."

"And what if the Silicon Kid shows up three days later?"

"Shit!" muttered the Iceman. "I forgot about him." He sighed. "You can take him if you're one hundred percent, but not if you're crippled up. I suppose we'll have to fake it."

"That sounds like a lot of faking for two men who aren't exactly professional actors," said Lomax.

"It'll work," said the Iceman. "By the time anyone pays much attention, it'll all be over. You'll walk out immediately—I'll instruct my men to let you go, and there will be a couple of them outside waiting to rush you to your ship, just in case someone wants to avenge me, or more likely add to his reputation by killing the man who killed me—and I'll be carried into my office before anyone can examine me. The word will get out by tomorrow morning, and Last Chance will issue formal denials for a few days and then admit that I was killed by the Gravedancer." He grinned. "Once I'm sure you're safe inside the Anointed One's sphere of influence, we might even put a price on your head, just to make it look legitimate."

"You're *sure* this is all necessary?" asked Lomax. "I mean, you could just go into hiding for awhile and I could pass the word that I've killed you."

The Iceman shook his head. "No, we've got to go through with it. Somebody told your boss that I was on Last Chance. That means somebody saw me here. For all we know, he's still on the planet, and if he is, he'll certainly be at the bar or the casino tonight; I mean, hell, there's nowhere else to go here. Whoever he is, he's *got* to see you kill me and confirm your story, or there's every chance the Anointed One won't believe it."

"All right," said Lomax, settling back in his chair and smiling. "I suppose I can live with being known as the man who killed the Iceman." He paused. "I wonder how many men died trying to get that title?"

"More than I hope you can imagine," said the Iceman grimly.

22

The End of the Line was crowded.

Lomax arrived after taking a Dryshower and dining in his room, and found himself in the midst of the usual miners, traders, explorers, adventurers, bounty hunters, whores, and misfits, some dressed in brilliantly colored silks and satins, some in outfits that would look more at home in the midst of a war. There was a fair-sized alien contingent there, too: a few Canphorites, some Lodinites and Robelians, an enormous Torqual, and even a pair of diminutive, faerie-like Andricans, the first of that species Lomax had ever seen.

The Iceman wasn't in evidence, so Lomax strolled over to the gaming tables. He passed up the roulette wheel and the blackjack games, and spent a few minutes losing a quick seventy credits at a *jabob* game. The Andrican who beat him looked so childishly pleased with itself, strutting and waving its money around with a laugh that sounded like the delicate tinkling of wind chimes, that even Lomax was amused, and finally he wandered back to the tavern.

Most of the tables were full. There were a pair available near the casino, but the last thing he needed to do was make his escape past half a dozen bounty hunters, some of whom might start wondering if a reward would be posted for the Iceman's murderer, and so he waited until one opened up by the outside door.

He sat down, ordered a bottle of Cygnian cognac, poured himself a glass, and once again surveyed the room. His path to the door was clear; he was in plain sight of the huge one-way mirror behind the bar, where the Iceman would have a couple of men stationed to protect him. He was partially in shadow, so if he didn't jerk his supposedly wounded arm just right, no one would see it. The best of the bounty hunters—by reputation, anyway—were some sixty feet away at the gaming tables, and they wouldn't risk hitting any customers as he walked out the door.

He gingerly felt his left arm with the fingers of his right hand. The artificial blood was there, right over his biceps, where the Iceman could slit it open with a knife. Then he checked his weaponry again: the projectile weapon, filled with blanks, sat on his right hip, where he could reach it with his "good" arm. And on his left hip was a laser pistol, just in case the Iceman's protection wasn't quite as promised.

Lomax forced his body to relax, content that he had done everything he could do to help carry off the ruse. Now it was just a matter of waiting for the Iceman, who in turn was undoubtedly waiting long enough to be sure that the Anointed One's informant was on the premises.

One of the whores sidled up to him, and he spoke to her for a few minutes. When she realized that he had no interest in transacting any business with her, she moved off to a likelier target, and something about her body language conveyed to the other whores the fact that the man in black wasn't in a buying mood.

Finally, after another hour had passed, the Iceman emerged from his office. He walked past Lomax's table with no sign of recognition, spent a few minutes glad-handing the customers, checked with his gamesmen and dealers to see how the casino was doing, then stopped by the bar for a beer. He downed it, asked for a refill, and carried his glass over to Lomax's table.

"You all set?" he asked softly.

Lomax nodded. "As ready as I'll ever be."

"Good. Let's wait a few more minutes, just in case our man is a late sleeper."

"Even if he is, you'll have a hundred eyewitnesses," noted Lomax.

"True," admitted the Iceman. "But I'm sure the Anointed One would rather have a firsthand report. *I* would."

"You're the boss," said Lomax, picking up his glass and taking yet another sip of his cognac.

They passed a few minutes in silence, and finally the Iceman spoke again.

"I'd say it's about time." He paused. "I almost hate to see

you leave Last Chance," he added wryly. "That's expensive stuff you're drinking."

"That's okay," said Lomax with a smile. "It's on my tab, which I have no intention of paying."

"The hell you're not paying it!" yelled the Iceman in a voice that rang out throughout the tavern. "When you come into my establishment, you're no different than anyone else!"

"You'd be surprised how different I am, old man," replied Lomax, not quite yelling, but making sure that he, too, could be heard.

"You bleed like anybody else!" snapped the Iceman, drawing a knife and slashing at Lomax's left arm, just below the elbow, and Lomax felt a bolt of pain surge through him, and blood—*real* blood—began discoloring his shirt sleeve.

"That was supposed to be my *upper* arm, you asshole!" he grated as the Iceman hurled his aging body at Lomax.

"I decided we couldn't take the chance," whispered the Iceman. "Now shoot me before someone pulls us apart!"

Lomax managed to withdraw his projectile weapon, and an instant later four loud explosions echoed through the tavern. The Iceman clutched at his chest, managed to slit open the blood bag with his knife, spun around once so that everyone could see that his chest and stomach were drenched in blood, and collapsed to the floor.

While the attention had been focused on the Iceman, Lomax had holstered the projectile weapon, painfully withdrawn his laser pistol, and transferred it to his good hand. Now he began backing out of the tavern very carefully, watchful for any indication that one of the customers might try to stop him. Nothing happened, and a moment later he found himself in the street.

"Let's go!" whispered a voice, and he was instantly surrounded by three men.

"In just a second," he said, his speech starting to slur. "I just have to get my bearings."

"What bearings?" whispered the voice. "You're standing right in front of the End of the Line."

"It must be raining," mumbled Lomax. "I'm all wet."

"What's the matter?" demanded another voice. "Just how much did you drink tonight?"

"Not much," answered Lomax. "What's the matter with me? I'm dizzy."

"Come on!" whispered the first voice. "Before someone comes after you!"

"Right," said Lomax. Suddenly he dropped to his knees. "I can't stand up," he murmured.

"Jesus!" hissed a third voice. "Look at his arm! I think the Iceman hit an artery. He's lost a lot of blood!"

"Then fix a tourniquet, but let's get out of here!"

"Hold him still! He's soaked with the stuff."

"Very good cognac," muttered Lomax, and passed out.

23

He remembered nothing about the next four hours. Evidently they patched him up, put him in his ship, and set the navigational computer to take him a few hundred light-years away and then brake to a stop in the void between star systems.

They could have doped him up a bit, he thought bitterly, as he tried to ignore the shooting pain whenever he moved his left arm, however slightly. They had cut his shirt off and bandaged his arm with the few strips of the cloth that weren't already blood-soaked, but the blood had congealed and he was in utter agony as he cut the material off. He had disinfectants galore in his medical kit, but nothing with which to sew up or cauterize the wound, and he instructed his ship to land at the first human outpost.

It was the Iceman's fault, he decided, trying to restrain his rage. Nobody could ever tell that fat old man anything. He had planned this from the start, and all that stuff during the afternoon about how he would fake a wound was just a smoke screen. He knew exactly what he was doing, old Mendoza; it was a deep and painful wound, and Lomax was weak enough from loss of blood that the Anointed One was sure to give him a few days to recuperate rather than send him out after the Prophet . . . and yet, with the experience of a lifetime, the Iceman had managed to miss most of the major nerves and tendons while opening the artery. It was an ugly wound, and a painful one, but it wouldn't incapacitate him if he had to go up against the Kid in a few days' time. A quick transfusion of blood and some painkillers and he'd be almost as good as new by the time the Kid showed up. He'd fake weakness, as the Iceman knew he would, rather than go after the Prophet, who seemed totally invincible to him, anyway, and probably the rumors of his brush with death and his weakened condition would be just the edge he needed against the Kid.

The goddamned Iceman thought of everything, and although he was undoubtedly right, Lomax couldn't stop feeling furious with him.

He faded in and out of consciousness for the next day, and finally awoke with a start when his computer signaled him that it had received permission to land on Pollux IV. He radioed ahead for medical service, was transferred to an ambulance and raced to a nearby medical center, and two days later, his arm bound in sterile packing and his blood count back to normal, he took off again.

He had no idea where the Anointed One was, but he contacted Korbekkian on Olympus via a scrambled channel, and was told that his leader was currently ensconced in a fortress on the desert world of Beta Stromberg, known locally as New Gobi. He loaded the coordinates into his computer, ate a light meal, and slept most of the way there. Once in orbit he used the secret frequency Korbekkian had given him to announce his presence, and a few moments later was directed to land at a small field on the equator.

He emerged from his ship into the incredibly hot sunlight, and felt a momentary dizziness as he carried his duffel bag to the tiny customs station, where he was immediately given a tall container of water and some salt tablets.

"It takes getting used to," confided one of the guards.

"No more than hell does, I'll wager," muttered Lomax, downing the water and a pair of tablets.

The guard laughed at that. "No bet," he said.

Lomax looked around, shading his eyes from the sun with his good hand.

"What now?" he asked.

"Come with me," said the guard, leading him off to a groundcar. "He's waiting for you."

"He is?"

"You're a hero, Gravedancer," said the guard. "He sent a lot of men out after the Iceman. You're the one who succeeded."

"You people know about that already?"

"Not much happens that the Anointed One doesn't know about," answered the guard as they climbed into the machine.

He ordered the ignition to activate, and suddenly Lomax felt a life-giving cold breeze hit him from all directions. "Better?" asked the guard.

"Much," answered Lomax. "I may never get out."

The guard laughed again and sped off along a narrow tract of ground that differed from the rest of the surrounding area only in that it possessed tire marks. They drove for about ten miles, circled an immense sand dune, and suddenly were confronted by an enormous fortress, capable of housing at least three thousand men.

"You guys didn't build *this* on the spur of the moment," remarked Lomax, studying the building, a huge, angular structure with tight molecular bonding that made the relatively thin walls almost impervious to attack.

"No," answered the guard. "It was standing here, deserted, when we first arrived a few years ago. Evidently there was a native race that resented Man's presence a few centuries ago. There are maybe two dozen fortresses like this all over the planet."

"And the native race?"

"Gone."

"What's so important about New Gobi that we had to kill off an entire race to possess it?" asked Lomax curiously.

"Beats me," said the guard. "Probably just because it was here."

Lomax nodded. "Sounds about right."

"Well," said the guard, "we might as well go in."

"It'd damned well better be climate-controlled," said Lomax as he reluctantly got out of the groundcar's cool compartment.

"It probably wouldn't bother the Anointed One if it wasn't," confided the guard. "He's totally beyond such mundane concerns as physical comfort. But he understands that the rest of us have human weaknesses and limitations, and he takes care of his followers."

"That means it's cool inside?" asked Lomax as the sun bore down upon his head and neck.

"Right."

"Then let's hurry," said Lomax, increasing his pace.

They reached the heavily guarded entrance and were passed through without question. The guard turned Lomax over to a pair of men in military uniforms, then left and began driving back to the spaceport. The two men accompanied Lomax down a long, high-ceilinged corridor until they came to a pair of ornate double doors.

"He's inside," said one of the men. "You're to go in alone."

"Thanks."

"You know the procedure?" asked the other.

"Well enough to get by," answered Lomax.

The man stared at him but offered no comment, and a moment later the two doors swung open just enough for Lomax to pass through them, then silently closed behind him.

Moses Mohammed Christ was on his self-styled throne, wearing the white robe and gold chain that seemed to be his trademark. His alien feline carnivore lay at his feet, as always.

"Welcome back, Mr. Lomax," he said, a smile of greeting crossing his ascetic face. "You have done well."

"Thank you, My Lord," said Lomax, approaching to within fifteen feet of him, then stopping as the carnivore's muscles began tensing.

"I understand that you did not emerge unscathed," continued the Anointed One.

"Not quite," said Lomax. He gestured to his left arm, which was hanging limp at his side. "The medics say that I'll be as good as new in three or four weeks."

"That's excellent news," said the Anointed One. "I would hate to lose the services of the man who killed Carlos Mendoza." He paused. "The remainder of your fee has been deposited in your account, as we agreed."

"I never doubted that it would be," said Lomax. "Everyone knows you are a man of your word, My Lord."

The Anointed One leaned forward. "Tell me about your adventure, Mr. Lomax."

"There's nothing much to tell, My Lord. I insulted him, he lost his temper, and I killed him. It was just another day's work."

"You're too modest, Mr. Lomax," said the Anointed One. "I sent four men to Last Chance ahead of you. Why did you succeed when they failed?"

"It's like I told you when we first met, My Lord," said Lomax. "I'm the best there is."

"And how did you escape? Surely the Iceman had bodyguards, men posted around his establishment."

You're a sharp son of a bitch, aren't you? thought Lomax

wryly. *You've heard the story from at least one confederate, and you still smell a rat.*

Aloud he said: "Partly it was the element of surprise, My Lord. The Iceman and I were old acquaintances, and his men probably weren't expecting anything. Also, I was positioned right by the front door, so I could make a quick exit."

"Surely they could recover their composure and shoot more rapidly than you could move out the door," suggested the Anointed One.

"I knew that his men were stationed in the casino and behind a one-way mirror that hung over the bar," answered Lomax. "I waited until enough patrons were blocking their view before I precipitated his attack on me." He paused. "It takes a long time to tell, but it was over in just a couple of seconds."

"And how did you make it to your ship, as badly wounded as you were?"

"I had a vehicle waiting outside," lied Lomax.

"That was a most remarkable escape," commented the Anointed One.

"Look," said Lomax heatedly, "if you think I'm lying, you can check with Last Chance; they'll confirm that the Iceman's dead. And you can check with the hospital on Pollux IV; they're the ones who patched me up."

"I already have," said the Anointed One.

Lomax stared at him. "Well, then?"

"I have a fondness for tales of derring-do," said the Anointed One with a smile.

"As long as you keep paying for them, I'll keep giving you new ones," said Lomax.

Am I doing it right? Did I get too mad too soon? Should I have been so defensive? Damn it, Iceman, I wish you were here. You're a hell of a lot better at lying and double-dealing than I am . . . and this is one smart bastard, this Anointed One. Almost as smart as you.

"You shall have ample opportunity to," said the Anointed One. "I have already selected your next target."

I'll just bet you have.

"But until you are fully healed, you will remain here on New Gobi with me." He paused. "I have long needed a man of your capabilities, Mr. Lomax. I think we shall have a long and fruitful relationship."

"I hope so, My Lord."

"If you are loyal to me, and fulfill your assignments, you can become one of the most powerful men in the galaxy."

"I can live with that, My Lord," said Lomax, forcing a smile to his face.

"I am sure that you can." The Anointed One paused and stared at him intently. "But if you betray my trust, I can promise you a death such as few men have ever experienced."

Lomax returned his stare. *He doesn't want to impress me with that. If he could scare me, I'm not the man he's seeking.*

"Save your threats, My Lord," he said in level tones. "I'm a businessman, and I've made a considered judgment that my best interests lie in serving you. If I should ever become convinced that I made a wrong decision, you'll be in no position to order my death."

The Anointed One smiled. "I like you, Mr. Lomax," he said. "You are forthright and uncomplicated. You wish to kill and become rich; I seek an executioner whose motivation is reasonable and predictable. I foresee that we shall work in harmony for many years to come."

"I see no reason why we shouldn't, My Lord."

"Good," said the Anointed One. "Now go to your quarters, unpack your gear, and relax. You will join me for supper tonight."

"Where?"

"I'll send some men to accompany you until you become better acquainted with your surroundings," answered the Anointed One. "It's a very large fortress."

"Thank you, My Lord," said Lomax, bowing and backing toward the doors, which opened just before he reached them.

He was escorted to his quarters—a large, airy room with a window overlooking a flowered courtyard—and immediately took another pain pill. Then he sent for his belongings, which the guard from the spaceport had left at the entrance of the fortress, took a Dryshower—being careful to keep his left arm free from the light chemical spray—and shaved. He considered taking more salt tablets, but the interior of the fortress was pleasantly cool, and he had no intention of going outside again, so he settled for drinking from the huge container of ice water he found at his bedside. Then, after too many days of napping in the cockpit of his ship, he lay down on the airbed, floating on the gentle currents, and was soon sound asleep.

He was awakened by a rasping sound, and realized that some-one was ringing the small bell outside his door. He got up off the bed groggily, wincing as he used his left arm to support some of his weight, and ordered the door to open.

"It's dinnertime, sir," said a uniformed guard.

"Five minutes," he muttered.

"The Anointed One doesn't like to be kept waiting," said the guard.

"Well, if the Anointed One doesn't want me passing out at the table, he can wait until I've taken my medication," said Lomax irritably.

He went into the bathroom, washed his face with cold water, ran a brush through his hair, and took another pain pill. He noticed some seepage coming through the dressing on his arm, but decided that it would lend verisimilitude to his story, and elected not to change the dressing until he returned to the room.

Then he approached the guard, who was fidgeting uncomfortably, and nodded. The man walked off rapidly, and Lomax followed him through a maze of cool, tiled corridors until they came to a large chamber where the Anointed One sat alone at one end of a long, polished table made of some alien hardwood. His pet was nowhere to be seen, and Lomax concluded that probably even the Anointed One couldn't control it when there was food present.

"You are late, Mr. Lomax," he said emotionlessly.

"I'm sorry, My Lord," responded Lomax as the guard silently left the chamber. "But I'm still on medication for my arm."

"I see," said the Anointed One. He paused for a moment, then inclined his head almost imperceptibly. "You are forgiven."

"Thank you, My Lord."

"While you are on medication, I will send for you a few minutes early."

"That's the most reasonable approach, My Lord."

A man and a woman, both clad in conservatively tailored beige robes, entered the chamber, bearing bowls of salad.

"We do not imbibe stimulants, Mr. Lomax," said the Anointed One as the two servers placed the bowls before them. "I hope this will not present a hardship for you."

"Not at all," said Lomax as another woman brought in a container of water and two large glasses. She filled them to the top and set one in front of each man.

"Good. For our main course, we will have roasted black-sheep."

"Blacksheep, My Lord?"

"A mutated sheep from Balok XIV," answered the Anointed One.

"Balok XIV, My Lord?" asked Lomax, frowning. "From the number, I'd have guessed it was a gas giant."

The Anointed One smiled. "Balok has thirty-one planets. The only habitable one is Balok XIV, an agricultural colony where they've done genetic experimentation with sheep and goats." He paused. "Blacksheep go about eight hundred pounds apiece and are said to be the most succulent meat on the Inner Frontier."

"Really?"

"I'm surprised you've never had any."

"I eat very little meat, My Lord," answered Lomax.

"Good. I like a man who watches his diet."

"And his blood pressure and his cholesterol level," added Lomax with a wry grin.

"Ah!" said the Anointed One with a smile. "Then you are not superhuman, after all."

"I'm afraid not, My Lord." Lomax paused, wondering if he should bring up the subject of Penelope Bailey or wait for the Anointed One to do so. Finally he decided to take advantage of the opening. "The only superhuman I'm aware of is the Prophet."

"Good!" said the Anointed One. "I had hoped that we might discuss her this evening." He paused. "Did Mendoza talk to you about her?"

"Not much," answered Lomax.

"He said nothing about her powers?"

Lomax shook his head. "No, My Lord. I was hoping *you* might tell me about her."

The Anointed One stared at him intently. "If you know nothing of her powers, why do you claim that she is superhuman?" he asked.

That's right, Lomax. Put your foot into it again, why don't you?

"The Iceman seemed to think she was," he said carefully. "And as for me, I can't believe he'd work for anyone who *wasn't* something out of the ordinary." He shrugged. "He said something about her predicting the future, but I don't put much stock in it."

"Oh? Why not?"

"Maybe she can read the backs of cards, or do party tricks, but if she could really see the future, why didn't she warn him that I had come to Last Chance to kill him?"

"Maybe she no longer had any use for him."

"Maybe," said Lomax, striving to look unconvinced. "But predicting the future? That's a little hard to swallow."

"Then what do *you* think makes her superhuman, Mr. Lomax?" persisted the Anointed One.

You'd better put an end to this before you say something else that he can pounce on, Lomax.

"I have a reason, My Lord, but I have a feeling it may offend you."

"Come," said the Anointed One. "You have my permission to speak frankly."

"All right," said Lomax, feigning reluctance. "I think you fear her, My Lord, and if a man who has no fear of the Democracy fears a single woman out of the Frontier, then she must be, in some way, superhuman."

"I fear no one!" snapped the Anointed One.

"Then I apologize, My Lord."

"No one, do you hear!"

"I hear, My Lord," said Lomax. "And since I was mistaken about that, then I am certain I was mistaken about the Prophet as well." He stared unblinking into the coal-black eyes of the Anointed One. "Once my arm is totally healed, I hope you will commission me to kill her . . . and because I have offended you, and I wish to convince you of my loyalty and my desire to remain in your service, I will accept such a commission for no fee at all."

Evidently it was the right answer, for the tension left the Anointed One's thin body, and he leaned back on his chair.

"That will not be necessary, Mr. Lomax," he said, his voice once more under control. "I will pay for value received."

"If you insist, My Lord," said Lomax. "But my offer stands."

The Anointed One continued staring at him. "You are a most unusual man, Mr. Lomax."

"I take that as a high compliment, My Lord."

"Perhaps," said the Anointed One. "At the moment, though, it is merely an observation."

They ate in silence, and then the servers took away their empty salad dishes and brought in the blacksheep.

Get here soon, Kid, thought Lomax as he cut himself a small piece of meat and chewed it thoughtfully. *This man is too god-damned sharp. Maybe the Iceman could handle him, but I sure as hell can't, not for any length of time. If you don't show up quick, I'm going to make one mistake too many.*

24

Two days passed, days in which Lomax did his best to keep to himself—or at least keep away from the Anointed One.

He complained that his medication made him groggy, then spent hours each afternoon feigning sleep on his bed, just in case his room was under surveillance. He insisted that the Anointed One's security was paramount, and spent more hours each day walking the perimeter of the castle and even the sun-baked grounds, checking every means of ingress, trying to imagine how he might gain access to the fortress if *he* was an assassin. He spent an hour a day cleaning and polishing his weapons, and another half hour taking target practice.

And still he found himself in the Anointed One's presence too often for his liking. He took lunches and dinners with him, and his presence was requested for the evening entertainments (a request no one dared refuse). Strangely, the Anointed One made no attempt to convert him to the One True Faith, probably because he made it clear early on that he had no interest in *any* religion, and this one—a combination of the harsher features of Christianity, Judaism, and Islam—made less sense to him than most.

He arose on the morning of the third day, allowed himself the luxury of a shower with actual water, shaved, dressed, and ordered his door to open. He no longer needed assistance finding his way around the fortress, though it was nonetheless frequently given, but on this particular morning there were no guards to be seen, and he walked to the enormous kitchen, where he usually had a glass of juice and a cup of coffee before the Anointed One could find him and invite him to breakfast.

This morning, though, there was no one working in the kitchen, and the coffee had not yet been made. Shrugging, he walked to the enormous refrigerator, pulled out a container of fruit juice, held it to his lips, and took a long swallow before replacing it.

As he was leaving the kitchen, he looked out the window, which overlooked the same garden as his bedroom, but from a different angle, and something caught his eye. Not a movement, for nothing was moving in the morning sun, but a patch of color that didn't seem to belong. He stared at it for a moment, then blinked his eyes and stared again—and suddenly the whole picture seemed to take shape, and he realized that he was staring at the leg of a dead man who had recently been the Anointed One's personal chef.

He drew his laser pistol and walked carefully to the kitchen door. It opened out to the dining room where the Anointed One took his meals, but the room was totally deserted, and Lomax quickly walked through it, into the high-ceilinged corridor beyond.

Here he came to two more bodies, both dead, both displaying the effects of sonic distortion. He couldn't remember if the Silicon Kid used a sonic pistol—in fact, he couldn't recall the Kid carrying a weapon at all—but there was no doubt in his mind that this was the Kid's doing. The Iceman had predicted it, and he had come to the conclusion that the cagey old man was damned near as good at predicting the future as was Penelope Bailey.

He stepped over the two bodies, then looked out into a nearby courtyard. There were no bodies there—but there also weren't any guards, and two men were usually positioned there, even in the heat of the day.

The Kid was good, he had to give him that. He'd killed at least three men, possibly more, and done it swiftly and silently, without alerting anyone to his presence. But he couldn't keep it up; there were close to a thousand armed men in and around the fortress, and any moment now he would have to hear the explosions of projectile weapons, the crackling of lasers, the eerie humming of sonic guns.

But he heard nothing as he proceeded along the corridor. He came to a turn, very near the front entrance to the fortress, and looked out a circular window. There were some thirty men in the courtyard, some standing at attention, a few in conversation with each other, four of them picking up tiny pieces of litter. He considered alerting them to the Kid's presence, but thought better of it: if he was to win the Anointed One's total confidence, he would have to go up against the Kid alone, as the Iceman had said. Calling in the army might save the day, but it wouldn't win the war.

Gun still in hand, walking in a semi-crouch, his left arm still hanging limply by his side, Lomax increased his pace to the "throne room," for it was there that the Anointed One conducted his morning business. He turned two more corners, then found himself facing the massive double doors. Four men lay dead in front of them.

He walked past them silently, then gave one of the doors a slight push. It didn't give.

"Open," he murmured.

The door swung open just enough for him to pass through, then closed behind him.

The Kid, his back to the door, was facing the Anointed One and three of his closest advisors, a sonic pistol in each hand. The three advisors had their hands above their heads, and the Anointed One's feline carnivore lay dead on the floor, but Moses Mohammed Christ sat passively upon his throne, staring at the Kid as if *he* somehow held the advantage.

"That wasn't so difficult at all," the Kid was saying. "She told me getting to you would be easy; I should have believed her."

"Did she tell you how you were going to get back out?" asked Lomax.

The Kid whirled to face him.

"She warned me about you, too, Gravedancer," he said. "You're the one to watch out for." He grinned. "I can't imagine why."

"Probably because I'm going to kill you," said Lomax in level tones.

"I'm the only one who's doing any killing today," said the Kid. "Because we were friends once, I'll give you five seconds to get out of here."

"I'm not going anywhere," said Lomax. "Now, drop your guns and you just might live long enough to leave the room in one piece."

The Kid laughed. "You've got a gun aimed at me, I've got a pair aimed at you. It's a standoff."

"No, it's not," said Lomax. "I'm prepared to die for the Anointed One. You've got your whole life ahead of you, Kid; are you ready to throw it away for a woman who hasn't got the guts to do her own dirty work?"

Just in case I come out of this alive, you'd damned well better have been listening to every word. I could just as easily have back-shot him, but the Iceman says I've got to be a hero for you.

"Neither of us has to die," said the Kid, and suddenly Lomax saw what he was looking for: the first tiny flickering of uncertainty.

"Oh?"

"You can throw in with me."

"Why should I want to?"

"So you can be on the winning side," said the Kid.

"What does she pay?"

"The sky's the limit," said the Kid enthusiastically. "You wouldn't believe it." He relaxed slightly. "What do you say, Gravedancer?"

"*This* is what I say," answered Lomax, firing his laser weapon and hurling himself to the ground, rolling rapidly to his left.

The Kid uttered a strangled gurgle and swept Lomax's vicinity with his sonic pistols, but they were aimed too high, and before he could lower them he had collapsed to the floor.

"This can't be happening," rasped the Kid, coughing up mouthfuls of blood. "I *can't* lose!"

Lomax walked over to him and kicked his weapons across the floor.

"I told you you should have stayed on Greycloud, Kid," he said.

The Kid tried to answer, but couldn't.

"You could have been a farmer or a chip manufacturer or half a hundred other things." Lomax paused and stared down at him. "Now you're just one more fool who came out to the Frontier and wound up in an unmarked grave."

The Kid glared at him for just an instant. Then a look of terror crossed his face, he tried to say something else, coughed again, and died.

"Are you all right, My Lord?" asked Lomax, turning to the Anointed One.

"I am, thanks to you," answered the Anointed One.

"I'm glad I arrived in time."

"You knew this man?"

"Yes, My Lord," replied Lomax. "He called himself the Silicon Kid. His real name was Neil Cayman." He paused. *A little distortion of the truth probably won't hurt.* "I took him in, fed him, gave him money. He used it to implant some biochips in his body, chips that made him a killer with phenomenal reflexes." He looked at the Anointed One. "Then he deserted me and went to work for the Prophet."

"He offered you your life," said the Anointed One.

"Yes, he did."

"Knowing that these chips made him a formidable opponent, and still recovering from your wounds as you are, why did you not accept his offer?"

Lomax's first instinct was to look him in the eye and say, "Because you are my leader, My Lord, and I am loyal only to you." He caught himself just in time. *Once you finish laughing at that, you just might decide to lop off my head.*

He paused for a moment and then spoke: "It was a value judgment, My Lord."

"A value judgment?"

Lomax nodded. "If I agreed to join him, it would be an admission to both him and to myself that I couldn't defeat him, and no matter how high I rose in the Prophet's organization, I would always take my orders from him." He paused and smiled a properly self-satisfied smile at the Anointed One. "But by taking him on and killing him, I've proved both my worth and my loyalty to you. I ask for no specific reward for my actions; I shall trust to your wisdom and generosity."

The Anointed One nodded. "You are a simple man, Mr. Lomax, but an honest one and a brave one." He smiled. "You shall have your reward."

"Thank you, My Lord."

The Anointed One sighed deeply. "I wish I could read the Prophet as easily as I can read you."

"Perhaps when you meet her, you'll discover that you can," answered Lomax.

"Perhaps," said the Anointed One. He turned to his three advisors, who had remained where they stood, silent and motionless. "Summon my military leaders."

The three men practically ran from the room and returned a

few minutes later with six uniformed soldiers.

"My Lord," began the largest of them. "I had no idea. I—"

"Silence!" commanded the Anointed One.

The man snapped to attention.

"While you and your subordinates were doing God only knows what, this man"—he indicated Lomax—"stood side by side with me and helped me dispatch the notorious assassin known as the Silicon Kid, the very same assassin who entered this fortress as if there were no guards at all!"

Well, thanks for admitting that I helped you, thought Lomax wryly.

"This man," he repeated, again pointing to Lomax, "and this man alone, was prepared to defend me with his life."

"That is not so, My Lord! We all—"

"Shut up!" snapped the Anointed One. "In all matters of security, this man, this Gravedancer, now speaks for me and must be obeyed as I would be obeyed. Is that clear?"

The six men stared sullenly at Lomax and muttered their acquiescence.

Wonderful. Six more men waiting to stick knives in my back. Just what I needed.

"I want you to conduct an immediate investigation and find out how this assassin was able to penetrate our defenses, how he came to sneak into the fortress past hundreds of armed men who were supposed to be protecting me from just such an occurrence." The Anointed One smiled a humorless smile. "When the report is in my hands, and I expect it no later than this evening, we shall mete out justice to those deserving of it."

The men's expression betrayed a certain uneasiness at his notion of justice.

"Your arm is bleeding again, Mr. Lomax," said the Anointed One, turning to Lomax. "Tend to it, and then join me in the dining room. We have many things to discuss."

"We do, My Lord?"

The Anointed One nodded. "She couldn't protect him. Perhaps she is *not* superhuman, after all." His eyes blazed with passion. "You may soon have your wish, Mr. Lomax."

"My wish?"

"You wish to kill her, do you not?"

"Yes, My Lord," said Lomax, wondering just what he was getting himself into.

"I think as soon as your arm is healed, I shall give you the opportunity."

"Thank you, My Lord," said Lomax, bowing and backing out of the room.

And just how do I get out of this one, Iceman?

25

Lomax returned to his room and noticed that his left arm was indeed bleeding. He went into the bathroom to change the dressing, then reached for his container of pain pills—and stopped.

He closed the door behind him and performed a thorough, inch-by-inch survey of the bathroom. Finally, satisfied that there were no security cameras embedded in the walls or ceiling, he took a pill and placed the container in his holster, just beneath his laser pistol.

Then he emerged from the bathroom, walked to the door of the bedroom, and ordered it to open. There were four guards this time, more, he assumed, for his security than because the Anointed One distrusted his motives.

"I've got to go to my ship," he announced.

"Is something wrong, sir?" asked one of the guards.

"I left the rest of my pills there," answered Lomax. "Anti-inflammatories and painkillers."

"I can send someone to get them for you, sir," offered the guard.

Lomax shook his head. "My ship's got a very complex security system. Your man would blow it up the second he tried to open the hatch." He paused. "Can you get me a ride there? I doubt that I could find it myself."

Which should assuage most of your doubts.

"Certainly, sir," answered the guard. "Let me just report to the Anointed One and tell him why you'll be late for your meeting."

"Of course," said Lomax.

The guard walked a few feet away, raised the Anointed One on his communicator, whispered something, listened for a moment, and returned to Lomax.

"It's all arranged, sir," he announced. "There will be a groundcar waiting for you at the main entrance. The Anointed One requests that you join him for lunch when you return."

"Thank you," said Lomax, heading off down the corridor.

A moment later he was racing across the hardened surface of the sun-baked desert, wondering what kind of native race had lived in such a place. The spaceport came into view the instant they rounded the huge dune that protected the fortress, but the light and the perspective played tricks with his estimate of the distance involved, and it took the groundcar five minutes longer than he anticipated to reach his ship.

"I'll wait right here for you, sir," said his driver.

"That won't be necessary," replied Lomax. "I may be a few minutes."

"Just to get some pills, sir?"

"I want to recharge my laser pistol."

"We have chargers at the fortress, sir."

"I trust my own," answered Lomax.

The driver shrugged. "Whatever you say, sir."

"It could take half an hour or so, and I don't want either you or the vehicle overheating," said Lomax. "Why don't you go over to the observation tower and have a cold drink? Keep an eye on the ship; when you see me come out of the hatch, drive by and pick me up."

"Whatever you say, sir," replied the driver, already uncomfortable as the hot air poured in through Lomax's open door. He sped over to the tower as Lomax opened the hatch of his ship, stepped through, and locked it behind him.

The interior of the ship was excruciatingly hot. He immediately activated the climate-control system, and in a short time the temperature dropped down to a comfortable level. He began charging his pistol's power pack—it wouldn't do to be caught charging it at the fortress that evening—then seated himself at the pilot's chair, activated the radio, masked his signal as best he could, and put through a subspace transmission on the Iceman's private scrambled code.

A moment later a voice, crackling with static, could be heard. "This is the Iceman."

"Lomax here."

"What's happening?"

"The Kid is dead, the Anointed One loves me, and I'm going to cut your arm open the next time I see you."

The Iceman chuckled. "I had to make it believable. I hope I didn't do any permanent damage."

"I'll live," answered Lomax. "At least, it won't be the arm that kills me," he amended. "But the Anointed One might, if I give him too many wrong answers."

"Are you in trouble there?" asked the Iceman.

"Not yet, but it could blow at any minute. I'm operating in the dark here. I don't know what you want, and I know just enough about the Prophet so that he thinks I know more."

"I see," said the Iceman. There was a brief pause in the transmission. "All right. I suppose it's time to move."

"Move where?" asked Lomax.

"Figure of speech," answered the Iceman. "*I* have to move. You're staying right where you are."

"What do you want me to do?"

"Somehow, you've got to convince the Anointed One to attack a planet called Mozart, and to attack in force."

"Mozart?" repeated Lomax, frowning. "Never heard of it."

"It's the third planet in the Symphony system. Alpha Montana III on your charts."

"What's so special about Mozart?"

"That's where Penelope Bailey is."

"Really, or is that just what we want him to think?"

"She's really there," said the Iceman.

"And you want him to attack in full force?"

"That's right."

"Does that include nukes and chemicals?"

"Everything he's got," said the Iceman. "Even antimatter, if he has any."

"I doubt it," replied Lomax. "Even so, there won't be much left of Mozart after he hits it."

"Don't kid yourself," said the Iceman. "He won't be able to harm a hair of her head."

Lomax frowned again. "Then what's this all about?"

"I need to get onto the planet."

"You plan to use an army of two hundred million men as a *distraction*?" exclaimed Lomax in disbelief.

"In a manner of speaking. They've got to keep her so busy that I can land."

"Just a minute, Iceman," said Lomax. "If she's what you say she is, she'll know you're going to land. I mean, she can see past the battle, can't she?"

"Of course she can. But she'll be so preoccupied with the immediate threat that she'll have to put me on hold, so to speak, and deal with me later."

"And what happens when she *does* deal with you?"

"That's *my* concern," said the Iceman. "You just see to it that the Anointed One attacks. You killed the Kid, and he thinks you killed me. Give him a good reason to attack, and he ought to trust you enough to do what you tell him."

"He's not the most trusting soul you'd ever want to meet," said Lomax dubiously.

"Then think of some reason why he *has* to trust you, and make it stick," said the Iceman.

"I'll do my best."

"Your best's been good enough so far," said the Iceman. He paused again. "Oh—I need to know one other thing."

"What is it?"

"Do his ships have any special military insignia? I don't want *them* blowing me to bits before I reach the planet."

"Not to my knowledge," replied Lomax. He considered the question. "No, I'm sure they don't. When the Democracy thinks you're planning to attack it, you don't advertise your presence by plastering an insignia all over your ships."

"You'd better be right," said the Iceman.

"If I find out otherwise, I'll try to get word to you," Lomax promised him. "Does your ship's radio respond to the same scramble code?"

"Yes."

"Good enough. I'll signal you if I'm wrong about the insignia."

"How soon do you think you can get him to attack?" said the Iceman. "You're a lot closer to Mozart than I am. I want to make sure that I don't get there too late."

"He's got his forces spread out all over the Democracy and the Inner Frontier," said Lomax. "If he gave the word right now, it would probably take them a couple of months to assemble and get into some kind of coherent formation—and he won't think he's got that kind of time." He paused thoughtfully, then continued. "My guess is he'll pull in whatever he can get from nearby systems—five thousand ships or so, maybe three to five million men—and attack within a week."

"Then I'd better take off in a couple of days and just stay a few systems away until my sensors pick up your fleet."

"Don't be in such a hurry," said Lomax. "I still have to convince him to attack. It's not as easy as you might think." He paused. "I'm not as quick as you, Iceman. Every time I start stretching the truth, he starts getting suspicious."

"Then don't tell him a thing," said the Iceman promptly.

"What are you talking about?"

"Let him discover the truth on his own," answered the Iceman. "The truth we want him to believe, that is."

Lomax stared at the blank viewscreen above the computer panel, lost in thought.

"Hello?" said the Iceman. "Hello? Are you still there?"

"Yeah, I'm here," said Lomax.

"You didn't transmit for almost two minutes," said the Iceman. "I thought I'd lost you."

"I came up with an idea," said Lomax.

"Oh?"

"I think I can make the Anointed One buy it—but I'm going to need your help."

"I'll help in any way I can," answered the Iceman. "But don't forget—the Anointed One thinks I'm dead."

"I know," said Lomax. "Are you recording this transmission?"

"Yes."

"All right." He rattled off a nine-digit code. "Did you get that?"

"Yeah. What is it?"

"It's a code that will reach a man named Milo Korbekkian on Olympus."

"Okay, what do I do with it?" asked the Iceman.

"Create a phony name and send him a message that can't be traced back to Last Chance or to your ship."

"No problem," said the Iceman. "What kind of message?"

"Tell him," said Lomax, barely able to suppress a smile, "that the Prophet's military machine won't be ready for war for another month or two, that she's relatively defenseless on Mozart, and that Korbekkian's assignment is to commission some assassinations, including mine, that will take the Anointed One's attention away from her vulnerability."

"You think that'll do it?" asked the Iceman.

"I think so," replied Lomax. "He sees conspiracies everywhere, so why not give him one? Korbekkian's just a contact man; there's no reason to assume he won't play both ends against the middle, supplying killers to both sides for a fee." Lomax paused. "Yeah, the more I think about it, the more I think it's just the kind of double cross the Anointed One will buy. And he if buys *that,* he'll buy the Prophet's being defenseless. It shouldn't take much to convince him to hit her before she builds up her forces."

"How much does he know about her?"

"Not much."

"Enough to know that she hasn't got any forces, or that she doesn't need any?"

"It would be inconceivable to him," answered Lomax. "Hell, I know all about her, and *I* have a hard time believing it."

"All right," said the Iceman. "You've had a busy day already, and we don't want to hit the Anointed One with too many things all at once. I'll send the message exactly two Standard days from now."

"Right."

"One word of advice, Gravedancer," said the Iceman.

"What is it?"

"Somebody always lives to tell the story. If you want it to be you, see to it that you're not in the attack fleet."

The Iceman broke the connection.

26

The Anointed One was waiting for him when he returned from the spaceport.

He entered the dining room, found a fruit plate already laid out for him, and promptly sat down. He took a long swallow from his water glass, then went to work on some citrus slices.

"Killing people seems to increase your appetite," remarked the Anointed One dryly.

Lomax smiled and shook his head. "No, My Lord. But being out in that heat makes me want to replenish some fluids."

"Did you remember your salt tablets?"

"No," said Lomax, surprised. "I totally forgot about them."

"As long as you remain on New Gobi, you must always keep them with you," said the Anointed One. "You have become one of my most valued men. I should hate to lose you to a case of heat prostration."

"I'd hate it every bit as much, My Lord," replied Lomax. "I'll make sure I'm not without the tablets again."

"Did you find your medication aboard your ship?" continued the Anointed One.

Lomax nodded. "And I recharged my power pack."

"I wouldn't have thought your weapon expended that much energy in this morning's altercation."

"It didn't, My Lord," answered Lomax. "But when you depend on your weapons for a living, you care for them the way a mother cares for her baby." He forced a smile to his lips. "I can survive forgetting my salt tablets . . . but if my weapons ever fail me, I'm not likely to get a second chance."

"Very sensible," said the Anointed One. "I approve."

Lomax didn't know what to say next, so he fell silent and concentrated on his food.

"Tell me, Mr. Lomax," said the Anointed One, breaking the silence after a moment, "how do you think the Silicon Kid gained entrance to the fortress?"

"He had to have a confederate on the inside," lied Lomax promptly.

"That is my conclusion, too. Have you any suggestions concerning who it might have been?"

Lomax shook his head. "I haven't been here long enough, My Lord." He paused. "But there's no question in my mind that an organization this size is riddled with traitors and double agents."

"A few, perhaps," admitted the Anointed One. "But *riddled*? I think not, Mr. Lomax."

"I hate to disagree, My Lord," said Lomax, "but whenever one man holds as much power and wealth as you do, it's an open invitation to, shall we say, disloyalty?"

"I am the Anointed One. My people follow me as a matter of faith and belief. Temporal rewards are secondary to them."

"They're no more secondary to your followers than they are to me, My Lord," said Lomax. "The only difference is that I make no bones about it." He stared across the table at the ascetic, white-robed man. "Take your man on Olympus, for example."

"Milo Korbekkian has served me loyally for seven years," responded the Anointed One.

"Milo Korbekkian has served you for seven years," responded Lomax.

"You are impugning his loyalty?" demanded the Anointed One.

"Let's say I'm trying to define it," answered Lomax. "I'm sure he's loyal—to Milo Korbekkian. And to Mrs. Korbekkian, if there is one. And to the capitalistic principle. But I know for a fact that Korbekkian has taken commissions from people other than yourself and has arranged various killings that you know nothing about." He shrugged. "That doesn't make him disloyal, My Lord. In all likelihood his other dealings have no effect on you or your plans."

"How do you know that he has accepted other commissions?" demanded the Anointed One.

"It's my business to know," said Lomax. "I'm the kind of man he hires."

"I don't believe you, Mr. Lomax."

"That's your prerogative, My Lord," said Lomax with an air of unconcern.

The Anointed One stared at him long and hard across the table. "Prove it," he said at last.

"How?" asked Lomax. "It would just be my word against his." He paused. "I suppose you could monitor his incoming and outgoing messages, if you wanted to go to the trouble."

"I do not," said the Anointed One. "The subject is closed."

But Lomax saw the shadow of doubt cross his face, and he knew the subject was far from closed. Satisfied, he devoured the rest of his fruit plate and spent the remainder of the meal offering wild speculations as to which guards had been paid to turn a blind eye to the Kid's presence that morning. Then word of still another body turned up—some hapless attendant that the Kid had killed and hidden earlier in the day—and the Anointed One, suddenly in a rage, went off to see the corpse and question his guards, while Lomax returned to his room and spent most of the afternoon feigning sleep for the benefit of any unseen observers.

Things proceeded uneventfully for the next two days. Lomax remained in his quarters as much as possible, spoke as little as possible during meals, concerned himself with examining the fortress's security, secretly tested his ever-stronger left arm and publicly favored it, and even began developing a taste for blacksheep.

Then, in late afternoon two days after he had spoken to the Iceman, Lomax was summoned once again to the throne room, where Moses Mohammed Christ sat alone on his chair, a look of triumph on his long, lean face.

"You were right, Mr. Lomax," said the Anointed One, "as you have been right all along."

"My Lord?" said Lomax, trying his best to look confused.

"Milo Korbekkian," said the Anointed One.

"What about him?"

"He was also in the employ of the Prophet, as you yourself suggested."

"I knew he was working for someone else besides you, My Lord," replied Lomax. "I never said it was the Prophet." He paused. "I assume you'll want me to eliminate him."

"That has already been taken care of," said the Anointed One.

"That's too bad," said Lomax. "I might have been able to pry some information about the Prophet out of him."

"I am in possession of all the information I need."

"Oh?"

The Anointed One leaned forward excitedly on his throne, his coal-black eyes shining with triumph. "She is hiding on a planet named Mozart in the Alpha Montana system—and she is practically defenseless!"

"You're sure of this?" asked Lomax.

"There is no doubt whatsoever!" exclaimed the Anointed One. "The Silicon Kid was sent here to divert my attention from her until she can build up her defenses. And from such information as I now possess, it is absolutely certain that Korbekkian also hired many others to wreak terror and confusion among us, to get us to look inward for traitors and conspirators rather than turning our eyes toward Mozart."

"If your information is correct," said Lomax carefully, "and if she is truly defenseless, then our next logical move is—"

"Attack!" cried the Anointed One, finishing his sentence for him. "I have summoned my forces here and given orders to my commanders: we attack Mozart in three days' time!"

"Can you mobilize that quickly, My Lord?" asked Lomax, amazed once again at the accuracy of the Iceman's assessment.

"Not all of my followers are warriors, and not all who *are* warriors are available to me," answered the Anointed One. "But we will attack in force, with almost four million men and women in close to eight thousand vessels that have been equipped for war."

"May I make a suggestion, My Lord?"

"Certainly."

"I don't think any of us know the full extent of the Prophet's powers, if indeed she has any powers at all," said Lomax. "But if we are to expose this many of our people to potential danger, then I think we should hit Mozart with everything we have. We should settle for nothing less than blowing it out of existence."

"My own thinking precisely," said the Anointed One, nodding his head in agreement. "We will spare no expense, withhold no weapon, and show no mercy."

"Good," said Lomax firmly. "I think you've made a wise decision, My Lord." He smiled. "Today the Prophet, tomorrow the Democracy."

"So it shall be," intoned the Anointed One. "And you, Mr. Lomax, will be beside me to share in the spoils."

"I wouldn't think there'd be anything left of Mozart to share in," replied Lomax.

"There will be the glory of victory over my enemy, a victory in which you will have played a fundamental part."

"I'm just doing what you pay me to do, My Lord," said Lomax. "Nothing more."

"Don't be modest, Mr. Lomax," said the Anointed One. "Without you, the Silicon Kid might well have killed me. And had you not expressed your doubts about Korbekkian, I might never have learned of the Prophet's whereabouts before she was ready to meet me in battle. You are truly one of the architects of our forthcoming victory."

"I'm flattered that you should think so, My Lord," answered Lomax.

"In fact," continued the Anointed One magnanimously, "it would be unfair to you not to allow you to participate in this Holy War. I have decided to give you your own ship to command."

"My own ship?" repeated Lomax, startled.

The Anointed One smiled. "I had my doubts about you initially, I confess it. But by your actions you have overcome every one of them. This is my way of rewarding you."

"You're quite sure, My Lord?" asked Lomax. "I mean, I've killed many men, but I've never commanded a ship or led men into battle."

"You will do both for the first of many times," said the Anointed One.

"But—"

"I will have no more of your false modesty, Mr. Lomax," said the Anointed One, still smiling. "It really does not become you." He got to his feet. "Our interview is over."

Lomax returned unhappily to his room, wondering exactly what the Anointed One's smile actually meant.

PART 5

The
Prophet's
Book

27

Penelope Bailey stood beside a wooden bench next to the pond behind her house, her eyes trained blindly on the sky, seeing what no one else on Mozart could see, what no more than a handful of sophisticated instruments on the planet could detect.

"You are a fool, Moses Mohammed Christ," she murmured. "Have you learned nothing from our prior encounters? Do you think my power is limited to destroying your churches?" She paused. "There is still time to turn back—but you will not retreat, will you? What lunacy has possessed you, what demons have goaded you into attacking me when the only possible result is your destruction?"

She sighed deeply, then went inside to make herself a cup of tea. The fleet was not yet in the formation she desired, and she knew that she had an hour or more to prepare herself. She sat down at a small table in the kitchen, added some lemon to the tea, stirred it absently, and continued looking out the window.

There were still factors to be sorted out, alternatives to be found, actions to be considered. Six of the Anointed One's ships had developed engine trouble; should she destroy them, or let them live to tell the story of his defeat, to spread tales of her power throughout the galaxy? There was another ship, too, one that she foresaw would not join the formation, that seemed somehow special though she could not yet determine why.

Then she turned her attention to the Democracy. The Plan took constant modification, incessant monitoring. This man must die; that woman must not. This world's economy must collapse; that lone miner must discover his planet's only diamond pipe. She twitched, she posed, she postured, she did all that was necessary to bring about the desired events, and then she began reading the permutations of those events, for each of them altered a million possible futures, and she was presented with a new set of choices, a new spate of alternatives, all of which must be read and analyzed and extrapolated.

She concentrated on the Plan for perhaps forty minutes. Then, satisfied that it was on track for another day, she made another cup of tea and walked out to the pond once more. Again she looked blindly up to the skies.

"Soon, Moses Mohammed Christ," she murmured. "Soon."

She finished her tea and set the cup and saucer down on the wooden bench.

"I would have given you another six years," she said softly, staring at the sky. "Eventually I would have defeated you in the Spica sector, but you would have enjoyed six more years of power and authority. Now I will have to rebuild your organization, will have to assert myself sooner. I will adjust and I will triumph, but I cannot fathom why you have chosen to throw your life away. When we met at Spica, I would have given you no alternative but to fight or run, and because you could not lose face before your followers, you would have fought." She paused, frowning. "But there is no reason for this confrontation today, no reason for you to die on the Inner Frontier. I must learn what brought you to this unhappy end, for it became likely only a week ago and certain only this morning."

And because she did not have the gift of reading the past, she turned her attention once more to the future, to the infinite number of futures confronting her, searching through them for a key to unlock the recent past, to determine the reason for her enemy's suicidal decision.

And, within a very few minutes, she found it.

"Of course," she said, with no feeling of surprise. "It had to be *you*."

She closed her eyes to better see the future.

"You learn well, Carlos Mendoza," she said, a half-smile on her lips. "You will not approach until the attack has begun, and at that time I shall be too busy neutralizing the doomsday weapons to bother with you. Their threat is immediate, while yours, though greater, is further removed in time, and I will have to let you land."

She concentrated harder, sifting through the futures. "You chose your position with foresight and intelligence," she continued. "No meteor, no asteroid, no debris can reach you before you join the battle. And yet," she said, "perhaps I can show you that I have more weapons in my arsenal than even *you* anticipate."

Suddenly she smiled. "A pacemaker? Blood thinners? You *are* prepared, are you not? Very well. You shall not die of a heart attack or a stroke before you can face me." She paused. "Some things even *I* cannot change. Evidently it has been ordained in the Book of Fate that I must confront you one last time."

And now her face contorted with rage. "I have never sought to make you my enemy. Twice I could have killed you, and twice I allowed you to live. I could have destroyed Last Chance in the twinkling of an eye, and yet I did not. And still you seek me out, you remain dedicated to my destruction. It is because of you that I have become a fugitive among my own people, that I have spent the past twenty years in hiding or in confinement. You are the architect of my unhappiness, and today, when I have done what I must do to the fleet that approaches, I shall face you one last time."

She paused, trying to control her emotions.

"I will show you no more mercy than you would show me," she whispered. "I have things to do in the galaxy, great things, things that are beyond your feeble comprehension. You will never hinder them again."

She looked up at the sky once more, not to where the fleet was gathered, but to where a lone ship, still light-years away, was speeding toward Mozart.

"You shall learn what it means to oppose me now that my powers are mature," she promised. "You shall learn why men fear the darkness, and why death itself can be a mercy. Prepare yourself, Carlos Mendoza, for this is your last day of life."

28

Lomax summoned his second in command to the bridge of the ship.

"Sir?" said the man.

"We have a serious problem here," he announced.

"Problem, sir?"

Lomax nodded. "One of the goddamned bombs has armed itself."

He stood aside so that the man could study his control panel, and especially the blinking red light on the left side of it.

"Could it be a malfunction on the board, sir?"

"I already thought of that," answered Lomax. "The board is working perfectly."

"Let me check the bomb itself, sir," said the man. "Perhaps it's emitting a false signal."

"Do so," said Lomax. "And be discreet. No sense upsetting the rest of the crew until we know what we're dealing with."

The man nodded and headed off toward the weapons bay. He returned some four minutes later.

"It's armed, sir," he reported.

"How much time do you think we have before it blows?"

"I don't know, sir. Maybe ten minutes, maybe ten hours. We've never carried this type of weapon before."

"It's new to me, too," complained Lomax. "Hell, the whole ship is new to me. I'm just a gunman that the Anointed One took a liking to."

"You saved his life, sir," protested the man with the passion of a fanatic. "We are prepared to carry out any orders that you give."

"The problem is that I don't know what orders are required in this situation," said Lomax grimly. "I suppose we should jettison the bomb, but according to my computer, it's in a position where we'd have to jettison the entire payload." He paused. "I hate to do that. We're attacking with a smaller force than I would have recommended had time not been a vital consideration. The Prophet is the most formidable antagonist in the galaxy; we may need every weapon we possess."

"There is an alternative, sir."

I was wondering when it would occur to you.

"What is that?" asked Lomax aloud.

"We can load the crew onto our landing craft and leave them to make their way to the planet behind the bulk of the fleet, while you and I stay aboard and try to deactivate the bomb."

"Excellent suggestion!" replied Lomax. "Pass the word. I want them all off the ship within fifteen minutes." He paused. "Yourself included."

"I request permission to remain on board, sir."

"Permission denied."

"I insist, sir. One of us is going to have to go down into the weapons bay and try to deactivate the bomb, and one of us is going to have to navigate the ship."

"I'll put it on automatic."

"That might work in deep space, sir, but we're in a war zone. You may come under attack."

"I doubt it," said Lomax.

"You yourself have stated that she is the most formidable foe we will ever face, sir."

Lomax realized that further argument could arouse the man's suspicions. Furthermore, it was essential that he get the crew off the ship as quickly as possible, before someone discovered what was really happening.

"All right," he said. "You can stay. Now see to the evacuation, and report to me when it's complete. I'll continue trying to deactivate the bomb from here."

The man saluted and left, and Lomax lit a small cigar and pretended to work the control panel until the bridge was totally deserted. He watched the viewscreen as the shuttlecraft left the mother ship one by one, until the last of the crew had gone and only Lomax and his second in command remained.

The man approached him and saluted. "The evacuation is completed, sir."

"Good," said Lomax.

"Now I'll go down and see if I can deactivate the bomb, sir."

"Be careful," said Lomax.

"Yes, sir."

The man departed, and Lomax lit another cigar and hoped the Prophet could see far enough into the future to know that his ship was no threat to her.

The man returned some ten minutes later, a puzzled frown on his face.

"Sir?" he said.

"Yes?"

"As nearly as I can tell, the bomb is not malfunctioning."

"You mean it's not armed?"

"It's armed, all right—but it seems to have been armed purposely, from *here*."

"You don't say."

"Yes, sir. From *your* panel."

Lomax pulled his pistol out. "You should have abandoned ship with the others."

"I don't understand, sir."

"You're a good man," said Lomax. "And I am truly sorry for what I must do."

He fired his gun. The man uttered a single surprised grunt and fell to the deck, dead.

Then, having done everything within his power to convince the Prophet that his ship wanted no part of the doomed battle, Lomax sat back to await the outcome.

29

In the first thirty seconds of the would-be battle, the life support systems of seventy-four of the Anointed One's ships lost all power; eighteen more were destroyed when their ordnance, unlike Lomax's, actually did activate and explode.

A meteor wiped out twenty-seven more ships. A comet, crazily careening off its eternal course, accounted for another nineteen. One ship's weapons computer malfunctioned and destroyed thirty-seven of its allies before it in turn was demolished.

"What is happening here?" demanded the Anointed One, his face contorted with rage and terror. "No one has fired upon us, and yet we are being decimated." He glowered at the planet Mozart, spinning, blue and green and serene, in his viewscreen. "She is just one woman! What is happening?"

And a million miles beneath him, Penelope Bailey, staring blindly at the sky, smiled and whispered, "Not yet, my foolish one. Not yet. First you must see the folly of attacking me. When all of your men have been killed, when all your ships float dead in the void, *then* I shall tend to you."

30

After receiving permission to land from a bored spaceport employee who had no idea that a war had erupted a million miles above his head, the Iceman's ship broke out of orbit and plunged down toward Mozart's surface. He wasn't worried about being fired upon, because he knew that whatever defenses Penelope possessed, they weren't military in nature. As for the local authorities, they caused him no concern whatsoever; he was willing to bet that no one else even knew that the Anointed One's fleet was out there, or that it was being torn to pieces.

When he got to within five miles of the surface he pressed a button and released a trio of parachutes, designed to save him just in case Penelope was able to stop concentrating on the heavily armed ships in orbit and devote a few seconds to him. But the landing was accomplished without mishap, and the Iceman climbed into the hold of his ship to prepare the cargo he had brought along.

It took him almost twenty minutes to assemble the components. Then he attached them to the loose vest he had brought, slipped the vest on, covered it with a bulky coat, and finally emerged from his ship.

A spaceport official was waiting for him.

"Welcome to Mozart," he said.

"Thank you," said the Iceman.

"You certainly took your time getting out of your ship," continued the official. "Is everything all right? Do you need any mechanical assistance?"

"No," answered the Iceman. "I was just rearranging some cargo."

"Will you require either fuel or a hangar?"

"Neither," said the Iceman. "My business here should be done before nightfall."

"If it isn't, there will be a two-hundred-credit fee for leaving your ship where it is."

The Iceman reached into a pocket and pulled out a wad of bills, then peeled off a pair of hundred-credit notes. "Here," he said, handing them to the official. "You can return them to me when I leave this evening."

"I'll make out a receipt while you're clearing customs," said the man, putting the bills between the pages of a small notebook.

"Where *is* customs?"

"At the base of the tower," replied the man, leading the Iceman into the lobby of the observation tower and over to the customs desk, where a handsome, uniformed woman looked up at him.

"Name, please?"

The Iceman pulled out his titanium passport card and laid it on her desk. "Carlos Mendoza."

She ran the card through a computer, waited a few seconds for it to scan his retina and verify his identity, and returned it to him.

"May I ask the purpose of your visit, Mr. Mendoza?"

"I'm here to conclude some very old business," he replied.

"And the name of the party you have come to see?"

"Penelope Bailey."

She looked up from her computer and stared at him for a moment. "Does Miss Bailey know you are coming to see her?"

"I'd be very surprised if she didn't," answered the Iceman.

"All right, Mr. Mendoza, you are cleared to stay on Mozart for fourteen days. Should you decide to extend your visit beyond that limit, please inform this office."

"Thank you."

"The Democracy credit is the official currency of Mozart, but we also accept New Stalin rubles, Maria Theresa dollars, New Zimbabwe dollars, and Far London pounds. If you possess any other form of currency, please declare it on this form"—she handed him an official-looking document—"and record all your currency conversion transactions."

The Iceman took the form, folded it neatly, and placed it in a pocket of his overcoat.

"Welcome to Mozart, Mr. Mendoza," she said. "Today's temperature is 28 degrees Celsius, which translates into 542 degrees

Rankine, 22 degrees Reaumur, and 83 degrees Fahrenheit." She paused. "You may find your overcoat rather warm."

"I won't be wearing it that long," he replied. "How do I get to town from here?"

"There is free public transportation every two hours." She checked her timepiece. "I'm afraid you just missed it. If you don't wish to wait, there are usually a few groundcars for hire in front of the spaceport."

"Thank you," said the Iceman. He turned and walked through the small lobby at the base of the observation tower and out the main entrance. A single groundcar was parked there, and he quickly climbed into it.

"Where to?" asked the driver.

"I'm looking for a private residence," answered the Iceman. "Have you got a directory here?"

The driver pressed a button, activating a holoscreen that hovered in the air about two feet from the Iceman.

"Just state the name of your party," said the driver. "His address will appear at the top of the screen, and the one-way and round-trip fares will be computed and appear in the lower right-hand corner."

"Penelope Bailey."

Instantly an address appeared. This was followed by a map that traced seven or eight routes, selected the quickest one, left it on display, and posted a rate of forty-eight credits one way or eighty-eight credits for a round trip.

"She's out in the sticks, isn't she?" remarked the driver as an identical screen appeared above his dash panel.

"I suppose so," answered the Iceman. "I haven't been there before. How long will it take?"

The driver stared at the map. "Maybe twenty minutes, twenty-five if we run into some traffic."

"Traffic? On this planet?"

"Harvesters or combines on the road, moving from one farm to another," explained the driver. "They can slow you down plenty." He paused. "Well, are we going?"

"Yes."

The groundcar pulled away from the spaceport.

"One way or round trip?"

"One way will do," answered the Iceman. "If I need a ride back, I'll call for one."

"Remember my tag number and ask for it," said the driver. "I can use the business."

"I'll do that," replied the Iceman.

They drove in silence for almost twenty minutes, passing through town and going out along the back roads, and finally the Iceman leaned forward. "How much longer?" he asked.

"Maybe another two miles."

"Stop when you're a mile away."

"You're sure?"

"Just trying to save you some engine trouble."

"I don't have any engine trouble."

"You never can tell," said the Iceman, handing a hundred-credit note to the driver.

"You're the boss," said the driver with a shrug.

A moment later the groundcar slowed down and pulled over to the side of the road, and the Iceman got out.

"If the map's right, it should be just around the next curve," said the driver. "You sure you don't want me to wait?"

"I'm sure."

"All right." He paused. "From what I hear around town, this is a very strange lady you're going to visit. I don't know what kind of business you've got with her, but good luck."

"Thanks," said the Iceman. "I'll probably need it."

The groundcar turned and headed back toward the spaceport, and the Iceman began walking along the edge of a mutated-corn field toward Penelope Bailey's house. When he finally was able to see the top of the geodesic dome, he removed his overcoat and left it lying in a ditch at roadside.

He stopped, lit a cigar, paused to enjoy the taste of the first puff, and then reached down to his vest and activated two tiny switches. Then he continued walking, and five minutes later he reached his destination.

He approached the front door and found that it was locked, and since he was no longer in any condition to pound it or pull at it, he gingerly walked around to the back, where he saw a young blonde woman, her back to him, standing beside a small pond, her eyes trained on the heavens, striking a new position every few seconds.

"Welcome, Iceman," she said without turning to face him. "I have been waiting for this moment for a long time."

"I don't doubt it," replied the Iceman, coming to a stop.

"I have only forty more ships to destroy," she announced, "and then I shall be able to give you my full attention." She paused. "Now twenty-three, now seventeen. You are very clever to have gotten this far, Iceman."

"I was fortunate."

"You would have been more fortunate had you elected to remain on your own world," she replied, still motionless. "Eleven, now seven, now four." She paused again. "And now there is only the Anointed One." Finally she turned to the Iceman. "Shall we let him live a little longer, so that he may grasp the full extent of his defeat?"

"It makes no difference to me," replied the Iceman.

"No, of course it does not," she said. "You care no more about Moses Mohammed Christ than I do." She paused and stared into the Iceman's eyes. "So it comes down to you and me, as I always knew it would."

31

The Iceman stared at the young woman confronting him.

"You were an appealing little girl, Penelope," he said, thinking back to the first time he had ever seen her. "Small, frightened, vulnerable." He paused. "I should have killed you then."

She smiled. "You would have failed."

"Probably," he admitted. "You were more than capable of protecting yourself even then."

"I still am," she replied. "I have grown stronger over the years."

"We've both grown, Penelope," said the Iceman, meeting her gaze. "You've grown stronger, and I've grown wiser."

"Wise enough to kill me?" she asked, amused.

"I think so," he replied seriously.

She laughed. "I don't even need my powers to destroy you. You haven't grown wiser, merely older. You are a fat, lame old man. Already you pant and sweat from the mere exertion of walking the last mile to my home. Your heart beats faster, your blood races through your body, you have trouble catching your breath. I could kill you with my bare hands, Iceman."

"Look ahead, and see what will happen if you do," suggested the Iceman.

"You will die."

"But not alone."

"You refer to the vest you wear, of course."

"If you hit me or shoot me, I'll fall down. And if I fall down, every map of Mozart is going to be obsolete half a second later. I'm carrying enough explosives to make this the center of a twenty-mile crater."

She stared at him. "So five million men died this morning merely to let you approach me with your plans and your explosives—and you call *me* a monster?"

"I don't call you anything, Penelope," he said. "I'm your executioner, not your judge."

"And did you really think it would be this easy?" she asked. "Did you think there wasn't a single future in which your switches failed to activate your explosives?"

The Iceman felt a sudden tension at the pit of his stomach.

"You're bluffing," he said with more confidence than he felt.

She shook her head serenely. "I never had any need to bluff. I could have disabled your explosives whenever I wanted to."

"But you didn't?" he said, frowning.

"No, Iceman, I didn't." She stared at him for a long moment. "You are prepared to die today, are you not?"

"I am."

"So am I," she replied. "Our deaths, like our lives, are intertwined." She paused. "But first I would like to talk to you."

He looked surprised. "What do you want to talk about?"

"Oh, about many things," she replied. "It is strange: I am bound to you by hatred, but I am also closer to you than to anyone now alive. And you alone have never lied to me." She paused. "The threat of invasion is over. We have all the time in the world to talk"—she smiled ironically—"the rest of our lives. And I have some questions for you."

"What kind of questions?" he said suspiciously.

"Simple ones."

"All right," he said. "Start asking."

"Why do all living things shun me?" she asked. "Not only people, but even animals." She paused. "Even puppies."

The Iceman was taken aback for a moment. It was not the type of question he had anticipated. Finally he spoke.

"Because you're different," he said. "Because you are no longer human."

"Men do not shun the crippled or the senile, the retarded or the deformed," said Penelope. "They take them into the bosom of their families and shower them with love and compassion. Why, of all the sons and daughters of your race, have I alone been cast out?"

"Because none of the unfortunates to whom you liken yourself have the power to destroy entire worlds at their whim. You not only have that power, but you have exercised it."

"Only to protect myself." She paused. "Do you know that no human being has touched me since the day the Mouse died some twenty years ago? Not a single one?"

"No," said the Iceman. "I didn't know that."

"Kittens hiss and puppies hide," she continued. "Birds fly away. Even the reptiles in my garden slither off into the shadows when I appear."

"I have no better answer," he replied uncomfortably. The sound of a tractor working in a nearby field came to his ears. "Have you any more questions?"

"You have hated me from the first day we met," she said. "Why? What had I ever done to you?"

"I don't hate you, Penelope," he replied. "You don't hate an ion storm that threatens your ship, or a meteor swarm that bombards your planet. If you're alone in a jungle, you don't hate the carnivores that stalk you in the night. None of them are good or evil. They're just hazards of nature that have to be overcome in order to survive." He paused. "I feel no hatred toward you at all. I bear you no malice. I blame you for only one thing—the death of the Mouse."

"She betrayed my trust."

"You were a child," he replied. "You had no grasp of subtleties. You couldn't fully comprehend what was happening." He paused again. "She loved you as if you were her own daughter. The only reason she's dead is because she never truly understood what you were. She thought she was saving you, as if you could be shot down like any ordinary human."

Penelope paused. "I have not thought of the Mouse in a long time," she said at last.

"I think of her every day," said the Iceman.

"Her death caused you that much pain?"

"It did."

"Then I have repaid you for some of the pain you have caused me."

He stared at her and made no reply.

"Did she really love me?" asked Penelope after a brief silence.

"Yes, she did."

"Will anyone ever love me again, I wonder?" she mused thoughtfully.

The Iceman shook his head. "No, they won't."

"I know," she replied. "Do you know what it is like to face a future in which not a single person will ever love you? A future in which every member of your race shuns you as if you were some beast to be avoided?"

"No," answered the Iceman. "And I don't envy anyone who does."

"I never asked for this gift, Iceman," she said. "All I ever wanted was to be a normal little girl, to play with other girls, to live with my family." She paused for a moment, lost in her memories. "My own mother was terrified of me. They took me away when I was six, and they killed my father when he tried to prevent it. Do you know how many times I played with children my own age after that, Iceman?"

"No," he said.

"One afternoon, when the Mouse and I were hiding from you," she said bitterly. "One afternoon in my entire life!" Suddenly she sighed. "And within twenty minutes they had all run away from me." She looked at him. "They will always run away from me, won't they?"

"Little girls?" he asked, confused.

"Everyone."

"Yes, I suppose they will."

She looked up at him, and for just a moment the emotionless, alien mask disappeared.

"I thought I was escaping from Westerly and Calliope and Killhaven and Hades," she said, "but there is never really any escape, is there? Mozart is just a bigger cell than the one I had on Hades, and the galaxy is just a bigger cell than Mozart."

"You can't escape who you are," he replied.

She paused. "Do you know something interesting, Iceman?"

"What?"

"Of all the Men I have known since I left Hades as a grown woman, only you have looked at me without repugnance. With fear, yes, as well you should, and with trepidation, but without disgust."

"I don't feel any disgust toward you," replied the Iceman. "Other things, yes. But not disgust."

"Every other man and woman has felt it. I even saw it on the Black Death's face, and in the eyes of your young spy." She sighed. "I have seen it every day of my life, even in the eyes of my own mother."

"I'm sorry," said the Iceman sincerely.

"You think me a monster," she continued. "But you are on the outside looking in. Believe me, Iceman, it is infinitely worse to *be* Penelope Bailey than to fear her. I inspire fear and hatred by virtue of my very existence. I am as much a prisoner as I ever was, trapped within this body as this body was trapped within a tiny cell on Hades." She paused. "My only consolation has been the Plan."

"The Plan?" he repeated.

"I have been working on it for years," she replied. "It began to form in my mind while I was in my cell on Hades, and I have been implementing it ever since I gained my freedom."

"What does it involve?" asked the Iceman. "Control of the Democracy? Its overthrow?"

"Even now, on this last day of our lives, in the middle of this conversation, you do not begin to understand me," said Penelope. "I have no desire to rule anyone. I have no army, I control no politicians, I have not garnered untold wealth."

"Then what *is* this Plan?" he persisted.

She stared at him with a level gaze. "Simply this," she answered. "That no child shall ever bear the curse of precognition again. There are some three hundred men and women with the genetic potential to produce another Soothsayer, another Oracle, another *me*. I have manipulated events, built and destroyed planetary economies, changed entire political systems, to make sure that none of those three hundred people ever meet." She paused. "That is my gift to your galaxy, Iceman. More important, that is my gift to the unborn. No child shall ever be cut off from his people as I was."

He returned her stare. "You *are* ready to die, aren't you?"

"Soon," she replied. "I have a few things yet to do." She closed her eyes for a moment, then opened them. "I have allowed Moses Mohammed Christ to live and fight another day. With his defeat this morning, he can no longer affect the outcome of the Plan." She shrugged. "Let your vaunted Democracy find out if it is fit to rule, or so corrupt that its time has passed."

"You don't know the answer?"

"I no longer care about the answer," she said. Suddenly she walked past him, circled the pond, and entered her house. She emerged a moment later with something small and furry cradled under one arm.

"I seem to remember that doll," said the Iceman.

She shook her head. "This is a new one. The one you remember fell apart while I was in prison on Hades, and of course I did not request another, because grown women do not lavish their attentions on dolls." She sighed. "Somewhere along the way I found out what others have always known: that I am not a woman." She stared at him again. "It is time, I think."

He carefully pulled his weapon out of its holster and aimed it at her.

"Say a prayer to your God," said Penelope calmly. "The surge of energy when you pull the trigger will activate your explosives."

"Just a minute," said the Iceman. "There is a better way."

"I thought you were prepared to die," she said. "I hope you were not lying, for neither of us will survive this day."

He carefully pulled one tiny explosive off his vest and attached it to his weapon's power pack.

"Let me take the vest off and deactivate it," he said.

"Why should I?"

"This bomb is more than enough to kill both of us. If the vest goes off, we'll wipe out ten thousand people."

"What are they to me?" asked Penelope.

"Let me do it, for what they *might* have been to you under other circumstances."

She considered his entreaty for a long moment, then nodded.

He deactivated the switches, removed the vest, and walked to the house with it, laying it carefully on a couch. Then he returned to the pond, where Penelope was waiting for him.

"Aim straight and true, Carlos Mendoza," she said.

"That's what I came here to do," he replied, raising the weapon and training it on her heart.

Suddenly he froze.

"I have a question," he said. "You're probably the only person that ever lived who might be able to answer it."

"What is it?"

"Can you see another life beyond this one?"

"God, I hope not," she said with a shudder of revulsion.

The Iceman pulled the trigger.

32

Lomax waited until the Anointed One's flagship retreated to New Gobi, leaving its disabled companions behind, before he jettisoned the body of the dead crewman. Then, because he was a cautious man who had every intention of surviving, he waited a few hours more.

Finally, when he was all through waiting, he requested permission to land and touched down at the tiny spaceport about two hundred yards from the Iceman's ship.

He spent a few minutes clearing customs, then made arrangements to refuel the ship and house it in a hangar. There were a pair of groundcars waiting outside the observation tower, and he got into the nearer of them.

"Where to?" asked the driver.

He summoned up Penelope Bailey's address from the computer's directory.

"I took someone out there yesterday," remarked the driver as they began racing past the endless pastures and fields that lined the road.

"Old fellow with a bad leg?" asked Lomax.

"That's the one."

"Do you know if he came back?"

"If he did, he didn't rent a vehicle to do it," replied the driver.

Lomax checked his laser weapon and made sure that the charge was full.

"Did he say anything to you?" he asked.

"Just that he had some personal business to take care of," said the driver. "Funny thing, though: he had me let him off about a mile short of where he was going. Guess he felt like taking a walk."

"Probably," said Lomax noncommittally.

They drove the rest of the way in silence, until at last the geodesic dome came into view.

"Well, there it is," said the driver. "Are you the walking type, too?"

"No, I like my comfort."

The groundcar pulled up to the house a moment later. "Should I wait for you?"

"It'd probably be better if you didn't," answered Lomax. "I'll call you if I need you."

He got out of the groundcar and walked up to the front door. It was locked, and the security system, which didn't recognize him, refused to let him in, so he cautiously walked around to the back of the house.

He found what was left of them by the pond. Not much, but enough to identify them. The back door of the house was unlocked, and inside it he found the Iceman's vest, loaded with explosives. Try as he would, he couldn't reconstruct what had happened, although the climax of it was there for anyone to read.

He found a toolshed hidden behind some bushes, broke the lock on it, killed the ensuing alarm siren with his laser pistol, and searched through the tiny building until he found a shovel. He picked a shady spot under a huge tree by the pond, dug a shallow grave, and buried what he could find of them.

He filled in the grave, then tried to decide how to mark it. He doubted that either of them wanted a religious symbol, and he had no intention of remaining on Mozart until a headstone could be created and delivered. Then his gaze fell on something small and fluffy lying on the ground. He walked over and picked it up; it was the shredded remains of a small doll.

He tried to imagine what the doll might have to do with either of them, and finally gave it up with a shrug. Besides, it didn't really matter: except for the vest, which was too dangerous to leave behind, it was the only object around with which to mark the grave, and so he skewered it on a short branch and stuck it into the ground.

It wasn't much of a marker, he knew, but it was the best he could do under the circumstances. He went into the house and summoned the groundcar via the vidphone, and twenty minutes later he was speeding back to the spaceport.

Epilogue

Five months had passed, and Lomax found himself, much to his surprise, on the world of Sweetwater, being served a mixed drink by a robot.

"That will be all, Sidney," said Robert Gibbs, and the robot bowed and left the room.

"All right, Mr. Gibbs," said Lomax. "You got me here. Now suppose you tell me what this is all about."

"It's about a crazed fanatic called the Anointed One," said Gibbs, "a man with whom I believe you have been associated in the past."

"What about him?"

"We want him."

"We?" repeated Lomax.

"The Democracy," answered Gibbs. "I've been reactivated and put in charge of my old department, although they've allowed me to operate out of my own home for the time being."

"Then let the Democracy go out and get him," answered Lomax. "He thinks I'm dead, and as far as I'm concerned, that's a healthy relationship."

"I don't think you understand the gravity of the situation, Mr. Lomax," persisted Gibbs. "This man is a threat to survival of our government."

"He's just a man," replied Lomax calmly. "You've already survived the most serious threat you're ever going to face."

"I beg your pardon?"

"Penelope Bailey."

Gibbs shook his head. "She's been dead for four years. She

died when Alpha Crepello III was destroyed."

"She died five months ago, when an old man with one leg hunted her down and killed her."

"You mean Mendoza?" asked Gibbs, startled. "He's dead?"

Lomax nodded, and took a sip of his drink. "He's dead. And so is she."

"But life goes on, Mr. Lomax, and right now more lives than you can imagine are being threatened by the man known as Moses Mohammed Christ."

"You survived *her,*" said Lomax. "You'll survive him."

"I am prepared to offer you five million credits for your services," said Gibbs. "One-third now, the remainder upon completion of your mission."

"Not interested."

"Then why did you come here?" asked Gibbs. "You must have known the kind of offer I was going to make."

"I just wanted to see the man who started all this."

"All what?"

"You kidnapped Penelope Bailey when she was six years old," said Lomax. "You weren't Robert Gibbs back then, but it was you." He paused. "You know, if you had left her alone or had made some effort to win her confidence, you wouldn't have had to depend on men like the Iceman and me to do your dirty work for you. She could have told you the outcome of every election, predicted the results of every battle, and if you didn't like the course events were taking, she'd have found a way to change them. You could have had all that, and because you never learned the secret of the stick and the carrot, you let it slip away."

"If she was so infallible," scoffed Gibbs, "how did the Iceman manage to kill her?"

"I don't think he did," answered Lomax thoughtfully. "I think she just got tired of fighting—like me."

"You're not quitting," said Gibbs. "Men like you and Carlos never quit."

"No, I'm not quitting," said Lomax. "But I'm not fighting *your* battles, Mr. Gibbs. If you've ever got a personal grudge against someone, you know where to find me. But don't expect me to fight every enemy the Democracy has created through its arrogance or its stupidity."

"We didn't create the Anointed One *or* the Bailey girl, damn it!" snapped Gibbs.

Lomax sighed. "Mr. Gibbs, you've created every enemy you've ever had."

"You've been with the Anointed One, spoken to him, seen him in action!" continued Gibbs. "Surely you realize that he must be eliminated!"

"He's a religious fanatic, and he's probably every bit as power hungry as you think," said Lomax. He paused and smiled. "Do you know who he reminds me of?"

"Penelope Bailey?" suggested Gibbs, surprised by the question.

"No, Mr. Gibbs," answered Lomax. "He reminds me of you, and I say a pox on both your houses." He set his drink down. "And now, if you'll excuse me, I have something important to do."

"You can't walk out of here!"

"Certainly I can," said Lomax. "Somewhere out there, on a world you've never heard of, there's a grave that's marked only with a rag doll. It doesn't mean a damned thing to you, not anymore, but I'm going to deliver a headstone to it."

"Seven million!" said Gibbs.

Lomax smiled and walked to the door.

"You'll be back," said Gibbs confidently. "Carlos always came back, and so will you."

"You have enemies, Mr. Gibbs," said Lomax. "I think you'd better hope I don't come back."

And then he was gone.